PRAISE FOR
DON'T DATE *Rosa Santos*

"A love song to family, diaspora, and to girls on the verge of discovering who they want to be."

—ZORAIDA CÓRDOVA, award-winning author of *Labyrinth Lost*

"*Don't Date Rosa Santos* blends two cultures brilliantly, seamlessly, and humorously. Rosa is a relatable American teenager guaranteed to make you smile."

—GLORIA CHAO, author of *American Panda*

"Maybe you shouldn't date Rosa Santos, but you should definitely read this book. This enchanting novel will sweep you up like the sea."

—STEPHANIE KATE STROHM, author of *Prince in Disguise* and *Love à la Mode*

"The delicate aroma of fresh-baked pastry combined with the heady intoxication of sea winds infiltrate the pages of this romantic debut novel. Pa'lante."

—JAYE ROBIN BROWN, author of *Georgia Peaches and Other Forbidden Fruit*

DON'T

Rosa

DATE *Santos*

NINA MORENO

HYPERION

Los Angeles New York

First Edition, May 2019
10 9 8 7 6 5 4 3 2 1
FAC-020093-19088
Printed in the United States of America

This book is set in Dante MT Pro/Monotype; Ernest and Emily,
Microbrew Soft Four/Fontspring
Designed by Mary Claire Cruz

Library of Congress Cataloging-in-Publication Data
Names: Moreno, Nina, author.
Title: Don't date Rosa Santos / by Nina Moreno.
Other titles: Do not date Rosa Santos
Description: First edition. • Los Angeles ; New York : Hyperion, 2019. •
Summary: Rosa Santos, a Cuban American, works to save her Florida town,
seeks admittance to study abroad in her homeland, and wonders if love can
break her family's curse.
Identifiers: LCCN 2018030125 (print) • LCCN 2018036360 (ebook) • ISBN
9781368046114 (e-book) • ISBN 9781368039703 (hardcover) • ISBN
9781368040860 (pbk.)
Subjects: • CYAC: Family life—Florida—Fiction. • Cuban Americans—Fiction.
• Blessing and cursing—Fiction. • Magic—Fiction. • Love—Fiction. •
Ocean—Fiction. • Florida—Fiction.
Classification: LCC PZ7.1.M66953 (ebook) • LCC PZ7.1.M66953 Don 2019 (print)
• DDC [Fic]—dc23
LC record available at https://lccn.loc.gov/2018030125

Reinforced binding

Visit www.hyperionteens.com

SUSTAINABLE FORESTRY INITIATIVE   Certified Sourcing
www.sfiprogram.org
SFI-00993

THIS LABEL APPLIES TO TEXT STOCK

For Dad

Imagining you reading this was part of the dream.
But we build new ones. You taught me that.
This story was always yours, and when I see you again
I'll tell you all about it.

1

The Santos women never go to the sea.

Once upon a lifetime ago a pregnant woman escaped Cuba with her husband by climbing into a boat he had built in secret with nothing but scrap and desperate hope. They left an entire life in the dead of night. They were still too late. The storm was sudden and violent, and the baby could not wait. As he fought a raging sea, she screamed into the angry winds and pulled her wailing daughter from her body.

When Milagro Santos reached the other side, it was only with her newborn baby.

My mom grew up in a new land and despite warnings, dared to love a boy who loved the sea. But the day before her eighteenth birthday, a spring storm formed out in open waters and shattered another dream. My father's boat was found but never his body. Mom waited at the dock, her screams etched into the town's memories as she clutched her middle, me growing inside.

That was the sea for us. And I am the bridge meant

to grow big enough to span their tragedies. The lullaby of my life is that to know the sea is to know love, but to love us is to lose everything. We're cursed, they still whisper, but whether it's by an island, the sea, or our own stubborn hearts, I don't know.

❖

"It's now or never." Ana-Maria sat on top of my desk as I paced the floor in front of her. She held up her phone and started the timer. I already wanted to quit this entire exercise in favor of verbally throwing up everything I'd been keeping to myself for months.

"So I think I've picked my college—"

Ana was already shaking her head. "Don't say 'I think.' You picked it. Be assertive or she won't take you seriously."

I bounced my shoulders in an effort to loosen up. My abuela wasn't even in the room, but my pulse was already hammering wildly. "Okay. Here it is, Mimi. I picked my college."

"¡Qué bueno!" Ana trilled in a thick Cuban accent that sounded frighteningly similar to my abuela.

"But it's out of state."

Ana let out a wail of despair. She was really getting into this. "Ay, mi amor, why do you want to leave me?"

I rolled my eyes at her. "It's only two states away. But I picked it because it has a study-abroad program—"

Ana sat up in a dramatic huff. "¿Cómo? A different country? ¡Eso no es college!"

I pinched the top corners of my blouse and pulled the fabric away from my already sweat-dampened skin. "It *is* college. They're actual classes with real credits that count toward my degree. And the program I've applied to . . ." I paused and Ana nodded. I squared my shoulders. "The program is in Cuba."

The College of Charleston accepted my transfer application last week. Right after I got that e-mail I celebrated by silently screaming in my bedroom before applying to their study-abroad program. A whole semester at the University of Havana. I would sit in on lectures taught by Cuban professors. There would be excursions and cultural visits. Old Havana, Viñales, Santiago. My Spanish would get better. I would have my own stories from the island that, for so long, had been an heirloom I couldn't touch.

Of course the program was expensive, but there wasn't time to hesitate. I was running against a clock ruled by politicians. I had financial aid, scholarships, and a shoe box of savings from working at the bodega. An education visa was one of the only ways to legally travel there now, and I didn't have family waiting for me in Cuba, so school was the answer.

At my declaration, Ana gasped and pushed herself off the desk, knocking me aside. She clutched her chest and crashed backward onto the bed, my throw pillows falling over the side. The performance was worthy of a telenovela. I sighed and dropped my hands to my hips. "And I suppose this is where my long-lost sister bursts into the room and tells me she's stealing my inheritance."

"Or better yet, your long-lost mother." It was just a joke, but it hit a nerve like always. If Mom still lived here full-time, maybe I wouldn't be so freaked out about telling Mimi I wanted to live and learn in the country she'd fled. I'd have a buffer for once, since Mom usually made Mimi mad enough to forget everything else.

Ana stood and grabbed me by the shoulders. Ana-Maria was Afro-Latina, and her parents were also from Cuba. Mrs. Peña left the island as a young child, when family in the States had the money and ability to claim her, but Mr. Peña escaped as a teen. Now they were here, together. My best friend was surrounded by cousins and siblings and didn't yearn to understand our island like I did. At least not outwardly. "You're as ready as your anxiety and many family issues will allow you to be," Ana offered with a loving squeeze as she pushed me out the door. "Go get 'em, tiger."

It was Friday evening at the Santos house, so I knew exactly where my abuela would be: sitting at our tiny laundry room window on the east side of our house, between two lemon trees, where neighbors came in search of answers, guidance, and a little bit of magic. The neighborhood curandera oversaw concerns about struggling gardens, bad dreams, career changes, and terrible luck, and she brewed hope from her window that smelled like herbs and dryer sheets.

I found her there now, corking a bottle. On the other side of the window stood our neighbor Dan carrying a baby in his arms. Dan and his husband, Malcolm—my college advisor and dual-enrollment guiding wizard—had recently finalized the adoption of their daughter, Penny. Mimi shook the bottle and studied the liquid against candlelight.

"What's the matter?" I asked Dan, momentarily distracted by the dark circles beneath his eyes. A paramedic currently on paternity leave, Dan handled his sleepless shifts pretty well, but he looked ready to fall over.

"Penny is teething," he said around a yawn. "And Malcolm's still at work, neck deep in appointments and paperwork right now." Malcolm was the most sought-after advisor at Port Coral Community College. He had a calm, thoughtful way about him and looked strikingly like Idris Elba. "But 'tis the season of college app deadlines."

"Why don't you just come inside?" I asked. Dan's family regularly came over for dinner.

"Because Mimi is working, and I won't make her play favorites like Malcolm does with you. Speaking of, didn't you—"

"See him earlier today? Why, yes. Yes, I did." Behind Mimi's back, I shot Dan a wide-eyed look. I'd met with Malcolm to see if we could find any last-minute scholarships for my study-abroad program. Dan was too tired to catch on

5

immediately. I cocked my head toward Mimi meaningfully until his drowsy gaze was finally replaced by a look of surprise. Everyone was shocked I hadn't told Mimi yet. But they didn't understand what it meant to talk to Mimi about Cuba.

"For you," Mimi said, ignoring us, as she handed Dan a tall, skinny blue bottle. "Drink it with tea one hour before bedtime."

"Bedtime?" Dan asked. "We've never heard of her." Penny laughed and kicked her feet.

Mimi grabbed a smaller bottle, its contents a golden-buttery color. She popped the top, and I caught the scent of apple pie. "For Penny and her gums. Pero un momento, I have something else for her, too." Mimi shuffled past me.

Dan held Penny as they waited on the other side of the window. His eyes fluttered closed. Penny grabbed his cheeks with a happy smack.

"I'll be right back," I told them and hurried after Mimi.

"Stir the sopa for me," she called over her shoulder as she moved through the warmly lit kitchen. It was usually only ever the two of us, but the house always made it feel like it was filled with more. More light, more people, more love. I lifted the lid of the pot on the stove and inhaled deeply. The stories about Mimi's soup ranged from bringing people back from the brink of death to healing broken hearts. The secret was in the caldo, which was carefully nurtured with herbs, vegetables, and bones. I stirred the simmering liquid and took another fortifying breath. "Mimi?"

"Aquí," she called from farther in the house.

I replaced the lid and went to stand at the threshold of her garden room on the far side of the kitchen. It was a terrible idea to try to talk to her while she was working, but I wanted to get this over with.

"Where are you?"

"Here!" she called again, but I still didn't see her. The space was technically called a Florida room and was meant for lounging with a cold glass of sweet tea. Mimi turned it into a greenhouse. Breezy and warm even when the windows were closed, it was the beating heart of our home. Lush green plants stretched and swayed in their pots. Well-read books and bottles filled with medicines and potions lined the shelves. There was a wood-and-steel wind chime that was steady when the day was nice, a little wilder with the rain, and as agitated as a scared kid when bad luck was coming. It was our safe, protected garden that sometimes growled like a tropical jungle. We lived in Port Coral, Florida, but this was Mimi's island now.

She popped out from between palm fronds, smiling. In her hands she carried a blue blanket—the color of a cloudless summer sky—that shimmered in the light. I slid my palm across the downy-soft fabric, a feeling of contentment stirring in me. Just like her soups. She headed past me, back to her window. I shook off the sunny feelings and followed.

"Mimi, I picked my college," I confessed as she handed

the baby blanket to Dan. They both looked at me. Dan was grinning.

"Pero you are already in college?"

"Well, yes, but that's dual enrollment." I was starting to sweat again. For the past two years I'd bussed my way between high school, community college, and summer classes. It hadn't been easy, especially with my part-time job at the bodega, but now I was only weeks away from graduating with a high-school diploma *and* a two-year degree. This fall I was transferring from our local community college to a university to finish my bachelor's in Latin American Studies.

"Ah, sí, I know. Okay, tell me." She crossed her arms, the jangle of her many bracelets as familiar as a song. It was how I learned to find her when she disappeared among her plants. My mouth opened, but silence stretched.

Mimi waited. And I couldn't do it.

"If you could go anywhere in the world, where would you go?" I threw the question out with panicked hands. Dan shook his head.

The candles beside Mimi flickered. "Hawaii," she decided.

"Wait, what?" I hadn't expected that. "*Anywhere* in the world, Mimi."

"I heard you." She smirked. "I like the Rock. He is very handsome."

Dan laughed. "Can't argue with that."

"But what if you could go to Cuba?"

Her smile disappeared.

Everything I knew about Cuba came from this coastal town, hundreds of miles from the island that was so unknown to me. I met my culture in the food I ate at our table, the songs that played on my abuela's record player, and the stories that flowed through the bodega and Ana-Maria's lively home. But I couldn't find my family in those stories. I couldn't find me.

"I would not go to Cuba," Mimi said simply, like it was enough. My abuela was patient and kind, but at the mention of her island, she became shuttered. So many people came to her asking for so much, and she gave them all answers and hope. But never me about this.

"Thank you for this," Dan said to Mimi. He paid her for the sleepy tea and teething balm. Penny buried her tiny fists in the blanket. He gave me a reassuring smile before heading home.

Mimi began to clean her table. I could smell the soup and hear the hum of music coming from my room.

"But things have changed," I said. Mimi's face jerked back to me. This was my first time pushing this. My racing heart stubbornly knocked at her closed window. "They've been changing for years."

My freshman year I watched my president step off a plane in Havana. Everyone at the bodega had frozen, watching in disbelief. Even at fourteen, I'd never expected to see the waters between us become crossable again. Soon after that I discovered study-abroad programs in Cuba and threw myself into dual enrollment.

Mimi exhaled sharply. "Ay, things change for you, but never for Cuba's people."

The gulf between Cuba and me deepened. "So even if you could go, you'd never return?"

"My spirit will, mi amor." The regret in her voice haunted me like an old ghost. "They care more about tourists than the Cuban people who still suffer. That is the only thing that never changes." Mimi snapped her window closed. She stepped up to me and raised a gentle hand to my cheek. "Where is your college, niña? Somewhere fancy?"

And that was that. I'd expected this. There was no reason to be surprised or disappointed. No reason to cry. "Never mind. I'm actually still deciding," I said, trying to keep my voice neutral.

"Ay, Rosa." Mimi sighed. "You will make a smart decision soon."

Soup simmered, wind chimes sang softly, and candles lit the way back to my room. I was home, and talking about Cuba had no place here. Mimi was never returning, my mother was always leaving, and I was a flightless bird left at her harbor, searching for answers that were buried at the bottom of a sea I could not know.

2

I opened my bedroom door, and Ana looked up from her phone. Her hopeful smile fell away at my expression. "How'd it go, champ?"

I fell into my desk chair, defeated.

"You gotta tell her soon. You might lose your spot if you don't secure it by May first."

I needed to do a lot of things. I clicked my pen and flipped through my journal. My goals were nicely packaged here. Sketched vines grew between calendar dates and bloomed into flowers. This notebook of doodles and tasks held all my plans that now felt like secrets.

My laptop whistled with a new e-mail. It was just two words—*Love you*—and a link to a photo album. I glanced over my mother's pictures this week. A cactus in the desert. A sketch of a daydreaming waitress on a diner napkin. A half-finished painting leaning against a brick wall. Next week, I'd likely get pictures showing the progress of that painting and glimpses of wherever my mom went next. I wondered if she would make it back to Port Coral before summer.

Ana's phone rang. "What's up, Mom?" She listened to whatever Mrs. Peña said before sitting up in a huff. "But why do I have to go? . . . Okay, okay, fine . . . I'll tell them. . . . Mom, I said okay! . . . I did not raise my voice. . . . I love you, too." She clicked off and rolled her eyes at me. "Emergency town meeting tonight."

We had meetings once a month, and the last one was only two weeks ago. "What happened?"

"She didn't say, but knowing this town, Simon changed the music at his diner without asking the viejitos. And my mom calls *me* dramatic."

I got to my feet and checked my reflection in the mirror above my side table and tiny altar. A couple of pastel candles and fresh flowers sat beside a faded sepia picture of my grandfather and the single Polaroid I had of my father. I reapplied my lipstick and popped a strawberry candy in my mouth.

Ana rolled off my bed and followed me out of my room. "Tell Mimi about college in Havana now. She won't yell at you in front of people."

I stopped in the hallway, and Ana stumbled into my back. "What? No way. That's not the plan." Mimi wasn't a yeller anyway. She grew quiet and closed off when she was upset. Her silence was lethal, and I was desperately trying to avoid it.

"Ah, sweet baby Rosa." It was a lifelong nickname. I hated it.

In the kitchen, we told Mimi about the emergency meeting and helped her pack up the soup, which she insisted on bringing. She hauled the pot from the stove to the table, then rubbed her back where it always seemed to bother her as we grabbed the containers and began filling them. Mimi was always healing others, but it was impossible to get her to visit her own doctor regularly. I didn't know if this was an old-folks thing or just a Cuban one, because the viejitos also acted like a person could live forever on coffee, rum, and cigars.

When all the containers were packed, Mimi slid a quick, disapproving glance over my outfit. "Nos vamos. But first, get out of your pajamas."

I grabbed a bag of soups. "These are not my pajamas. It's a romper." I headed past her and out the door, knowing she would follow, bearing potions and opinions like always.

"¿Qué es un romper?" Mimi asked Ana, who laughed.

The town square was only two blocks away, and the April evening was a warm gold as the sun dipped low in the sky. Flowering trees lined sidewalks, and shop doors sang greetings with friendly bells. We headed toward the library's meeting room.

Mimi handed out her soups inside while Ana and I took our seats beside her mother. Mrs. Peña was on break, her apron across her lap and pens still stuck in her curls. We all still called it the bodega, but el Mercado, once a neighbor-hood quick stop for lotto, snacks, and coffee, had expanded into the bigger grocery and deli restaurant it was now, thanks to Mr. Peña's food. He was an amazing cook but hated talking to people, so it was always his wife at these meetings and deli counter.

"Don't forget to put your drums in the van. You have jazz band tomorrow," Mrs. Peña told her daughter as she handed us a bag of chips to share.

Ana sank into her seat. "God, don't say that so loud."

"What's the matter with jazz band?" I asked as I did jazz hands.

Ana nearly growled. "I'm tired of wearing sequins and playing congas." What Ana was tired of was school band. Her father was an amazing trumpet player—from what I'd heard—who never played anymore, but her family gave her a hard time whenever her drumming took her off their idea of an established path. To them, band equaled scholarships, which equaled college, which equaled a degree that wasn't in music.

A bigger crowd than usual milled into the room for the meeting. A row over, Malcolm and Dan grabbed two seats. Penny was bouncing happily on Malcolm's lap, looking nowhere near interested in a bedtime. Dan's head dropped onto his husband's shoulder. I knew a power nap when I saw one. Ana and I shared the chips while everyone said quick hellos and got settled. The four viejitos sat in the front row like always. They were the old Latinos of the neighborhood who mostly hung outside of the bodega drinking coffee, playing dominos, and gossiping. They considered it their duty to be at every meeting for their blog and had recently started an Instagram account, which meant their new response to everything was, *Check our story.* I recognized every face as the room filled—until I didn't. My next chip stopped halfway to my mouth.

"Who is that?" I whispered to Ana. She sat up a little and checked out the boy who had just sat down ahead of us. I stared at the backs of his two very tattooed arms. "I don't know," she admitted. We knew most everyone by their name or relative, so it was a surprise that neither of us recognized him. He ducked his head to listen to the woman beside him. "He's sitting beside Mrs. Aquino, though, so maybe he works for her." The Aquino family ran the marina. I had never been there, of course, but I knew her from these meetings. I wondered if Tattoo Guy was new to town as I studied the blue, nearly luminescent waves that swelled from his wrists and up his forearms, before disappearing beneath the short sleeve of his shirt that pulled tight around his bicep. I leaned forward to get a better look.

And jerked right back when Mimi stepped into my line of sight.

She slid into the seat beside me and reached over to brush my hair out of my face. I gently batted her hand away, but she just switched to fussing with my clothes. "Look at

15

how short these are. I can see everything." She tsked with disapproval and whispered in Spanish, "I don't understand this romper business."

I tugged at my shorts. "You're making me all tiki-tiki." It was the sound of frazzled nerves and Cuban for *You're stressing me out.*

Simon Yang, our mayor, stepped up to the front of the room. He wore the beach-bum version of office casual: a white button-up with the sleeves rolled and khaki shorts. In addition to his mayoral duties, he ran a breakfast place on the boardwalk. His service dog, Shepard, sat by him.

"What's the big news?" Gladys asked, sounding annoyed. "My league meets in fifteen minutes." Her gray hair was a frizzy mess, and her red-and-yellow bowling shirt read NO GUTTER GLADYS on the back. She was retired but wouldn't tell anyone from what.

Simon sighed. "Unfortunately, we have to cancel Spring Fest."

The room fell quiet. Beside me, Ana sat up from her slouch. Spring Fest was less than two weeks away. It started as a way for local fishermen and nearby citrus groves to share harvests, but had expanded into a sort of homecoming for the town that included food, music, and even fireworks over the harbor. This year's was especially important because two of our neighbors were getting married.

The viejitos hurried to take out their phones.

"Canceled? Why?" Mr. Gomez demanded.

Jonas Moon got to his feet. "Because of the harbor." Jonas was a soft-spoken fisherman with curly red hair. He was engaged to Clara from the bookshop on the board-walk; theirs was the upcoming wedding. "We're getting bought out."

At this revelation, the room exploded with noise.

Tattoo Guy moved to stand beside Jonas at the front of the room. As he turned to face us, I caught sight of his short dark beard and watchful brown eyes. He looked standoffish with his colorful arms crossed.

Ana ducked her head and whispered, "Oh my god, that's Alex."

I leaned in. "Who's Alex?"

"Mr. Tall, Dark, and Mad. That's Alex Aquino!" She gaped at me, waiting for me to confirm the apparently unbe lievable news.

"I don't know who that is," I confessed.

"He was a year or two ahead of us. I had an art class with him and he never spoke. He was so lanky, I swear he just disappeared sometimes. Kind of awkward."

I shook my head, unable to connect the name, let alone her description, to the stranger with the huge, brightly painted arms currently standing in front of us.

"I heard he left town after he graduated, but I guess he's back."

"Well, he looks mad about it," I said, my voice small.

Jonas raised his hands for quiet. "A developer made an

offer. They plan to turn the area into a mixed-use district. Condos will go up, and the marina will most likely become a private one for residents."

"And you're just gonna roll over and let that happen?" Gladys demanded.

"No, ma'am. We were working with Simon on applying for grants to protect the surrounding land from sale. Right up the coast, the university has helped smaller fishing towns with new methods of aquaculture, mostly clams, and they see the potential to certify us as a new conservation district. It would halt the sale."

"Sounds smart," Mr. Gomez said.

"Unfortunately, the university just cut funding for further outreach."

Jonas's crestfallen look reminded me of how it felt when I first saw the price for my study-abroad program. I sat up. "What would the university program do, exactly?"

Alex's gaze shot to me before skipping away. Jonas explained, "They bring in teams of students and teachers to cultivate clam farms and retrain our fishermen to work them. Convert boats and open hatcheries. It creates a new, steady, and sustainable line of work." Jonas gestured to Alex. A slight frown tugged his dark brows lower. "Alex has been restoring oyster reefs out in the Gulf and knows some of these folks, so he's been helping us with the application process. But we got word today about the cut to funding, and without the project, we can't stop this sale in time."

Simon stood off to the side. With his hands in his pockets, he shrugged. "And without the harbor, there's no festival."

"Without the harbor, there's no Port Coral," Clara said, voicing all of our fears. She was a British Nigerian woman with a cardigan collection I envied. Clara's soft, broken tone reminded me what losing the festival meant this year. Our weekend of flowering trees, feasts, and music to celebrate the season had all the makings for a whimsical spring wedding, so when Jonas had proposed, we all knew their Spring Fest nuptials would be perfect. Her mother, who lived in Nigeria, had even gotten a visa and plane ticket.

"But your wedding!" I said.

"There will be other days," Clara said, shoring herself up. Jonas twisted his hands.

"Maybe even other marriages," Gladys offered. "Get a hobby instead." She patted the bowling bag beside her. "Marriage is for the birds."

People broke off into smaller, resigned conversations. Jonas and Alex turned away to talk to a dejected Simon. Mrs. Peña sighed, like she could already see a CLOSED sign on the bodega.

I shot to my feet. "No!"

"What are you doing?" Ana asked, startled.

"Give me a second," I said, my mind racing.

Jonas watched me with a curious expression. Alex's sharp glance was dark and irritated. He looked impatient for this meeting to end. Standing in front of his imposing glare made my stomach spike with nerves, even as I straightened my shoulders. I had recently watched a video about power poses.

"A grant, right? That's what all of this hinges on? If we fund the project, then we're square and it crosses that problem off the list."

"What list?" Jonas asked.

"There's always a list. How much money was the grant for?"

Jonas rubbed his brow. "The one to establish the project here was for twenty thousand."

Gladys whistled. Twenty thousand wasn't shoe box money. But I was a scholarship kid with her eyes on a study-abroad program that cost nearly as much. It was time to get creative.

"We need a big idea, fast, because we can't raise that much among ourselves in this time frame. We need to bring the money in from others."

Mr. Gomez held his phone up and pointed it at me.

"How do we do that?" Jonas asked.

I caught sight of Clara. "We have Spring Fest anyway," I declared with sudden certainty. The idea was forming too fast in my head.

"You don't have enough time."

I glanced at Alex, surprised to hear his input. His very gruff, negative input. It was disconcerting coming from someone so aggressively tall. I stubbornly stayed put even as Ana tugged on my romper. "We have enough to try."

"To try to have a party?" His tone was serious, not teasing.

My eyes narrowed as a hot, embarrassed flush burned up my neck. "It wouldn't be *just* a party. It could be a community fund-raiser, big enough to possibly raise that amount of money." Everyone was used to my big ideas—even coddled them when I was younger and would nose my way into conversations, asking too many questions. They were not used to seeing someone so unimpressed by them. Or maybe I wasn't. But I couldn't let this go.

Ana tugged on my clothes again, whispering, "You can, like, not do this, you know."

I glanced at Mimi. This was about all the layers of home to me. People and politics had broken my abuela's heart. We couldn't lose Port Coral.

"Unfortunately, the marina can't afford to sponsor the festival with all of this going on," Mrs. Aquino spoke up. Alex's hard gaze softened.

Mrs. Peña stood. "El Mercado will sponsor the festival this year."

"*What?*" Ana demanded.

Relief flooded me so fast I had to grab the seat in front of me.

"Rosa is right. We can do this. My husband makes the best Cuban sandwiches and croquetas this side of Miami.

We'll advertise the festival and what we're trying to do, and then we sell those tourists some lechón asado that will have them throwing money at us. We play some salsa, serve some mojitos, and bada bing, bada boom, we save our town."

"¿Bada qué?" Mr. Gomez asked.

"I love it." Xiomara, the owner of the dance school, shot to her feet. "I can do the show for free and give away lessons. Between all of our businesses, we have something to offer."

"And we won't have to cancel your wedding," I said to Clara and Jonas. They didn't look convinced, but I locked onto the hope shining in both their gazes. "We can still totally do this, and your mom will be here, and it will be just as romantic as you hoped."

"But how?" Clara wondered. "We already canceled everything, and if we turn the festival into a fund-raiser, Jonas has to work on convincing the university of our success. A wedding doesn't fit into all of that."

"It will. I'll make sure of it." They shared doubtful looks. I refused to glance at Surly Oyster Reef Alex. "I can do this. I'm super organized and all my classes are online this semester. Let me show you my bullet journal. The layouts alone will show you what I'm about."

"Please don't," Ana said.

"I say it's for the birds," Gladys grumbled.

Clara grinned and playfully bumped her shoulder into Jonas's side. "I'm still in if you are."

He kissed her hand. "Always."

Something passed between them before they turned to me with hearts in their eyes. "Let's do this."

I grinned at Ana, who was shaking her head. "Do you have any idea what you're doing?" she asked.

"Of course not," I said. "But that's never stopped me before."

3

The next morning, I sat outside the bodega to eat breakfast with the viejitos. My final semester was all online, allowing me to pick up extra shifts at the bodega, but it was weird to not *go* to school every day. I ate my pan tostado and café con leche as the four old men bickered over last night's spring training baseball game. Within seconds, I'd finished the warm slice of bread smothered in sweet butter.

Mr. Saavedra took one look at my face before reaching into his shirt pocket and offering me antacids. I downed the rest of my cooling coffee and popped one. Mr. Gomez, Mr. Saavedra, Mr. Restrepo, and Mr. Alvarez always wore pressed slacks, button-up shirts, and smelled of sharp aftershave and cigars. Together they were an entire town's abuelo.

"We need to start getting word out there about the festival and fund-raiser," I told them.

"Claro," Mr. Saavedra said. "We already posted about it." He handed me his phone and I checked their most recent post. It was a picture of the marina with the caption *Spring Fest, dale!*

"Dale?" I asked.

"People like Pitbull," Mr. Gomez said and tapped his temple. "You gotta be smart about advertising, Rosa."

"I like it. I have some ideas to share with Mrs. Peña, too."

Mr. Gomez harrumphed. "You're too busy for this. You worry about college."

"Trust me, I've got worrying about that under control."

"Not like that Aquino boy." Mr. Restrepo sucked his teeth with disapproval. "He comes back with all those tattoos? Qué oso. It's always the quiet ones."

"Yeah, what's his deal?" I leaned closer. The only time Alex had spoken up of his own accord at the town meeting had been to criticize my awesome idea.

Mr. Saavedra shot me a sharp look. I knew that look. It was the one I got every time I escaped the kids' table to interrupt grown folks. "Don't worry about him. You worry about college." Then he added, "And no tattoos."

"College, college." I got to my feet. "Ay, forget it."

"Have you picked a university?" Mr. Gomez asked me, not for the first time. Only a handful of people knew about Charleston, but I definitely needed to tell Mimi before I told the viejitos.

"Not yet," I lied. "And stop posting about it."

They returned to their game of dominos. I headed around to the back where the big gates were rolled up.

25

Inside, Ana's cousin Junior was unloading a delivery. "Hey, valedictorian," he called as I walked past.

"I'm not valedictorian," I returned. Lamont Morris beat me out for the title. He'd also done dual enrollment and was transferring to Duke in the fall.

"Okay, nerd." Junior was a few years older than me and managed stock. He used to sell weed, but now he was focused on getting his mix tape to go viral.

The back room of the bodega was a big space where they handled deliveries on one side, and set up tables and chairs on the other. It was more than a break room, it was the second living room where the Peña kids all grew up while their parents worked long hours. There was a handwoven throw rug, a TV that still depended on an antenna, and a small painting of the store on the corkboard among the schedules and Mrs. Peña's many reminders. The painting was a long-ago gift from Mom.

I dropped my backpack on the table beside Benny. His leg was stretched out on the chair in front of him with an ice pack on his knee. Ana's brother was a star soccer player, a year younger than us, and really popular at school. His injury meant that not only was soccer on hold, but so was his social life. He'd been bumming around with us a lot more lately.

"Thanks to you, I'm now an errand boy." He shot me a look of disgust as he held up a to-do list.

"Your mom is the one who nominated the bodega." I sat and unzipped my backpack.

"After *your* dramatic monologue. I saw Mr. Gomez's Insta. Now Mom says we're going to Cuban the whole thing up. Oil a pig and make a contest of catching it before roasting it."

My smile disappeared. "What?"

He shrugged. "That's what my tío says they had to do before they were allowed to marry a girl in their village."

I slipped out my notebook, only half wondering if that was true.

"But, listen, I had a better idea. We should search for the Golden Turtle."

"Oh my god, this again?" The viejitos had posted an old picture of the lost artifact for throwback Thursday, and Benny became obsessed. According to local legend, the Golden Turtle had first been discovered in a sunken pirate ship by a bunch of teenagers who, instead of handing it over to their parents, or I don't know, a museum, hid the small statue of a turtle for their friends to find. A tradition was born, and every outgoing senior class hid it for the next one until it was lost forever about two decades ago.

"It's still out there, so why not try to find it?" he asked, sounding earnest and determined, and not at all like the usually carefree Benny.

I slid his to-do list closer to him. "Because we're all busy. You have to do all of that, and I've got to finish one more scholarship application, write a paper for my humanities class, and help plan a small wedding."

"What happened to Rosa the dreamer?"

I tapped my journal. "She's in here."

Junior walked over to us, sighing louder with every pen and piece of paper I pulled out of my bag. "How many times I gotta tell you all those book smarts don't help in the real world?" he said. "You need some life skills, little sis. How to make real deals. You need some street smarts."

Benny laughed. "The hell do you know about any streets?"

"I'm from Miami. Three-oh-five till I die."

"You were born in Palm Bay, bro."

The door to the inside of the store flew open, and Ana exploded into the break room. She pointed her drumstick in Benny's face. "You have to give me a ride to jazz band. Mom's busy now, thanks to Rosa."

I clicked my pen. "If you mean thanks to Rosa for saving the day, you're welcome."

"I got things to do today," Benny said with a resentful wave of his list. "I don't have time to take you to go bang on your shitty drums."

"Hey!" Ana's stick flew back up. "Those drums cost more than your shitty car." Ana was a year older, but her brother was the one with the car, since she'd spent her savings on a drum set instead. Her parents were still pissed about that.

"Watch your mouths, coño!" Mrs. Peña demanded as she entered the break room, her phone up to her ear. She was frazzled, but she always operated that way. She shared

28

my affinity for organization and vintage tropical aesthetics, and she ran the bodega like someone who knew all about making real deals. In her hands, this could work. God, I hoped it would work. It was starting to feel like everything hinged on this one weekend.

"Mrs. Peña, I wrote up some ideas last night—"

Junior interrupted. "Your head is gonna get as big as that nerdy book bag you carry everywhere, Rosa."

I scowled at him. I loved my backpack. When I grew up I wanted to *be* my backpack. It was sturdy, with a colorful, busy fabric. Mimi had sewn it before I started high school, enchanting it with powerful words so it would always carry whatever I needed and never get lost.

"Don't be a dick, Junior," Ana said. She only let her family tease me up to a point.

Mrs. Peña pulled her phone away from her ear. "¡Oye! I have ears! ¡Carajo!"

"Ma," Ana deadpanned. "Everyone here speaks Spanish. We know you curse as much as us, if not worse."

Her mother ignored her and looked at Benny. "Please take your sister to jazz band."

Benny sighed loudly and made a big show of getting to his feet, but he kissed his mom's head on his way out the door. "Let's go, bongo girl."

"I'm gonna kill him," Ana said as she followed.

Mrs. Peña sat down and continued talking on the phone. She quickly scribbled something down on her clipboard. I pushed my notebook closer to her. In a break in the conversation, she looked at me, and said, "I'm on hold. Go ahead."

I hurried to say, "I listed all the businesses on the square and the neighboring ones between it and the harbor—"

Mrs. Peña smacked her forehead. "I forgot! I have a bread delivery I'm supposed to make. I was going to ask one of the kids."

"I can do it!" I offered and jumped to my feet. They never let me do deliveries, and I needed in on the tips. Benny had flashed some serious dollars last week before blowing it all on a video game.

"Are you sure?" Mrs. Peña asked me.

"Totally. You look at those lists and tell me everything you think when I get back. Don't worry, I got this." I swept out of the room before she could change her mind.

In the kitchen, Mr. Peña sliced pork, preparing for the upcoming lunch hour. Garlic, peppers, onions, and bacon hissed together in the big pot that would soon hold arroz congrí, according to the menu board.

"Good morning, sir. How are you?" I stepped up close beside Mr. Peña. Ana's dad wasn't a talker. The deli was his kingdom and his food the gift he bestowed on the rest of us—as long as we didn't bother him.

"Rosa?" he asked, looking past me to see if anyone else was coming.

"Yes, me. I'm on delivery duty today." I saluted him, my eyes closing at the smell of roasted pork. "Sorry, I can't think past the smell of the lechón. Whenever Mimi cooks it, I become this hungry, growling zombie and—"

"Rosa," he interrupted, and his knife came to a quick stop. My waving, storytelling hands stopped, too. Mimi teased that they were the most Cuban thing about me. "Take that bread to the marina's restaurant. Please go now."

My dreams of making it rain instantly dried up.

I'd never been to the marina. No one in my family had been in years. I never went farther than the bookshop, and that was the second business on the boardwalk. But even then I always stuck to the right side, away from the railing on the left and the beach beyond it. When I was ten, my friend Mike jumped from it and broke his ankle. I'd cried harder than him.

Mr. Peña looked at me, waiting. He was probably the one person in town who wouldn't stop to consider old stories and superstitions, because he was too busy. He gestured to the pile of freshly baked loaves tucked into their paper sleeves. How was I going to help save the harbor if I was too scared to go there? It wasn't like I planned on jumping off the boardwalk. I could do this. I had to do this if I wanted out of the kids' table. I scooped the bread into my arms, pressed my nose to the bouquet, and inhaled deeply. A happy sigh floated from me. I could do this. It was just a delivery.

Mr. Peña cleared his throat.

"I'm going." I shuffled around him, arms full of my bounty, and headed out the back door.

"You know how to ride the bike, right?" Doubt crept into his voice.

"Of course I do," I called just before the door closed behind me.

Of course I didn't know how to ride the delivery bike, because no one ever let me do deliveries, but that wasn't going to stop me now. The giant basket in the back was a concern, but I dropped the bread into it, dusted my hands, and surveyed the dragon I was going to slay.

"Listen, we can do this." I pointed east to the sea. "You help me, I don't crash you. Teamwork."

"Who are you talking to?" Junior came around the corner, startling me.

I glanced around for an excuse, but I was alone and my phone was back in my bag. "Myself." That didn't make me sound any better. "Mostly the bicycle. A pep talk before I ride it."

His brows shot up, and he stopped chewing on the toothpick between his teeth. "You're doing the delivery?"

"I know how to ride a bike," I argued.

"Not what I asked, but I gotta say, Rosa, your defensiveness worries me."

"Just get out of here. And don't tell your uncle I was talking to the bike."

I climbed onto the seat and carefully situated my skirt around me. Not the best outfit for today's venture, but with enough care no one would see anything good. Mike rode a skateboard, and after watching him, I became so fascinated he built me a longboard for my fifteenth birthday. I covered it in college and bookish stickers and used it to get around town most days, so a bike shouldn't be any different.

With a murmured prayer, I kicked off the curb and set off.

"Whoa." The handlebars grew wild in my hands. "Do not. Do *not*." The wheels dipped into a curve in the road, my stomach falling from the near fall. "What did I *just* tell you?" I pleaded. After a few shaky readjustments, the wind, wheels, and I aligned. Finding my balance was exhilarating. I cycled past the post office and library, and wished for a friendly little bell to announce my victory. Or better, a guttural air horn, because I'd just become queen of a freaking dragon.

It got dicey again over the cobblestones. This part of downtown was not as cute on a bicycle with this much junk in its trunk. At the boardwalk, people watched me heading their way with growing concern. Frankie stopped sweeping the barbershop's entryway. Simon looked up from his paper. His dog, Shepard, watched me stoically. Clara dropped the books she was organizing in the small cart outside her bookshop.

I couldn't let go of the handlebars to wave and coolly reassure them, so instead, I shouted, "I'm good! This is fine!" When I reached the last of the wooden planks, where the boardwalk ended at the marina, I slammed on the brakes and jumped off, grateful to be alive.

I bent at the waist and let out a heavy breath. "I did it. Victory is mine."

"What?"

I straightened. An older man in brown rain boots and a green vest decorated with fishing hooks stopped in front of me, wearing a look of concern. "You okay, miss?"

I tried to catch my breath. "I brought bread."

"That's . . . nice."

"Not for me." I squeezed the pinch in my side. "Not actually sure who it's for. I don't ever do deliveries and they didn't give me specifics beyond 'Take this to the marina,' when I've never even been to the end of the boardwalk." I glanced toward the bookshop, trying to estimate the exact distance. The man was still standing in front of me. "There's a restaurant here, right?"

"The Starfish." His eyes narrowed slightly as he searched my face. His frown deepened. "You're Liliana's girl." He didn't say it nicely. I sighed. This was partly why I didn't come here. Still, I didn't expect to get heat from the first person I saw.

"Rosa Santos," I said, because I had a name. He backed up a step. One hand went to the stair's handrail while the other jerked up in a gesture I didn't recognize. He turned away and took off toward the docks. "Rude," I muttered, then flinched when a bird cried out above me. I tracked its path before it disappeared into the gray sky. My gaze fell to the horizon, and the world quieted as I faced the sea.

It wasn't that I'd never seen it before. It was always there, somewhere in the distance doing its thing. But after finally making it to the end of the boardwalk and the marina where my dad once worked, it was like finding the heartbeat of Port Coral. The lifeblood of our palm trees, sandy sidewalks, and sun-bleached houses. The start of every breeze that rustled Mimi's lemon trees.

To my right was a two-story building that looked like an overgrown shack painted in varying shades of blue. The wide wraparound porch confidently stood above the water on stilts. A few smaller buildings continued past it, safe on the harbor's shore. Rows of boats waited out in the water. People walked along the docks without fear. I watched from my perch on the edge of the boardwalk, above sea level. Beside me, stairs led down to the hustle and bustle, but I was locked in place.

There was a reason this was my first time here. The last time my family stood on those docks, my teenage mother was pregnant with me, screaming at the sea for stealing her love. My father didn't have a tombstone. Only the tiny altar I'd created in my room.

I gripped the railing in front of me. Santos women never went to the sea. But we were also stubborn. Mimi avoided the ocean, never returning to the waters she once loved, yet she settled in a sleepy coastal town, because perhaps my abuela couldn't bear to stray too far from her lost husband or island. Mom was always leaving this town, yet she painted snapshots of it everywhere she went. And now here I stood, stuck.

A strong gust of air swept over me, sending strands of hair into my face. I couldn't do this. If I went down there, people would notice me like that fisherman had. I would stir old painful stories that would get back to Mimi. I needed people to take me seriously and I needed to tell Mimi about my study-abroad plans, and this was not the way to do that. I spun around to leave and slammed into a solid wall.

Unfortunately, the wall was a person.

4

"**I'm so sorry!**" I didn't mean to shout in Alex's face or grab his shirt, but unfortunately I did both. The memory of Mike's broken ankle flashed through my mind. I tightened my grip, and Alex's dark brows inched up a little. Forget broken bones, this embarrassment was going to kill me.

Alex looked concerned, but he said nothing. He held a small plant in one hand, my upper arm in the other. The unexpectedness of the potted plant struck me. Mint? He let go of me, and I released his shirt. "It's my first time coming here," I explained. Above us, seagulls cawed again, startling me. "That wasn't a call to attack, right?"

He checked the sky.

Another horn blared. A bell rang and someone down on the docks called out about the fresh catch. The sharp lines of Alex's face, shadowed by the beard, were distracting. His thumb and forefinger idly rubbed one of the mint leaves. The green scent reached me, and I leaned closer before I could stop myself.

Alex looked down at me. "Why are you here?" he asked with that same rough edge in his voice as last night. Hearing it bothered me more than the rude old fisherman.

"It's not like I can't come here," I said.

"I didn't mean—" He stopped and tried again. "You graduate next month, right?"

Before I could ask him how he knew that, I remembered *everyone* knew that. I wondered if he followed the viejitos' blogs, too.

"Yes," I said, and a miracle happened: He didn't ask me where I was going. The cool sea breeze moved between us, making the tiny sprigs of his mint plant flutter in his hand.

Not being asked where I was going was so novel and refreshing that I couldn't help but blurt, "I'm going to Havana." It was exhilarating to say it so definitively, and almost worth the panic my bold confession induced in me. "For a semester of study abroad," I hurried to add.

Alex appeared mildly impressed.

"I technically haven't— Oh my god, the bread!" I yelped and rushed back to the bike where the loaves were still thankfully in the basket. I hugged them to my chest. Alex still stood by the stairs. "Do you know who gets bread delivered here?"

He pointed at the open door a few feet away. "The Starfish. Ask for Maria."

It *would* be right behind me. "Sorry again for barreling into you. Maybe I'll see you at tomorrow night's meeting."

"There's another meeting?"

He sounded so aggrieved, I grinned. "Of course there is. Welcome back." I headed inside the building with my bread.

The restaurant was painted in soft, washed-out blues, and the tables were made of distressed wood. A chalkboard menu advertised the day's fresh catch, and the wide windows were open to the salty, cool air. Behind the bar stood a short dark woman with an easy smile for the patron seated in front of her. When she noticed me, though, her smile froze. Mrs. Aquino. We'd never spoken beyond quick hellos.

"I believe this is for you," I said and handed the bread over. She ripped me off a receipt, while not-so-subtly studying me. I sighed. "Yes, I'm at the marina. Big news. It'll be the viejitos' top story, I'm sure."

Her laugh was sudden and pleased. "You're as sarcastic as your dad."

The simple acknowledgment knocked me off my axis. It was offered easily, like maybe my dad still existed here. When I was younger, and it was just Mom and me, living miles from Port Coral, Mom spoke about my father easily, too. Ricky Garcia was a foster kid who loved comics and fishing, and was short like me. But the older I got, the less Mom told me. Stories didn't roll off her tongue but were instead carefully bargained from a collection she safeguarded.

I wanted to ask this woman about him but couldn't find my voice.

39

"He was a good guy. You look like him." Mrs. Aquino now looked lost for words, too. She handed me two bakery boxes. "Pastelitos for the bread. Let Mrs. Peña know our baker is happy to make plenty for the festival."

I took the boxes and was almost to the door when I stopped and turned back. "My . . . father, he had a boat slip, right?" I knew he'd worked and kept his small boat here.

Mrs. Aquino nodded. "The last one on C dock. It's still his." My surprise must have been obvious, because she smiled. "Sailors are a superstitious lot."

I knew a thing or two about that.

Outside, the harbor continued to move with life and energy. I spotted Alex on a boat where he carried a rope, and I wondered what he did with his mint plant. He dropped the rope on top of a box, and when he looked up again, he glanced my way. I realized I hadn't told him not to tell anyone about Havana. The gray sky rumbled and the first drops of rain fell. I scurried to my bike and raced the rain all the way to work.

Back at the bodega, I grabbed my apron and headed to the registers, disappointed that Ana was at jazz band. Paula, another one of Ana's cousins, was at the other register.

"What's up, nerd?" she said with a friendly grin. Paula was twenty and only worked here part-time while going to school to become a veterinarian. She treated me like a little sister but didn't baby me, so I mostly didn't mind it from her. "Where have you been?"

"I was running a delivery." I considered texting Ana, but she was probably in the midst of kicking over a conga.

Paula had the radio turned low on a reggaeton song. She unwrapped one of the tamarind lollipops and popped it into her mouth. Her short curls bounced a little as she considered me. "Where was the delivery?"

"The marina," I answered without thinking.

Paula's smile grew. She slipped the candy from her mouth and pointed at me with it. "*You* were at the *harbor*?" It sounded like an accusation.

"And it didn't sink into the Gulf. I can't believe it either. Do you know the Aquino family?" Ana had said they were older than us.

She shrugged. "I went to school with Emily. I heard she works for some big resort now. And I know Alex came home." She smirked at whatever she saw on my face. I crossed and uncrossed my arms before retying my apron. "Wow. So Rosa was trolling the docks for dudes. Never thought I'd see the day."

Frankie stepped up to the register with a basket. His short hair was bright purple this week. "See what day?"

"Rosa asking about guys," she told him.

I rolled my eyes. "I didn't ask about guys."

Paula scanned the steaks and cereals, and Frankie turned to look at me. "What guy?"

"Oh my god, there's no guy," I said. "Also, I'm not ten anymore. I *could* talk to a guy." It was true that I didn't date.

I didn't have the time. There had been kisses at parties and group movie things, but nothing to write home about.

"Does Mimi know about this?"

"Of course she doesn't," Paula said. "Rosa met him at the *harbor*." She said it like a dirty secret, and Frankie looked shocked.

"I saw you on that bike. I thought you had a delivery, not a date."

I leaned over my register and looked toward the store aisles, desperately calling out, "Is anyone ready to check out?"

"Don't listen to us," Paula said, laughing. "Date whomever you want."

Frankie half-heartedly nodded. I could tell it totally pained him to agree. "Just, to be safe, maybe not boys with boats."

Sometimes it felt like the idea of being cursed was all in my head. Like it was a fabled warning to remind me to work hard and focus on my goals. The women before me had lost too much for me to be anything but firmly focused on the future. I was meant to achieve and make all of the loss, heartache, and sacrifices mean something.

But the curse looked back at me from their worried gazes. It turned an entire town into an anxious parent who feared I might fall into the water at any moment. Even the idea of me being near the sea frightened old fishermen and stressed my friends. Maybe going to the sea tempted something older and wilder than me. Something that collected bones like seashells and birthed hurricanes. I was bound to find my own heartache out there, too, like my mother and abuela before me.

And yet, after being there, I was filled with an edgy sort of wonder. I knew where my father had last set off from. No one ever talked about him without pain, but out there he was remembered fondly. I envied their ease with ghosts.

It was still raining when my shift ended. The wind picked up as I got closer to home. I grabbed my board and ran the last block, a crash of lightning startling a yelp from me just before I reached the front steps.

When I looked up, my mother was waiting for me by the door.

5

My mother was here, but she wasn't home. She didn't have one. She might have given birth to me in the small hospital on the other side of town, and once upon a time she might have sung me to sleep in the rocking chair on the front porch with songs of magical seashells, but this wasn't home to her. I never doubted she loved us, but whether she was a cursed mermaid or a falling star we couldn't keep, I didn't know.

"Hey, you," she said, waiting beneath the glow of the porch light.

I nodded my acknowledgment and headed past, unlocking the door with my key. She didn't carry one anymore. She didn't call either. Phones always dropped her calls home. She and the house were like warring siblings, and it always knew when she returned, because it stopped working. Food burned, candles wouldn't stay lit, and worst of all, my laptop always struggled to find the Wi-Fi signal. Mom coming home was as troublesome as Mercury going retrograde.

"I finished that mural in Arizona. They wanted these awful sunflowers in their dining room, so awful sunflowers is what they got." She shook the rain from her yellow coat in the entryway as I continued inside, turning on lights as I went. She gathered her long dark hair into a topknot. "When did you cut your hair?" she asked me, curious.

I dropped my bag on the kitchen table and exhaled sharply. "I didn't."

She slipped her bag off her shoulder and onto the couch. "Oh," she said, her voice small.

Yeah, *oh.* I opened my laptop and clicked my mouse pad. I needed the internet for class and as a portal out of this kitchen. And yet, at the same time, I wanted to be here. I wanted it to be as simple as throwing my arms around my mother and burrowing into the smell of violets and sunshine. She would ask me a hundred questions about my day and listen to every single wandering answer with rapt attention. Because that was my mother.

I had spent the first seven years of my life following her in her search for home. We tried cities and mountains, but always avoided the sea. I missed Port Coral every time we left after a short trip to visit Mimi. Mom finally decided we could stay here for good after I turned seven. We shared a room like always. She walked me to my first day of third grade.

She was gone by middle school.

Her visits were once as steady as the tides. But the older

I got, the less the calendar and moon were able to track her. A storm on the horizon, my mother on the front porch. She always knocked, and I hated that. She returned, bursting with affection and stories, bringing gifts that grew up with me as she explained birth control or helped me buy a bigger bra, before disappearing yet again.

Love and mothers weren't simple. So I stayed at the kitchen table while Mom lingered in the other room.

The door opened and Mimi strolled inside. She didn't appear to be surprised by Mom's arrival. Maybe the rain had clued her in. Perhaps she could tell the difference between typical precipitation and the foreshadowing kind, in the same way her wind chimes knew the difference between a strong breeze and looming danger.

"Hola," she said and brought her errand bags to the kitchen. She paused and lifted her cheek for a kiss from Mom. "¿Tienes hambre?"

"Yeah, I'm starving." Mom sat at the counter as Mimi began to cook. This was our normal routine whenever Mom returned to Port Coral between jobs. Her career had taken off after she painted a mural of a starlit Parisian café inside the Philadelphia coffeehouse where she worked as a barista when I was five. She had a simple website where people bought her artwork, and she traveled the country to do commissioned work. Knowing her, she did graffiti in between. Being in constant motion was the rhythm of my mother's life.

"Mimi, what does this mean?" I imitated the older fisherman's gesture from earlier. It was hard to google a gesture.

My abuela gasped, offended. My mother laughed.

"What?" I demanded.

"It's an old warding sign," Mom explained. "To keep evil away."

"An old man did it to me."

With an almost audible click, both their gazes narrowed at once. "Which old man?" Mom asked, sounding like she was a single name away from sharpening a knife or brewing a hex.

"Over by the boardwalk," I said.

Mom's expression turned curious. "Where on the board-walk?"

I squinted. "Like, the end of it?"

"You mean, the marina?" Mom asked.

Mimi's thunderous gaze snapped to Mom. "Did you go, too?"

Mom muttered a curse under her breath. "I just got here, and for the record, I am not seventeen anymore."

Mimi looked at me again. "Why were you there?"

"I did a delivery." I went to the fridge and grabbed a can of pineapple soda. "For the bodega." I watched her as I took a sip.

Mimi and Mom shared a loaded look. I frowned, feeling like baby Rosa all over again. "I might have to go back for festival planning," I blurted.

Mom's brows shot up. "You're planning Spring Fest?"

"Mrs. Peña is pretty much in charge, but the whole town is pitching in. We're turning it into a fund-raiser to raise money to save the harbor from being bought by some developer."

"Wow." Mom looked surprised. "So things *can* change in Port Coral."

Mimi began pounding a steak on the counter with a mallet. The steaks had been marinating all day. Onions sizzled with crushed garlic in olive oil. My stomach grumbled.

Mom leveled a look at Mimi. "If everyone's helping, what are you doing for the festival? Some secret bruja stuff?"

Mom used the word purposely to ruffle Mimi, who didn't take the bait, instead dropping the first breaded steak in the sizzling hot oil. Mimi was a curandera. She grew her own medicine in her garden and created teas, tinctures, and tonics, but she never called herself a bruja. The term was still used negatively by older generations, if it was uttered at all. But I'd heard them whisper it about Mom. Sometimes there was a knock at the door, late at night when she was home, and a sad-eyed soul waiting on the other side. Mom would sit with them, cards spread across the old wood table. My mother was a storyteller fluent in spells and heartache.

"Was there anything you wanted to do in particular?" I asked Mimi. "I was thinking about setting up a stand with some sage bundles and tinctures."

"No sé, mi amor. We will see."

"It's, like, three weeks away, Mimi."

Mimi smacked Mom's hand, which had been wandering toward the first fried steak. "Oye, but don't rush me."

Mom slipped the small piece of steak she'd stolen into her mouth. "And what's your pet project for it?" she asked me.

"Not sure yet. Everyone keeps reminding me to do my homework, like I haven't been on top of that since kindergarten."

"My honor-roll Rosa," Mom said affectionately. I tried not to let it bother me.

"We can set up a dominos tournament with lessons hosted by the viejitos. Xiomara can teach salsa and bachata. We'll serve pastelitos and Cubano sandwiches. A spin on Hemingway with a Catch the Biggest Fish contest."

"This all sounds very . . . Cuban," Mom pointed out.

My smile fell away. The urge to defend my idea made me uncomfortable. I cleared my throat. "Well, the bodega is sponsoring it and we have a lot of Latinx people in this town, not just Cuban, and we should celebrate that."

"Latinx?" Mimi asked, hand on her hip.

"It's an inclusive term," Mom explained.

Mimi rolled her eyes. "Eso no es una palabra."

"It is a word, get over it," Mom said, then grinned. "You see her hands flying when she gets excited? If she's not careful, she'll signal an airplane."

Mimi laughed. I had to bite back a smile.

We ate our bistec empanizado together. Mom sat across

from me, curled into her chair, smiling between bites as Mimi updated her on all our neighbors. The rain eased outside, and I settled into the comfort of being together. I wondered how long she would stay this time.

"Which class do you have tomorrow?" Mom asked me as she got up to make coffee. Mimi took our plates to the sink.

"Tomorrow is Sunday," I told Mom. "But it doesn't really matter now because they're all online."

"I would be terrible with that. I need the accountability," she said without a trace of irony in her voice.

Mimi's harsh laugh tumbled out too fast and loud to stay under her breath.

The easy peace shattered like a thrown plate. Forks and knives clattered sharply together as Mimi washed them in the sink. Mom poured sugar into a metal cup, spilling some onto the counter, a gritty mess to be cleaned later. She splashed the first spit of coffee into the cup and tapped her spoon fast and hard against the metal, agitating the hot espresso and sugar together, creating an angry foam for the rest of the Cuban coffee. Mimi's lips pressed together in a familiar thin line of displeasure.

The kitchen was about to burst. Home sweet home.

I grabbed my laptop and got to my feet. "I'm going to finish some work."

In my bedroom, I paced in front of the small nightstand that held my altar. Deeper in the house, my mother and abuela had begun arguing. "She's back," I told the photos of my father and abuelo. Nothing. But what did I expect in return from these men on my table?

I knew as much about them as I knew about Cuba.

"Where is that ugly yellow blanket? The one with the daisies?" Mom's tired voice called from the hallway. The linen closet door squeaked open. "It's my favorite one."

"¡No me grites! It's there!" Mimi shouted from the kitchen. I turned my radio on low.

"No, it's not," Mom said, quieter. She knocked against the neighboring wall as she searched the closet, her frustration evident. I pulled open my drawer and grabbed a soft shirt to sleep in. Mom called out, "I don't see it!"

I cleaned my face with a makeup-remover wipe.

"Oye, pero it's there. I saw it!" Mimi returned.

"It's not here." Mom sighed, the sound of it heavy and tired. "It's fine, I'll just use this blue one." I turned off my bedside lamp and crawled into bed, curling beneath the yellow daisy blanket that always smelled like violets and sunshine.

6

I woke to salt on my floor. I sat at the edge of my bed, wiping sleep from my eyes, trying to comprehend the coarse mess sprinkled around my bed.

Mom leaned in my doorway. Her dark hair was down around her shoulders and her honey-yellow crop top exposed her tanned midriff. "Be careful. Mimi is mopping."

I caught the potent scent of lemon and rosemary. Mimi was *cleansing*. Now I could make out the music that woke me. It had the crackle of an old Cuban song and a beat you could swirl and dance to, even as the lyrics referenced saints, orishas, and salvation. One of Mimi's records. Her player was so ancient it had to be cranked, but she considered that part of the ritual.

Her cleansing days were calming to me. The fresh smells and sounds grounded me, but looking at my mother's tense pose, I wondered how it felt to always have your homecoming marked like this.

"It's my bad juju." She shrugged and turned away.

"I stopped taking it personally when I was, like, twelve. Coffee's in the kitchen."

I walked along the grout lines between the tiles. Mimi was halfway to the front door, which meant she was almost done. When she saw me she immediately leaned down to check whether I was wearing socks, like this was my first time in a house with an abuela and a mop.

Sandalwood incense burned, and the sweet, earthy scent of sage she always started with still hung in the air. I poured myself a cup of coffee and opened my laptop. It took longer to wake up than I did, and with Mom being home, it would take a few minutes to find Wi-Fi and get my e-mails to sync. I settled in.

"Show me your pictures," I asked Mom. She was terrible with phones—lost them incessantly—but she always carried a digital camera on her. She turned it on and handed it to me. I scrolled through the most recent images. Among them were paintings and murals she had uploaded to her online photo album, but there were more here. The monstrous sunflowers in someone's dining room. A field of wildflowers outside of an art studio. Tired, smiling cowboys with their hats in their hands. A dock that invited you out to sea. Lemon trees bursting with fruit, stars shimmering over calm waters, shady sidewalks covered in fallen petals.

I looked up, and Mom was watching me, waiting. She chewed on her thumbnail.

"They're all beautiful," I told her. "And the cowboys are pretty cute."

She laughed, sounding relieved. "That was for a high school in Austin. Their mascot was in desperate need of a makeover. I heard they won their next basketball game."

Mimi walked into the kitchen, a bushel of sweet-smelling herbs and a knit bag in one hand and a black metal pot in the other. She dropped them onto the counter with a heave. She looked at us and complained, "Nadie me ayuda."

"I made the coffee," Mom said.

"I just woke up," I argued.

Mimi looked unimpressed with our excuses. She lit a charcoal and dropped it into the pot. "The hierba is full of weeds. Go pull them."

"Do we get an allowance?" Mom teased.

Mimi scoffed, but her lips twitched. She dropped in a few dried leaves, flowers, and roots, and fragrant smoke rose out of the pot. We all took a moment to enjoy the calming scent of her homemade incense blend.

"Are we going to get high in here?" Mom asked.

"Out!" Mimi called, and we slid out of the room, laughing.

Outside, we half-heartedly began to pull weeds in the front yard, but after five minutes, my stomach growled. "I'm hungry."

Mom dropped back on her heels. "Me too. Let's go down to the bodega. She's fired up her cauldron and won't even notice we're gone."

Ten minutes later, we stopped in front of a display of freshly baked desserts at the bodega. I had never seen them carry desserts. "What is all this?" I asked Junior with my nose nearly pressed against the glass. It was like an episode of my favorite baking show. Triple chocolate with ripe strawberries. Lemon curd sponge cakes with raspberry and rose. Passion fruit with cream. Coffee cake swirled through with cinnamon and mocha. I spotted the pastelitos. "Is all of this from the marina restaurant, too?"

Junior walked over to us and nodded. "Yup."

I pointed at the remaining pastelitos made with the flakiest dough, sprinkled with sugar, impossibly light with sweet guava and creamy cheese.

"I want all of them."

"Damn, girl."

"I wish I could get one of everything," Mom told him with a warm laugh.

Junior's gaze turned dreamy—and not from the desserts. He packaged up the rest of the pastelitos and added a coffee cake with a wink. Gross.

"Where's your tía?" Mom asked.

Junior shrugged. "She's been out all day."

Mom looked disappointed as we left.

We ate while we walked, neither of us filling the easy silence, and Port Coral stirred awake as we headed across the town square. The crape myrtles were flowering white and pink while the jacarandas spilled purple blooms onto the grass. Papá El was out with his Popsicles. The flavors rotated every day, but there was always something tropical and sweet. Spring was blossoming and my mother was back, but I only knew how long one of those would last. I took a big bite of my pastelito, sinking my teeth into the guava and cheese.

"Why were you looking for Mrs. Peña?" I asked.

"To see her," she said, sounding embarrassed and defensive. "If you came back to town, you'd look up Ana-Maria, wouldn't you?" Sometimes I forgot they grew up together. I hoped Ana and I never became as distant as our mothers.

At the boardwalk, Mom's steps didn't hesitate. But when we reached the bookshop, I chickened out like always. Before she could move beyond my personal point of no return, I rushed to say, "Let's go inside."

She dusted the sugar from her hands before following me. The bell rang and I was embraced by the sounds of a crackling fire and smell of chocolate-chip cookies, warm from the oven. Clara lived her hygge life to the fullest.

"I'm going to try to find some art books. Emphasis on *try*." Mom headed toward the back.

I wandered the cluttered shelves closer to the front. The shelves were terribly disorganized, their contents changing constantly. It was a fretful game of hide-and-seek sometimes. Between a paperback romance and a manga series that was all out of order, I looked up and saw Alex.

Panic struck and I dropped out of sight.

I pressed back against the shelf, my skirt a tent over

my curled-up knees. But wait. Why was I hiding? I had a perfectly legitimate reason for being here. I was shopping with my mother . . . Oh god, my mother was also here while wearing a crop top. I leaned up just far enough to see Alex.

He was turned to the side, reading the back of a book's cover. The shop grew warmer from the fire. Dust swept into my lungs on my next inhale and I coughed, hard. Alex turned and I dropped lower. He slipped the book he'd been reading back in place on the shelf. I couldn't see his face from this angle. I hurriedly searched between spines for a better view.

He bent to pick up the box by his feet and hefted it into his arms. The blue lines of his tattoo moved in gentle waves. He said something to Clara I didn't hear because my heart was beating too loud. When he moved toward the door, I silently slipped around the shelf. The last thing I saw was his smile before I crashed onto a pile of books.

"Are you okay?" Mom and Clara both asked as they jumped to help me to my feet.

My head shot up, but there was only the friendly ring of the bell as the door closed behind Alex.

I pressed my hand to my racing heart and glanced at the mess around me. The smell of old books and warm sugar hung in the air. "I'm so sorry about all of this," I said to Clara. "I'll pick it up."

"Oh, don't worry about that." Clara offered me a cookie. I was never getting away from the kids' table. I took the cookie, feeling all of ten years old. Mom glanced out the window, and when her gaze came back to me, it was thoughtful.

After we each bought two books and I ate another cookie, we were back outside.

"I thought it was supposed to be the other way around," Mom said with a teasing lilt to her voice. "You just crashed and burned, when we're the ones meant to lead boys to *their* doom."

It wasn't the joke that stole my breath, but how easily it fell from her lips. I turned and marched back down the boardwalk, far from the marina. Mom caught up to me and slipped her arm through mine, squeezing me tight to her side.

"I'm sorry," she said. This close, she was overwhelming. Wild hair, soft perfume, her arm tangled in mine. "Come on, tell me about him. You haven't had a crush in forever."

I actually had. On an older guy in my calculus class at Port Coral Community who always held the door open for me, and a girl from the ice-cream shop who never wore the same name tag and told me I smelled like strawberries. My mother just hadn't been around to know about my crushes. "There's no him," I told her.

"Well, he was really cute. His tattoos are amazing."

"His tattoos are of the *sea*," I said, incredulous. "He has a boat, Mom."

"Yeah? What kind?" she asked.

I barked a disbelieving laugh. "Oh my god, how you can be so flippant about it?"

"Flippant? God, you've lived here too long." She sighed and stepped off the curb. We crossed the street. "I'm so tired of this curse and everyone who believes in it. Things will be better when you leave Port Coral. You'll see."

I didn't like the way she said it. Like I was leaving for good.

"Speaking of," she went on. "Your last e-mail said you would hear back soon about your college applications. What's the latest?"

I hadn't considered how Mom might take my news. She must still wonder about Cuba, too. We hadn't talked about it since policies between the US and Cuba began to change. And then changed again. "I was accepted to the College of Charleston."

"Really? Wow, that's great." Mom smiled. "What about the others?"

"Others? Oh, I got into Florida, Miami, and UCF."

"Nice." She grinned. "Why is the Florida girl headed to South Carolina, though?"

"They have a really great study-abroad program." That was a good place to start.

"That's exciting." Of course my wanderlust-afflicted mother would approve.

The next part was the tough one. I blew out a sharp breath and jumped. "In Cuba."

Silence fell between us.

I felt validated by her heavy pause. It *was* a big deal for me to go to Cuba. My family's island was complicated. There were exiles who wanted nothing to do with Cuba until those in power were totally gone, and others who wanted the embargo to end and to rebuild relations again. I wasn't sure where I fell, but I knew I wanted to understand the place my family fled, as well as those who lived there now.

"So you want to go to Cuba," she said. It wasn't a question, but a revelation. Soft pink petals fell against the sidewalk between us. I gently kicked up the ones in front of me. "What do you plan to study while you're there?" she asked me.

"Spanish and history classes focused on the island."

"And they apply to your major?"

"Of course," I said. "I'm majoring in Latin American Studies."

"Still?"

I stopped walking. A streetlight separated us. "What do you mean *still?*"

She leaned against the post. "I figured you'd change your mind at least a few times. Didn't Florida have that environmental program you liked?"

I'd mentioned it over a year ago after a science class lit a curious fire in me, and I became fascinated with biodiversity and sustainability. "The coursework was kind of intimidating and didn't leave a lot of room for the cultural stuff. Plus their undergrad program doesn't have any upcoming trips to Cuba."

"So? Are you only going to college to go to Cuba?"

"Of course not." The enormity of studying in Cuba was so overwhelming, but the ultimate goal had to be graduating and earning a degree. A future career. "This is just one of the only ways I can go, and it makes sense if I'm majoring in Latin American Studies."

"You don't have to get a degree in being Latina, Rosa. That's not how this works."

Annoyance sparked through me like a match. "Are you serious right now?"

She tactfully changed course. "Have you told Mimi about any of this?"

"God, no. Look how much fun it is just talking to you about it."

"I just want to make sure you're not so hyperfocused on Cuba that you miss everything else you want to study. There are a lot of roads that can take you where you want to go."

"I *want* to study this. That's the whole point." Of the past two years of my life.

"Just remember school isn't the only way there. Look at me, I've been a few places. And, hell, we could go one day," she said. "We used to talk about that, remember?"

Maybe that's where this idea had first been planted, tended by my mother's infectious optimism in the face of the impossible. Cuba? Sure. One day.

My phone whistled—a text from Mrs. Peña informing

me the planning meeting was moved to her garage after the book club had refused to budge from the library's room.

"You think I could do something for the festival?"

My head jerked up. My surprise must have been obvious, because Mom gave me an almost shy smile. "I was thinking I could paint something. A very not-flippant mural."

I looked at her for a beat. How we had gone from her questioning my college choices to her painting a mural, I would never understand. "You catch me off guard some-times. Like a gust of wind."

"Your poet's heart is too kind to me," she said, sounding almost guilty. But she was the poet, not me. As we walked I remembered my favorite story of hers, where a young, scrappy girl found a huge bright pink seashell that could take her anywhere she wished. The girl traveled to so many places thanks to that seashell, and whenever we moved somewhere new, Mom always reminded me we were still looking for ours.

"How long are you staying?" I asked carefully.

She was quiet for a long moment. I braced myself. "For as long as I can."

It was as simple and complicated as that. Tired of talking, I slipped my phone out and scrolled over to my music. I offered her an earbud, and she took it. I hit shuffle. Another one of Mimi's favorite Sunday morning songs, the guajira beat of an old country song. We walked, side by side, and I imagined the bustling streets of Havana. To the left somewhere the seawall would be standing strong against wild, breaking waves. Cars honking as friendly, familiar Spanish that rolled with a Caribbean tongue spilled out of open windows. Maybe sometimes going home again could be as simple as listening to a song.

7

A small crowd was already milling around the Peñas' open garage door. It was a typical sight, since Ana's house was home base for everyone: friends, cousins, anyone with scattered families or who'd recently migrated here. We gathered for birthdays, holidays, and every Christmas Eve for Noche Buena. When Mr. Peña cooked, people showed up.

At the bottom of the driveway, Mom returned my earbud and I headed inside to find Ana, then all but crashed to a stop in front of the poster boards in the garage. One was the map I'd drawn of the square that Mrs. Peña had blown up. The other was a list organizing tasks along a very detailed timeline. The days were color-coordinated with a beautiful key along the side.

I held a hand against my heart. "This is art."

Mrs. Peña's bright smile faltered when she noticed Mom behind me. "Hey, Liliana." There was a moment of hesitation before they greeted each other with a quick hug and kiss on the cheek. "When'd you get back into town?"

"Last night. I popped into the bodega this morning."

Mike arrived and I ducked away from the awkwardness of Mom and Mrs. Peña attempting small talk. Whenever Mom came back, she rarely attended town meetings, and her presence stirred curious glances now.

"Hey, I heard this was all your idea." Mike grinned at me. "Just like you to get everyone assigned extra credit." Black, geeky, and super crafty, Mike lived with his parents and grandmother across the street. He was a skater kid with old-man hobbies like whittling and puzzles, and he apprenticed for Oscar the Hermit Carpenter. Oscar lived in the old fire station, and everyone in town owned something made by him. Our kitchen table, for instance. Oscar trailed behind Mike before stopping in front of the poster board. He silently studied it.

Ana strolled into the garage, tapping her purple drumsticks. She smiled at Mike. "You got Oscar out of his workshop? Very impressive."

"Mrs. Peña needs new tables and signs," Mike explained. "Also set pieces for the stage."

Mimi arrived with Malcolm, Dan, and Penny, whose feet were swinging from the wrap her dad wore across his chest. Mimi smelled of the peppermint water she sprayed her plants with sometimes. "Doña Santos," Mike said as he approached my abuela. She offered her cheek, and he kissed it like a pro. He liked practicing his Spanish with other people's abuelitas, and Mimi ate it up.

The last to arrive were Jonas and Clara. And Alex. He glanced my way and I smiled, but his dark gaze skipped over me. My smile crumpled and fell away like an undelivered note.

He looked like the surly fisherman again. The mint plant and box of books had nearly made me forget.

Mrs. Peña moved into the center of the garage, the poster boards a beautiful backdrop behind her. "Thanks for coming, everybody. We've got a lot of work to do in not a lot of time." She paused and everyone looked at me. I offered a quick wave.

"It's spring and I know we all love our carnival season." A murmur of agreement went through the garage. I tried to pay attention as Mrs. Peña went on about vendor applications, a silent auction, musical acts, and my dominos tournament idea that had taken off, but I was busy being way too conscious of how I was standing. I shifted my hip out a little. From my peripheral vision, I spied Alex scanning the room. He was a head taller than Jonas even as he leaned against the wall. My eyes started to hurt from the strain of looking sideways. I really hoped I didn't have guava on my cardigan from my earlier pastelito.

". . . and the sailors will put on the regatta . . ."

I pictured the harbor and imagined the spray of salt water flying toward the horizon. A wave of dizziness washed over me.

"I would like to paint a mural," Mom announced. The

room quieted. Everyone was looking everywhere except at her.

"I do this kind of work, and I'd like to do one here. You could present it at the festival." Her voice wavered. I wondered if anyone else noticed. I glanced at Mimi, who watched her curiously.

The silence was getting weird. Mrs. Peña looked at her notes.

"Where?" Mimi asked. "You have no wall here."

Mom didn't look at her. Her gaze stayed defiantly on Mrs. Peña, waiting for her answer.

"She can have mine." Oscar's growly voice startled me. He dragged a hand through dark hair that was going gray at the temples. "She can have the side of the fire station. The brick is faded, but it could work." He shrugged. "If you want."

Mom's answering smile was soft with relief. "Thanks, Oscar."

Mrs. Peña perked up. "Okay, great, so Liliana will paint a mural, and the marina will host. . . ." She went on with her list, but my attention was zeroed in on Mom and Oscar. Were they friends? The quiet carpenter was someone else who left Port Coral, only to return. I knew Oscar had shipped out after high school and returned a retired Navy SEAL who built furniture, but had he known Mom when they were kids? Or my father?

"How does that sound, Rosa?" Mrs. Peña asked, jerking me out of my thoughts and back to the garage.

"Great," I told her. Across the room, Alex seemed surprised. Mimi shot me a sharp look of concern, while Mom was grinning like she knew a secret.

"Oh god, I wasn't listening," I murmured to Mike. Beside us, Ana laughed behind her hand. "What happened?"

He ducked his head. "Jonas volunteered that dude Alex over there to help you with their wedding."

"Wait, *what?*"

Alex's glower burning a hole into the poster board told me how he felt about it.

"I told you," Ana said. "You have no idea what you're doing."

When Mrs. Peña was finished handing out assignments and the meeting wrapped up, I hurried to catch Clara on the sidewalk.

"Rosa!" She beamed, the blushing bride again. "I really didn't see how we could pull this off after canceling everything, but this is going to be even better! We never needed a big production, and with everyone coming together for the festival and harbor, it's kind of an adventure now. It's just so romantic, Jonas and me having our little moment with my mum here. I'm so excited!"

"That's great, Clara. But, uh, I was just wondering if I could have a recap, maybe? Over what we just decided back there."

"Oh! Of course, well—"

"I can do food."

I spun back to see Alex right behind me. His arms crossed, he looked at Clara. "The cake. I'll get that," he offered.

"Wonderful!" Clara said. "I have my dress, of course, and our personal details like vows, but with everything else going on we just need a bit of help with setting up and executing the moment." Clara turned her heart-eyes on me. I could almost see the cartoon baby birds chirping around her.

"Don't worry about a thing," I said. "We got this."

She held up her hands like she was framing Alex and me in a picture. "The dream team," she said before handing me several lists of favorite flowers, songs, and cake flavors. "I'm off to Gainesville in the morning with Jonas to meet with the university. Wish us luck!" She clapped again before turning to go. I wasn't the best person to impart any kind of luck.

Mr. Gomez aimed a watchful glare at Alex and me. He pointed from his eyes to mine. Yeah, I got the message.

"Looks like we're planning that party together, then," I said lightly. "I figured you'd be headed with them to Gainesville, though."

"I'm not one for meetings."

"Yeah, I can understand. Look how it turns out when you do go to one," I joked, and then something amazing happened: He smiled. Well, almost. It was a soft twitch of his lips, and it was gone in a blink, but a tiny ray of sunlight had broken through the clouds of this shadowy boy. I had to be careful; a full smile from him might be lethal.

"Uh, so, yeah." I cleared my throat and read over the papers in my hands. "It says here they would love a short ceremony at sunset. The exact location isn't important to them, so I'll take care of that and flowers, and you can handle the cake and wine. Easy breezy. Sound good?"

He nodded and slipped his hands into his pockets.

"And if I need you for anything else?" I ventured.

"You can find me on my boat."

I laughed, the sound too high to be comfortable or cool. It was the most outrageous thing anyone had ever said to me. "Most people have phone numbers."

There it was again. An almost smile. I selfishly wanted a real one. "If you call it, I can't answer it."

Um, rude. "Why not?"

He shrugged. "I dropped it in the ocean and haven't bought another one yet." He turned and, with a backward wave, headed down the sidewalk, toward the marina.

Ana walked over to me. "Be careful with that one."

In a whisper, I asked, "Is my mom looking at me?"

"She's been watching you this whole time."

I sighed. It felt like I was proving her right about something, and I didn't like it. I had no business talking to boys with boats. I silently repeated that to myself as I watched him go.

8

The next morning I worked on finishing my last essay for the study-abroad scholarship. Well, I worked on starting it. I crunched down on a strawberry candy as I ruminated over the blinking cursor and blank screen. It was a demanding thing, the cursor. *Come on, Rosa, tell us again why we should give you money.* I'd answered every variation of the *Why you?* question presented to me so far, but here I was, unable to string together a sentence. Maybe I was burnt out. Dual enrollment had fried me. Someone alert the viejitos, Rosa Santos had peaked. I glanced at the date on my calendar to count the days until May, but my attention snagged on today's date. The day before Mom's birthday. The day my father's boat didn't return. I closed my laptop and went to find Mimi.

The windows were open to the warm, citrus-sweet breeze. I moved through the garden room, drinking in the lush green scent. There was sacred knowledge in these living, breathing roots. Remedies and secret recipes.

71

A collection handed down from one mother to the next. I followed the heartbeat of the house out the screen door and into the backyard garden, where Mimi plucked peppers into a basket before straightening. She pressed her hands into her back and leaned into a stretch. Her eyes closed and she tipped her face to the sun. I wondered over her soft smile and the sudden twinge of guilt that tangled with my good mood.

Reconnecting with my mother felt like trying to balance a set of scales. Did going to Cuba mean I would hurt her, too? I didn't know how to balance my love for her with my need to leave.

"Do you need help?" I called, coming closer.

Mimi grabbed her basket. When she noticed I was still in my sleep shirt, she said, "Oye, pero did you just wake up?"

I swallowed my sigh. "I've been working on an essay in my room."

Frustration at my tone tightened her expression. She quickly banished it and cupped my cheek. After a moment of hesitation, she said, "Voy a hacer una medicina para la tos."

"Who's coughing?"

She laughed. "Everyone. Our flowers are very pretty, pero carajo, the allergies."

She dropped her hand, and we returned to the garden room where we worked side by side like always. Mimi chopped and measured without following any written instructions. I followed along, peeking over her shoulder, scribbling notes in my journal littered with leaves and pencil shavings. She showed me where to properly cut the peppers. I peeled and chopped ginger, and listened as she hummed to herself and poured golden honey into the bottle, a healing concoction that would soothe a scratchy throat and quiet a persistent cough. I didn't know if I was a healer like Mimi, but making this syrup with her felt like being let in on another secret, another story about home and family.

When she went inside to make us some tea, I glanced over the clutter of her table. Mimi's organizational system was nearly as bad as the bookshop's. Beneath the dried mint was an open notebook filled with Mimi's cursive handwriting. There were ingredients listed for different oils and potions. Messy footnotes written in quick scrawls and different inks. Orders and reminders about coughs and achy backs. The name Tía Nela stopped me.

I'd never heard of a tía. All I knew of our family was the three of us. Whoever was left in Cuba was gone. Right? But notes about Nela chased one another across pages, written between tonics and plants Mimi noted she couldn't find outside of her island. She listed Cuban cities, and I hurriedly read each note to see if there were more names or even addresses, but instead I read different accounts of healing. In Camagüey, a sick boy who woke from his death bed. Healed oxen in Pinar del Río that saved a family farm. A mother who found her lost daughter in Holguín. A trail of miracles. How in the world did Mimi know what was happening in Cuba?

"Honey?" Mimi called and I started. I hurried to put the notebook back.

"Please," I shouted, though my heart was currently stuck in my throat.

Mimi returned with two mugs. I watched her as I took a careful sip, hoping I didn't look as guilty as I felt, but as the tea warmed my chest, my hand itched to grab the notebook so I could read more. I wanted—no, needed—to know more. I just needed a way in.

"I'm going to the hardware store today with Oscar and Mike. They're helping me with the wedding."

"Qué bueno." Mimi grabbed her spray bottle and turned away to tend the basil.

"What was your wedding like?"

She paused, the bottle in her hand stilling. After a moment, she sprayed the basil. "Small. I also married in the spring."

I waited on the edge of my seat. "Did you guys get married in Havana?"

"Oh, no." She laughed. "Papi would have killed me. Alvaro and I married in Viñales, at the church. Alvaro still lived in Havana as a student, but he knew it was important to my family to marry near our farm."

"Wait, he was a student?"

She nodded. "At the university."

"The University of Havana?"

"That's what I just said."

"But why have you never said it before?"

At this, her defenses crept safely back into place. She focused on the green leaves in front of her. "Ay, mira, this one is wilting."

I'm going to attend the same college as my abuelo. The words demanded out. I wished I could set them free as my abuela happily shaped memories for me. I would find meaning in the ruins of a language I only knew in scattered, unfinished pieces. But, like a ghost, she drifted away into her plants. My confession settled back into its hiding place, perched on my ribs. A bird with nowhere to go.

Was it lack of bravery holding me back? I was scared of hurting her. And of her breaking my heart in return over something this important to us both.

"Where's Mom?" I asked, and worried over the scale again. Mimi sighed as the wind chimes sang softly.

"She's at her new wall. Go and remind her what tomorrow is."

❖

On the way to the hardware store, I stopped beside the old fire station. My mother stood, her arms crossed, as she studied her empty canvas. The white paint looked fresh. Her jeans were faded and spotted with flecks of color. She tipped her head back, looking so much like Mimi, and I wondered if they recognized their similarities. "What are you picturing?" I asked as I drew closer.

Mom didn't startle. "Not sure yet." She glanced at me before looking back at the wall, like she was sizing up an opponent.

On the sidewalk between the buildings, Gladys stopped. She wore her bowling shirt and carried her bag. She looked at us, then at the wall. "What are you going to paint?"

Mom didn't stop her contemplation. "Not sure yet."

"Well, make it good," she said. "The rest of us will have to look at it every day, you know." She continued on her way. Mom looked like she'd taken a sucker punch.

Once she was gone, Mom said, "It would blow her mind to know people from other places actually pay me to do this."

"They've never seen your work." She only ever sent her photo albums to me.

"They're too busy setting wards against my supposed evil." She sounded tired. Her hair looked darker in the shadow. "People in other places don't look at me like I'm bad luck. But nowhere else feels right, either." She tapped her paintbrush against her palm. "It's easy to have a hometown when you don't have to leave."

It was the first time I'd ever heard my mother say it so plainly.

"*Have* to leave?" I asked, but she continued to stare at the wall. I was so tired of everyone's silence. I tried again. "Well, you can stay for a while. See what that does for your reputation." Mom didn't say anything to that either. She was as stubborn as Mimi.

"What do you want to do for your birthday tomorrow?" I asked, frustrated with both of them and their never-ending battle. This was the first time she'd ever been home for this day.

Mom looked confused for a moment, like she was trying to find where she was in time and place. It clicked together with a look of anguish.

My mother's birthday was complicated. Her father had died to save her. Mimi had become a mother and widow in her bid for freedom. And eighteen years ago—on the day *before* her birthday—my father hurriedly set out to finish a day of work, so he could buy her a gift. Make new memories on a difficult day. But he never returned, and now her life was bookmarked by two tragedies.

"I forgot," she murmured. She paced in front of the wall for an agitated moment. Her gaze jumped from the colors at her feet to the blank space in front of her. "I've never forgotten before."

Surprise swallowed whatever I was about to say. Mom remembered everything down to the tiniest detail. When she gave you a gift it was always spun from a memory you'd half-forgotten, and the rush of remembering again meant as much as the gift itself. She looked skittish now, like she was one spook away from taking off again.

"His boat slip is still his," I said, and she finally looked at me. I knew something too now. It was selfishly gratifying to carry coveted information.

"How do you know?"

"You never asked?" She said nothing. "Mrs. Aquino told me."

How could you love someone so much and never talk about the important things? The silent question felt so loud, it practically bounced off the wall beside us. Time was supposed to make grief easier, but it seemed to work the opposite way in my family. The more distance we had from a tragedy, the deeper we buried it, and the harder it haunted us.

Mom considered the blank wall in front of her. She bent down to pack up her paint, and sun glare spilled into the alley behind her, blinding me for a second. "I have to go."

Panic and frustration struck. "Already?"

"I'll be back tonight."

"Where are you going?"

Instead of answering, she said, "We'll have dinner tomorrow for my birthday. As a family."

If only she sounded happy about coming back.

9

"I just feel really caught between them all of a sudden," I confessed, clutching my notebook to my chest. "But where is all this guilt coming from? It's because I'm keeping a secret, isn't it?"

Oscar and Mike waited, both of them holding up pieces of lumber. The hardware store was busy around us.

Mike looked between the wood and me. "Caught between these two?"

We'd been here for the past half hour, Mike rushing from school, but I was so distracted, I was totally wasting their time.

"Sorry. You're both just really easy to talk to," I said, and Oscar grunted like I'd accused him of something terrible.

"Which one did you want, Rosa?" he asked, gruff but patient.

I glanced at the page my journal was open to and noted my doodle of Clara and Jonas's wooden arch. "The lighter wood, I think. And maybe we could add some driftwood to it? What do you think, Mike?"

"I think you bit off way more than you can chew, but, sure, the birch is nice."

I flipped to the next page and my secret project for Clara. "Am I good for the lighting, you think?" I asked Oscar and handed him my notebook.

He checked over the sketch I'd drawn of my plans again. "Yeah, let me go double-check with Mr. Cordova, but this should work."

The whine of an electric saw rang out, and the sharp, almost sweet scent of fresh-cut lumber was heavy in the air. Mike and I went to search through tiny drawers of bolts and hinges. He rolled his sleeves up his forearms and stuck a pencil behind his ear. I didn't know what I was meant to be helping him look for, despite him explaining it seven times, so I just sat on a box and took out my phone to check my e-mails.

"What's with the hyper-distraction?" he asked after a moment.

"I still haven't told Mimi I'm going to Charleston."

"What?" He looked shocked. "You better do it soon. Damn, if my grandma found out she was the last to know something . . . I don't even want to think about it. Everything I said from the time I found out and didn't tell her would be considered a lie. Grandmas are too much."

"I'm not lying, though. I'm just not telling her about it yet."

He gave me a look that said, *Yeah, sure.*

"I just want to go to Cuba—it should not be this difficult. It's not like I'm skipping college or running away with a sailor from Argentina."

"Why Argentina?"

"I don't know, Mimi always roots against them in soccer." I sighed. "This is all my mother's fault. She went and fell in love with a boy with a boat, and now she's this wandering vagabond, constantly upsetting her mother and making me too scared to do anything to rock the boat." I frowned. "Bad analogy."

"Terrible. But I doubt she fell in love with your dad to piss off Mimi."

"Out of everyone, she just had to fall for him? Seems fake."

He smiled at my weary sarcasm. "Let's see, change of topic. What's new with your buddy Mike? Oh! You have to see this boat I'm working on." He glowed with excitement. "The spruce Oscar found for me is straight out of my dreams. I mean, right now it's basically a canoe, but it's gonna sail, baby."

"You too?" I whined. "Why am I suddenly surrounded by boys with boats?"

Mike paused his digging through the brass bolts. "Riiiiight. You and Alex planning your wedding." I scowled and Mike grinned. "Wait, *are* you running away with an Argentinian sailor?"

"Would you date me?"

"*What?*" he burst out. Honestly, the question was a surprise to me, too, but the panic on his face was a little much.

"I didn't ask you out, Michael," I protested. "I was just curious if you'd ever thought about me like that."

"Why? Are you thinking about *me* like that?"

First Paula's and Frankie's laughter and awkward pity at the bodega, and now Mike's shock. *Was* I still in middle school? "Forget it." I got to my feet. I wasn't even sure what I was asking. "I've got to— Oh my god." I spun back to Mike. Alex was behind me at the very end of the aisle searching through the other baskets. I moved in super close to Mike and lowered my voice. "Talk to me normal."

"You first," he shot back, then glanced behind me. "Ah, your fiancé."

"Don't," I gritted out.

Mike continued to watch Alex, despite all the screaming in my head for him to stop. He looked at me with sudden understanding. I didn't like it one bit. "This is why you're all hyper and guilty. You have a crush."

"*What?* No." I shook my head. "I do not."

"You do. Dude is your type: mysterious and brooding."

"I do not have a type or a crush. Having a crush on him would be a terrible idea."

"And yet here we are," he said, grinning.

"No, we are not. We are not there."

"Excuse me."

82

Mike and I snapped our heads to the right. Alex stood, waiting. He gestured to the shelf behind us. Without a word, we slid out of his way. He stepped forward and grabbed a box of screws. The silence was so sharp it nearly whistled.

"Hey, Alex," I said, too brightly. "Good to see you."

Mike offered a hand to Alex, and they shook in greeting while I slowly died in the hardware store.

"This is super fun, but I need to finish helping Oscar. See y'all around." Mike patted my shoulder twice, and then just left me there, drowning.

I could *not* get a read on Alex, because where I expected him to rush off like before, he instead stayed where he was. The moment grew tense with expectation. He brushed a hand down his dusty blue shirt, which looked soft. "Are you buying something?" he asked.

Relieved to have something to say, I told him, "No, I came to plan out the pergola for Jonas and Clara. Oscar is building it for me."

"Nice." He didn't move.

Silence stretched. "Did you have any questions about the cake or anything?"

He looked at me strangely. "Uh, no. I'm good."

"Cool, cool. Well, I have to go ask Mr. Cordova about a light situation."

"I'm headed that way, too." He tapped the box in his hand. "I need to pay."

"Right, of course." I tried not to wail from embarrassment as we made our way to the register. Alex slipped a worn leather wallet out of his back pocket and paid for his stuff. Mr. Cordova, the owner of the hardware store, looked at us curiously as he took Alex's money and bagged his purchase. Mr. Cordova had also been my fifth grade math teacher.

"Did Oscar show you what I needed?"

Mr. Cordova smiled. "The order's already in, should be here early next week." His smile fell as he passed a searching gaze between Alex and me. I tried leaning up on my toes a little.

"You're both working on the wedding?" he asked, looking at Alex.

"Yes," I replied. "Different parts of it."

Mr. Cordova grunted. "Good."

Alex said nothing. He grabbed his bag and went to the door. He held it open and glanced back at me. I followed him outside into the bright sunshine.

Alone on the sidewalk, I blurted, "I saw you in the bookshop."

He looked confused. "Today?"

"No, yesterday . . . before the meeting. You picked up a book and then put it back." Oh my god, why was I telling him this? I sounded like a tiny stalker. "I love that shop."

"I was looking at a book about knot work."

"Knot work?"

He hesitated for a beat. "Boat stuff," he explained. The scent of burnt caramel and vanilla hit me, and I wondered what kind of coffee he drank.

"I'm sorry for calling your idea for the festival a party." The surprising apology was given with swift but grave determination. "I should have already apologized for that."

"If you knew me, you'd know I take projects very seriously."

"But I do. . . ." He stopped and finally looked at me. "You don't remember me. From before."

"Before?" He looked startled by my surprise, like he'd been running on the assumption that I remembered something I didn't, but I couldn't have known him before the town meeting. "There's no way. I have a very good memory, and plus, I'm a Santos." The *and you're a very cute sailor tattooed with the sea* was implied.

"Well, I didn't have a boat back then."

Back then? My mind raced back years, through my high school hallways, looking for him. "Did we have classes together?"

"No. But you ate lunch near me."

Sophomore year flashed to mind. I didn't have the same lunch period as my friends so I sat alone at a bench. The one beneath the live oaks where I could do homework in the shade. In my memory, I glanced to the right of that bench, and there, leaning against the brick wall, he sat, wearing headphones and holding a notebook like me.

He looked at me now, smiling as I found him. Alex, a little older and bearded, molded into the quiet boy who once sat a few feet away from me for an entire semester, both of us inhabiting the same space, neither breaching the other's boundary.

"Alejandro," I said. The memories bloomed with color. The faded red brick wall and freshly cut patch of grass. My favorite perfume of raspberries, and the wild clatter of lunchtime chaos. But in front of me was a boy with messy dark hair whose focus I envied so much, I decided to save to buy myself better headphones. I thought him tall, as most people are to me, and he always had a book leaned up against his long legs. The only time I ever heard him speak was on the phone to someone else.

"You spoke Spanish."

He nodded. "Both my parents do. You met my mother."

Right. Mrs. Aquino. "She knew my dad." The sunlit moment felt cosmic. There was something here. Something curious and unfinished. I wanted to know more about him. Maybe there were more places our lives connected, more memories we both held. But my alarm sang out from my phone.

"I have to go," I told him as I silenced it in a hurried rush. "But I want to know about—"

You. Could I just say that? I had no idea how to continue this conversation. It had been so long since I met someone. Maybe that's all this was. Nerves over a new friendship with someone so much bigger they blocked out the sun.

"—the oyster reefs." I grabbed my notebook again. "Can I schedule a conversation for us to do that?"

"Sure," he said after a beat. I clicked my pen, ready to write. "I'm free most afternoons."

"Great." I wrote that down quickly. "And where would you be at that time?"

"My boat."

My pen slipped. I jerked my head up from the stray line of ink. As I watched him leave, once again headed toward the harbor, I realized two things. First, he wasn't much for good-byes. And the second? Someone alert the viejitos—just kidding, please don't—but I was pretty sure I was on my way to having a crush on a boy with a boat.

10

Mom still hadn't returned that evening. Frustrated, I bypassed the empty living room and climbed into bed with Mimi to watch her telenovela beside her.

"¿Qué es eso?" she asked, looking at my face.

"A sheet mask," I explained, and propped her throw pillows behind my back.

"Sheet mask, qué es sheet mask?" Mimi leaned over to her nightstand and grabbed her familiar little tub of cold cream. "Me encanta esta crema."

"Mimi, I'm eighteen. I don't need night cream yet."

She opened the tub and smoothed more down her neck. "¿Qué pasó?"

"Nothing, I'm fine."

"¿Y tu madre?"

"I don't know where she went. She forgot about her birthday, which of course meant she forgot what today is."

"Ay, mi niña." Her sigh was heavy and sad and surprisingly maternal.

"Why don't you sound like that when you talk to her?"

"Sound like what?" she asked, but before I could argue, the commercial ended and she shushed me. We watched the episode together, and a little while later we heard the sound of the front door opening and closing. After a few more moments, Mom poked her head into the bedroom.

"What are you guys doing?"

"Miguel is about to find out he is actually his dead twin, Diego," I said, relieved to see her. She sat down at the end of the bed. Mimi handed her the night cream. Mom twisted it open without saying a word and smoothed a little over her cheekbones.

"Where'd you go?" I asked, because I had to know. I was tired of the three of us never asking the real questions.

Mom flicked a glance between us. "You two make a hell of a sight."

"It's relaxing and moisturizes my inherited dry skin," I said.

"Right. Well, let's see . . . I bought a bottle of wine and sat at the end of the dock where I drank the whole thing before slipping a note inside and chucking it into the water."

"Really?" I asked. I had not expected that.

"I do it every year."

Mimi simmered beside me.

"But this is the first time you've been home on this day," I pointed out.

Mom swayed a little. "I'm always somewhere on the

Gulf. Last year I was in . . ." She frowned in concentration, but it softened as she remembered. "Louisiana."

"You're drunk," I said, annoyed. She did this every year. And I never knew.

She waved her hand back and forth. "I walked home from the marina."

"They saw you at the marina?"

"Who saw me?"

Mimi reached for her saint medallion on her nightstand and muttered a prayer.

"People, Mom. The fishermen and sailors who say we're cursed with bad luck."

"Yes, they probably saw me." She handed the night cream back to Mimi after several tries of getting the lid back on right. "Never figured out how to swallow my grief in such a presentable way like you, Mami."

"Borracha," Mimi accused mildly.

"Y diciendo verdades," Mom shot back and stood. She wobbled a little but managed to stay upright.

"And that doesn't sound messy to you?" I asked.

"Well, I suppose it would be considered littering."

"No, Mom. Emotionally messy."

She barked a harsh laugh and reached out for the wall, feeling for it to find her way back to the door.

I climbed out of bed. "Come on, I'll get you some water."

"But I thought the water cursed us," Mom muttered.

90

When she stumbled into the door, she glanced back at me and said, "I'm not drunk. Only clumsy."

I grabbed her arm and led her into the kitchen, dropping her off at a chair. I filled a glass with water and handed it to her. She considered it.

"My mom never let me see her cry," she admitted thoughtfully. "I was always so afraid of being sad, because I thought it would swallow me whole." She looked at me, her brown eyes shining with emotion. "I want you to know it's okay to be sad." She smiled and touched my face. I realized I still had on my sheet mask, so I pulled it off. Mom watched me and said, "You look like a ghost who came back to life. Oh, baby. I shouldn't have left you here. You got all . . . serious."

"You didn't leave me, Mom. I chose to stay."

Mom looked at me now as if she was remembering. "You and her were always good together," she whispered. She drank her water, kissed me on my cheek, and stumbled onto the couch.

I helped her out of her shoes and went to grab her favorite blanket from my bed, but when I returned to her side, she was already covered with the quilt from Mimi's room. I glanced up. My abuela stood in the doorway to her bedroom. Her face was weary with heartache. She said nothing before closing her door.

I watched my mother sleep and wondered what she wrote in her notes to the sea.

Mom slept in the next morning. Spread across the couch with her mouth half-open, she would probably wake with a righteous hangover, but that was between her and Mimi.

"Happy birthday, Mom," I whispered. She was out.

With five minutes until I had to clock in for work, I burst into the back room of the bodega, grateful to catch Ana in time. It was a weekday, so she'd only come into the bodega to grab free food on her lunch break before returning to school. Bright cartoons bounced around on the TV. Junior and Paula sat across from her with their plates of ham croquetas and crackers.

I sank into the chair beside Ana. "I have to talk to you."

"Well, here she is." Junior looked up from his phone with a cheeky grin. "You Santos girls are good at stirring up chisme." My impatience to talk to Ana disappeared in the wave of fear over what my mother had done now. "Hold on, there's a picture."

I was going to die. Or kill her. Oh god, someone saw her drunk at the docks. Ana, Paula, and I leaned forward to look at the picture. Relief washed over me only to be immediately doused by outrage. It was me standing on the sidewalk outside the hardware store with Alex yesterday afternoon.

I gasped. "Are you spying on me, you sleazebag?"

Paula smacked her brother's shoulder.

"No! This is the viejitos' Insta account."

"Those chismosos," I hissed. It was a good picture, though. The sunlight was all soft and gold, highlighting my brown skin and floral A-line skirt that gave my short, curvy frame a nice silhouette. Alex's head was bent toward me.

Paula snatched the phone out of her brother's hand. "Damn, *that's* Alex now? Dude got fine." She swiped to scroll, but Junior wrestled it back.

"This is real friendly." Junior pointed at his phone. "You guys are looking real hard at each other, if you know what I mean."

Of course I didn't know what he meant, but I wanted to look at the picture again. I focused on Ana. She was giving me *such* an *I told you* look. "You're making time to sneak around with this dude and I bet you still haven't told Mimi."

"About Alex?"

"No, about college!"

"Listen," I said. "I'm not sneaking around. Every time I've seen him I've been on task. It all started when I almost crashed the delivery bike—"

Junior's laugh became strangled. "The hell are you doing talking to strange dudes when you got that much merchandise? What'd I tell you?" He tapped his temple. "No street smarts."

"And then I saw him at the bookshop and he was reading about knots—"

"Knots?" Ana practically yelped. "You know who reads about knots? Kidnappers and murderers, Rosa."

"You listen to way too many podcasts," I accused. "It's for boat stuff."

Ana jabbed a finger into the table. "That's just what a murderer would say."

The door to the inside of the store opened. It was Mrs. Peña, and Lamont Morris trailed behind her. He wore dark jeans and a short-sleeved button-up decorated with tiny pineapples. His backpack was slung over his shoulder. His tense expression relaxed into a smile when he saw me. "Hey, Rosa."

"What's up, valedictorian," I said, smiling. Our competition for the top spot had been a friendly one.

Mrs. Peña snatched the clipboard off her table. "Teenagers will be the death of me. So now you're telling me I have no band?" she asked Lamont.

His face was pinched. "I guess Tyler and I could just do an acoustic set, but to be completely honest, we really suck at those."

"Dios mío." Mrs. Peña rubbed her temple.

"What happened?" I asked Lamont. I knew he was the bassist in the Electric.

"Brad just moved to Nashville," he said. At my blank look, he explained, "Our asshole drummer. Well, former asshole drummer."

Beside me, Ana perked up. "I'm a drummer."

Mrs. Peña's head jerked in her daughter's direction. She considered her and then looked at Lamont. "She is a drummer."

"Cool. Do you have a set?"

Before Ana could answer, Mrs. Peña said, both aggrieved and relieved, "Yes, she does. One that cost too much money." She pointed back at Ana with her clipboard. "If I give you a drummer, you give me a band again, right?"

"Works for me." Lamont turned to Ana. "Meet us at Tyler's garage tonight to practice."

Ana agreed coolly, but once he left, her eyes lit with excitement and she let out a wild laugh. "Can you believe this? A band! A real band and a show and oh my god, *finally*." She grabbed my shoulders and shook me.

"Ana!" Mrs. Peña called from somewhere inside the store. "School! Now!"

Ana's grin didn't budge. "We've got a band and festival to save." She let go and slipped her purple drumsticks off the table, tapping a rat-a-tat on her way out of the room.

"Don't forget, my mother's birthday dinner is tonight," I announced before everyone scattered. Mom's shameless honesty last night had inspired me. She drunkenly told Mimi she'd been tossing bottles into the sea every year, and the world hadn't ended. Mimi even covered her with a quilt and looked at her fondly after the confession. I wanted that. We might argue after I told her about Havana, but after the uncomfortable argument, we would be okay. And Ana was right—Mimi probably wouldn't yell at me in public.

"Don't sharpen the knives tonight," Paula said.

"Also, I might need help defusing us when we start arguing."

"Are you a granddaughter or referee?" Junior asked.

"Is there ever a difference?" I grabbed my apron and went to stock cereals and practice how I would tell Mimi my news. Finally.

11

At the end of my shift, I met Mom and Mimi in the newly renovated outdoor dining area. The tables, painted in bold, bright shades, were now lit by hanging tin lanterns. Mimi took in all of the recent changes with a curious look. By the margarita at her elbow, Mom was clearly moving on from her hangover. The viejitos covertly watched us, ready to report the inevitable fight.

Benny stopped beside our table. "Tonight, we have appetizers."

"Stop lying. We never have appetizers," I said. Mr. Peña cooked dinner and that was it. He didn't understand why people expected snacks before their food.

"Mom is trying something new." Benny waved a hand at the lights and chairs. "There was a lot of yelling in the kitchen, so please don't order any of it even though it looks decent."

"You're a terrible waiter," I told him.

"So I keep telling them."

Mimi tsked. "You are a good boy who works to help his

97

familia." The praise was for him, but the loaded implication was a birthday gift for Mom.

"Tell your mother to keep the tequila coming," Mom said with a shake of her ice.

Benny, obviously noting the tension, took a step back before spinning away. It hadn't always been this way. When it was just Mom and me we always did something fun and ridiculous for both of our big days. For my seventh birthday we ate pizza for every meal and rented all the Star Wars movies, and the next year we went to a roller rink in Georgia that sold frozen pickle juice and played nonstop disco. We always gorged on food and laughed, which made getting older feel like a perfect thing to do. But when we moved to Port Coral, the day—just like everything else between us—had changed.

Mrs. Peña delivered a shrimp-and-scallop ceviche served alongside plátano chips still warm from the fryer and crispy chicharrones. It was plated very cool and not at all like Mr. Peña usually did. Because Mrs. Peña waited at the table, we holstered our issues and took our first bite.

"Good?" she asked, and Mom and I both shot her a thumbs-up. Mimi leaned into the fried pork belly with gusto. "Good," Mrs. Peña said, delighted. "I'm going to go tell my stubborn husband and then maybe kill him."

She left, and I spooned a mountain of ceviche onto a plátano and shoved it in my mouth. The lime and salt sang together in concert.

"I saw your wall today," Mimi said to Mom. "It's white. Is that it? If you want to paint houses, ours could use a coat."

"I don't paint houses."

"Pero you could. That would be steady work, no?"

"I'm not looking for steady work."

I popped three chips into my mouth.

Mimi made a haughty sound under her breath.

I continued to dig into the ceviche while another argument rolled over them. It was mild and mostly passive-aggressive, but we pulled a few glances. Mr. Gomez was pretending to take a selfie, but I could see the screen and it was pointed at Mom and Mimi. Mr. Saavedra was getting the latest Wi-Fi password from Benny. I idly wondered if they'd figured out how to do live streaming. Mom and Mimi's fights were like a summer storm—sudden, inevitable, and impossible for me to plan my day around.

I wondered what this table might be like with two more people. If this family were whole instead of broken into pieces, would our edges still be so sharp?

"Mimi, I have to tell you something." There was no going back this time. I had practiced this all afternoon, and the boxes of cereal had taken it well enough.

Mimi readjusted the bracelets at her wrist. "¿Qué pasó, mi amor?" she asked me.

"I got into a university in South Carolina, and I'm going to accept, because they have a study-abroad program in Cuba—with the University of Havana, actually—and I intend on going." I ripped off the Band-Aid like a total pro. The ensuing silence would possibly kill me, but still. I'd done it.

Mimi set her glass of water down. "¿Qué?" she asked softly, her gaze sharp.

"I want to go to Cuba," I told her. "For school. I want to go to school there."

Mimi looked at Mom. "What did you do?"

Mom signaled Benny for another drink. "This is Rosa's decision, not mine. Or yours."

"You can't go back." Mimi's voice sounded small and haunted.

"But I've never been in the first place. I want to see it now that we can."

Mimi shook her head.

"Why not?" I asked, desperate and frustrated.

Her hands swung up, her bracelets hissing. "The farm is gone, our family is dead, everyone is hungry, and a Castro is still alive, but you want to go to school there? Dime qué quieres."

Tension swam from our table like a storm cloud that swallowed the rest of the dining area. A domino did not move at the viejitos' table, and chairs refused to squeak beneath their uncomfortable patrons. Even the breeze stilled.

What *did* I want? I wanted the reassurance that it was okay to dump all of my questions about family and culture on someone who'd lost both. I wanted her to be proud of

100

me, to let me in, but instead she guarded me from all of it. Our past was a wound that would not heal, and I didn't know how to make her understand I just wanted to make it better. For all of us.

Mimi watched me with an old fire banked in her steady brown eyes.

Tucked away in my bag, a notification sang out from my phone, breaking the standoff. I fished it out, because it was the sound assigned to incoming messages from my school e-mail. My heart skipped when I read it was from the study-abroad program director. I clicked it open without reading the subject line.

So it took several tries to understand the first sentences.

Thank you for your interest . . . recent changes in national policies with regards to American students traveling to Cuba . . . need to review. The rest of the e-mail blurred into a watercolor mess.

"What's the matter? What happened?" Mom asked.

It took a few tries to collect my fractured thoughts. "Um, well." I put my phone away, my throat tight. "I actually just got word that the study-abroad program to Havana has been . . . canceled for the foreseeable future." As Mom and Mimi looked back at me with stoic expressions, I realized I should have expected this. There was no reason to be surprised or disappointed. No reason to cry. The timing of the e-mail didn't even strike me as strange—of course this would happen to the cursed girl as soon as she had finally worked up the courage.

"See?" Mimi said after a beat. "You can't go. You try to go and they'll keep you. Throw you in jail, and when they take you to jail, you don't come back."

Mom lowered her voice. "She's not going to go to jail, Mami."

Mimi gritted out in Spanish, "You weren't there. They show up and take you because you said the wrong thing to the wrong person. And you don't come back again."

"Is that why you left?" My heart was somewhere in my throat, and it felt too big to fit back into place. I felt both starved and selfish. "Were you going to be arrested?"

"It was not safe," Mimi said, her eyes haunted. "We were not safe." She blinked at the familiar window of el Mercado. She scanned the space around us, taking in the viejitos at their table, the town square lit by gas lamps just beyond her. She looked strung tight and ready to snap or flee. With a shaky hand she picked up her ice water. "They promise one thing before taking it away again.

"Carajo, qué mierda," she cursed. Mom choked on her next sip, erupting into coughs.

Benny dropped off our plates of arroz con pollo with tostones and yucca drenched in mojo. "There's flan when you guys are done." He slid me a sad look. He'd overheard my news, then.

I pushed my fork into my rice but couldn't find my appetite. An ultimately impossible idea had proved itself as such. It was as simple and inevitable as that. Look at the three of us. Mimi was secretly chasing miracles on an island she would never see again, while Mom was throwing bottles into the sea with letters no one would read. And now there was me, the dutiful daughter who still couldn't win.

"It's okay to be sad," Mom told me quietly as I grieved for a future that had never been mine.

12

Once Mimi was tucked away in bed with her novelas, I slipped into the garden room and grabbed the notebook. On my way out, I stopped at her bedroom door and said, "I have to finish some homework with Ana." Focused on her TV and night cream, Mimi waved me off.

On the front porch I quietly closed the door behind me.

"When I used to leave at night, I had to use the window."

Startled, I dropped the notebook. Mom glanced from it to me. She knew it wasn't my notebook, but I didn't explain, and she didn't ask. She continued to lazily rock back and forth in the rocking chair.

"Well, she trusts me," I said.

Mom nodded with a thoughtful look. Her gaze returned to the night sky.

With nothing to say, I turned to go.

"Be safe," she called after me.

I followed the sound of drumming to Ana's garage. The room was empty save for Ana and her set. Her family was probably upstairs, cursing her right now, but Peña house rules said Ana had until nine to play. When she spotted me, she acknowledged me with a nod, but continued to play whatever song she was drumming along to in her headphones. I settled onto the old orange couch. When she was done, she pushed back the headphones.

"How did it sound?"

"Awesome."

She narrowed her eyes. "What song was I playing?"

"You know I don't know."

"I practiced with the band today, and oh my god. It was so much better than jazz band. I mean, as soon as I got there, the lead singer dude, Tyler, is all . . . What's the matter?"

"What? Nothing! Tell me about band practice." It was getting harder to hold my smile in place.

"You look like you're about to cry."

I laughed. It sounded a little unhinged. "I always look like that."

She wasn't convinced. "What happened?"

My voice careful, I confessed, "They canceled the program to Havana."

Ana got to her feet and pulled me into a fierce hug. My tears spilled against her shoulder. Ana wasn't soft, but she tried when I needed it. "You'll find a way," she whispered, sounding so sure. But I wasn't. "It's right down there, and hell, even cruise ships are going now. It's not like it is for Mimi or our parents. *You* can go, school or not."

I stepped back and wiped my face. "I'm so bummed, but I'm also freaking out, because now . . . I don't know what I want. And I *always* know what I want. Do I still want to go to Charleston? Did I really consider Florida? Miami? Or even a different major? It all just lined up as this perfect, legitimate way of studying in Cuba in the face of everything that said I couldn't."

We stared at each other in the ensuing quiet. Ana raised her brows. "The indomitable Rosa Santos is in the midst of a small crisis."

I held my thumb and forefinger up, and tried to measure my panic in centimeters.

She tugged my hand down to my side. "You're getting tiki-tiki."

"I am not."

"You are," she said. "You're stressed because you're used to impressing." I tried to argue, but Ana wouldn't hear it. She lived in a house full of Latinos, so it was hard to talk over her. "You are. You're afraid of disappointing everyone. You prepared yourself to death, but you don't owe anyone a success story."

"Success story? Ana, I am *not* offering one. If anything, I'm being super selfish and was wholly prepared to take all of Mimi's work and sacrifices and break her heart."

Ana was shaking her head. "You weren't being obvious about it, trying to become a lawyer or doctor. But you're barely stopping to consider what *you* want, because your diaspora dream has always been to grow up and stop questioning whether you're Latina enough or deserving of what Mimi lost."

"That's not . . ." I trailed off.

Enough. I was still trying to work that one out. I was a collection of hyphens and bilingual words. Always caught in between. Two schools, two languages, two countries. Never quite right or enough for either. My dreams were funded by a loan made long before me, and I paid it back in guilt and success. I paid it back by tending a garden whose roots I could not reach.

"I do want to see Cuba," I said, my voice quiet but firm.

"I know."

"And I want Mimi to be happy and proud of me, and"— I sighed, willing only to admit the next vulnerability here—"I want Mom to come home."

Ana tapped the notebook in my hands. "Let me guess, you already wrote out a new plan to make all that happen."

"Actually, no. This is Mimi's notebook. I wanted to see if you'd help me with a cleansing spell, because I need to get this new batch of bad energy away from me after this disappointing plot twist."

"Rosa Santos, are you saying you came over, past your bedtime, to ask me to do some brujería with you?"

I could almost feel Mimi hissing at me. "Yes, I am."

Ana grinned. "Awesome."

I flipped through the notebook. "I should do some sort of

ritual," I decided, thinking of Mimi and Mom. Memories of them working together flashed in my mind so clearly I could smell the pungent green herbs and the sweet citrus of Florida Water. "A cleansing or something. Light some candles, say the right words, and I kick this bad juju out the door."

Ana was nodding. "Remember that time we tied a string to a doorknob?"

"That was for San Dimas because I lost my notebook and needed him to help me find it."

"Or when we wrote down our wishes and left them in bowls of water under our bed?"

My dream had been to become taller. I sighed. "Did you get your wish?"

"Uh, does it look like I've been discovered by Janelle Monáe and am now playing in her band for her next big tour?" She hit a cymbal, then pointed her stick at me. "Hey, Walter Mercado, can you find my horoscope in there?"

"No, but I might have found a long-lost tía."

"Whaaaaat?" Ana gaped at me. "Wow. Maybe this really will turn out to be like a telenovela."

I found Nela's name on a new page beside the city of Santiago and another miraculous healing. "I don't even know if Mimi has sisters; she's only ever mentioned her dead parents. Maybe Alvaro had sisters?"

I flipped to a new page and found a small sketch of a root. I never took Mimi for someone who liked to draw, but it looked like a botany piece with the parts of the root broken down. Next to it were instructions to burn the root and throw the ashes into the sea along with seven pennies. The ashes were for release and the pennies an offering, asking for protection. The second made sense. Things were always done in odd numbers, and pennies carried a lot of energy—people infusing them with wishes before tossing them away. Mimi advised me never to pick them up out in the wild. When they crossed her hand, she cleansed and kept them for future offerings.

"I think I found something." I described the ritual to Ana. Before I did anything, I needed to make sure I was grounded. "I'll do a limpieza and then I'll go do this." I didn't have time tonight for a spiritual bath—though I should really do one soon—and I definitely didn't have cigar smoke, but there were other things I knew how to do.

"You don't have that root, though," Ana said.

"No, but I bet Mimi will."

We hurried back to my house and snuck into the garden room through one of the open windows. "I really hope I don't run into my mom," I whispered.

"Because you'll get in trouble?"

"No, because I'll be proving her right." Trying for super stealth mode, we quietly searched through Mimi's tables and shelves. The glass jars were different sizes that held all sorts of ingredients. Darker bottles were tucked in the back with aging tinctures. I moved aside the hanging, drying bushels of herbs and searched the jars.

"Check us out, snooping through Mimi's witchy stuff." Ana laughed under her breath. "It's like we're in middle school again. I'm not going to find, like, eyeballs or anything, right?" A ceramic bowl clattered against the table before she hurried to right it. "Sorry," she said.

Finally on the third shelf I found a root that looked similar to the one Mimi had drawn. I uncorked the jar and noted how it smelled like licorice. I slipped the root out. "Got it."

Before we left I checked her desk and found a little stack of pennies. There were exactly seven. *When the right number presents itself to you, it is an invitation,* Mimi had told me once. I grabbed the coins.

Ana jumped out of the window, and I followed, trying not to laugh.

Back at her house, her mom asked if I needed dinner. I told her that I was fine as Ana snuck an egg from the fridge behind her back. We ran upstairs and hid in her room.

We dropped our pilfered goods on her bed. "I forgot to grab oil," I muttered.

Ana plucked a scented blue candle off her shelf. "What kind?"

I wanted one of Mimi's anointment oils but didn't want to sneak back in and try my terrible luck again. "I'm not sure."

"I've got some coconut oil in the bathroom, hold on." Ana left the room and banged on the bathroom door. "You've been in there for an hour," she yelled. Benny shouted something back. Ana pounded down the stairs before racing back up a moment later. She swept into the room and closed the door behind her, raising a small bottle. "I got olive oil."

I warmed a few drops in my palm before circling the candle's wick with the oil. "Wait, I forgot . . ." I muttered, feeling nervous as I tapped the candle against the desk three times. I exhaled a shaky breath before asking for protection and guidance. Ana dimmed the lights, watching me. With the swipe of a match, I lit the wick and held the egg over the flickering candlelight for a few seconds before closing my eyes and mindfully holding it to the top of my head. I circled my scalp before lowering it to the back of my neck, over my throat, and around my shoulders. I opened one eye and whispered, "Rub this over the rest of me."

"If only Mike could hear us," Ana murmured before taking the egg and doing as I asked. When she was done, she got to her feet. "Now what?"

The door rattled, startling us both. Benny poked his head in. "Hey, what are you guys—"

Ana leapt forward and slammed it in his face.

"I'm going to tell Mom you're doing brujería," he threatened against the closed door. We exchanged glances. Ana whipped the door open and let him in, shooting him a death glare.

I grabbed her glass of water from the nightstand and cracked the egg into it.

"Remind me not to finish drinking that," Ana said.

"The hell are you guys doing?" Benny asked.

I studied the yolk. It looked okay. Nothing was floating. No signs of anything wild or dangerous was hanging over me.

"Okay," I said, relieved. "I just need to burn that root, toss the ashes into the sea, and then I should be good and ready to know what to do about college."

Benny raised his brows. "You are *really* intense about school."

13

It was a quiet walk back to the marina, where I stopped at the stairs again. My new point of no return. In my denim jacket's pockets were a bag of ash and the seven pennies. I took the first step down to the docks. It was so dark, windy, and wild. How was I still in Port Coral? My cozy, soft hometown was gone, swallowed by a hungry, growling ocean I couldn't see. When a black cat pulled away from the shadows and stopped in my path, someone else might have seen bad luck, but this brujita saw a familiar.

"Which way is C dock?" I asked under my breath.

The cat began to bathe itself. I waited, pathetic and desperate.

Finally it stretched and slunk down the dock. I hurried to follow. The boats all looked tucked in for the evening. I checked around for some sort of signage or map, but there was nothing, only the string lights that decorated the back porch of the Starfish like stars.

It was just past nine now. I ought to be home and on my

way to bed with a book, lemon balm tea, and a face mask. That new golden shimmery one that smelled like honey.

Feeling utterly lost, I sighed at the stars. "What am I doing here?"

"Rosa?"

I screamed.

Alex froze, one foot on the dock beside me, one still on the boat behind him. "What *are* you doing here?"

I pointed accusingly at the cat.

He frowned, his gaze skipping between us as he stepped all the way off his boat. "Luna?"

"You know her?" I squeaked out.

"She hangs around a lot. Rosa, seriously. What are you doing here?"

I didn't know how my devil-may-care mother swept through town with paintbrushes and wine bottles when I felt foolish and out of my depth just standing here. It didn't help that Alex sounded so brash and grumpy. My eyes pricked with embarrassing tears. There was no way I could expose myself any further and bring up my mom or father right now. Poor baby Rosa, so lost she was chasing after stray cats.

"You're the one who told me to find you on your boat," I said.

Alex looked at me like I had three heads. "I didn't mean at night."

"Well, my bad," I said haughtily and spun on my heel

to leave, fully knowing I was possibly going in the wrong direction.

"Rosa, wait."

I stopped and glanced over my shoulder. Alex stood just behind me. He rubbed his brow. "I don't mean to be rude." He sounded so earnest and anxious I turned all the way back to him. He pushed a hand through his hair, and it swooped over his forehead in almost a wave. He gestured to a bench I hadn't seen. "You want to sit?"

I considered leaving, but I needed a moment, and this little seed of a crush really wanted me to sit with him. We sat on opposite ends and stared out into the dark. He leaned forward to study his hands. His thumbs circled each other in calming patterns. Luna curled up by our feet. It was almost cozy.

"I came to see where my father last set off from." Saying it out loud was like taking a dare. I felt bold and, yes, a little messy. It wasn't terrible, though.

"But why come when it's dark?"

I laughed, both tired and a little delirious. "I didn't want anyone to see me." I stared straight ahead, unwilling to see whatever was on his face. There was no way I could explain what I carried in my pockets.

Alex pointed ahead of us. "It's the one at the end of this dock."

I studied the empty spot with a knot in my throat. So that's where it all went wrong. Again. "It's so ordinary,"

I said. I'd spent most of my life trying not to become my mother, for Mimi's sake, and yet it wasn't until I acted a little like her that I found something this important.

"They mentioned it when I docked my boat here. This part of the dock isn't the most . . . popular."

"You're not superstitious?"

"I'm mostly broke," he admitted. "It's humbling to have to pay off a year of college you didn't finish."

"Why didn't you?" I asked, then cringed. "Sorry, you don't have to answer that."

"It's fine. I'm surprised the viejitos haven't done a full report on it yet."

His smooth Spanish accent distracted me for one very warm moment. It was curiously easy to talk sitting like this, both of us facing forward, glancing at each other only in small, careful bites. In the shadows, we were like two kids whispering after everyone else had fallen asleep at a slumber party.

"College was more of a necessary hurdle to prove I knew what does and doesn't work for me," Alex admitted. "I hated school and was a terrible student. College didn't change that."

"Did you hate it for any particular reason?" I loved being a student and sometimes feared it was all I was good at.

"I had learning difficulties." He said it mechanically, like he'd heard the words applied to him a million times. "School was mostly a pain of trying to learn things in a way my brain didn't work, so I was in a lot of self-contained classes in high school. Probably one of the reasons you didn't remember me."

"Maybe, but you also have a beard now."

He looked confused so I pointed at my chin and then his. "The beard makes you look older than nineteen."

Alex ran a curious hand over the lower half of his face. I found myself wondering how it might feel to run *my* hand across his beard and maybe press my face to his neck. I frowned, surprised at myself. Talking by moonlight softened a *lot* of edges.

"Where did you go for school?"

"Texas. It's where my dad's family is from. Where we lived until I was ten and my mom moved us back here to help run the Starfish after her mom died. I always meant to return." He looked out at the water like he was searching for his hometown on the other side of the Gulf.

"Not a fan of Port Coral?"

"Not a fan of change." At some point in our conversation he had gotten hold of a small piece of rope, and his hands were now busy tying knots as he talked. I watched, fascinated. It looked worn and soft.

He looked up and his hand stopped. I immediately felt intrusive.

"Sorry, I didn't mean to—" I started to apologize, but he shook his head.

"It's a coping thing," he admitted with a frown. "Calms me down when I get nervous."

Was he nervous right now? Had I done that to him? The tiny thrill electrified me.

His fingers tugged, and the knot in his hands untangled. "My dad gave me this rope to teach me different kinds of knots when I was younger. A way to keep me busy or distracted while he worked on the boats in the marina. After a while, it became a way to keep my hands busy and chill out."

"And you still have the same rope?"

"And I still have the same rope," he said with a hint of pride in his voice.

I wondered over the touchstones and talismans we all carried, and the energy they held from enough handling and hoping. My hand slipped into my pocket and counted the pennies again. "Did it help with school?"

"Lots of things helped, but it never got easier. The rope reminds me that despite failing physics I became a hell of a sailor."

I glanced at where he'd appeared from the dark earlier tonight. "Is that your boat?"

"Yeah. If you ask my dad, it's why I quit college. It's not true, but I don't regret it. I love my boat. Hell, I live on my boat."

I stared at the sailboat with renewed fascination and noticed the light on inside. He lived on that tiny little house that could take him anywhere.

"The one good thing that came out of my year was interning for the biology department. Since I knew my way around boats I helped with their projects out in the Gulf."

"And now you're back to help Jonas?"

"I'm back to eat crow served by my dad *and* help Jonas. The marina is important to me. I've been doing some cool stuff, and I want to be able to do that here, too."

"So, you *do* like Port Coral?"

He studied the stars for a moment before looking back at me. "Sometimes I like it very much. What about you? Where are you headed after you graduate? Havana, right?"

I no longer had a sure answer. It was as disorienting as finding myself out here at night. "I just found out the program with University of Havana was canceled, and now I don't really know. I've been accepted to a few places. I have until May to decide." I squinted as if I was counting. "In other words, I have a few weeks to figure this out."

"A lot can happen in a few weeks." Alex crossed his arms and the moonlight caught his tattoos. I realized with renewed alarm that he was a sailor with a boat *right over there.*

I jumped to my feet. "It's late. I should go."

Alex stood and I had to tip my face up to meet his gaze. He studied me for a moment with an open, curious look. "Well, you know where to find me now."

He returned to his boat and Luna followed. I waited until I was alone before moving on to the empty boat slip. My hair whipped across my face as I confronted the dark water and took measured breaths of the cooler, salty air.

My father was both forever gone and still somewhere out there. Maybe that's why Mom could never stay put. Did I want to be free from bad luck or from being in love? I reached into my pocket and tossed the ashes and pennies into the sea.

14

"Late night?"

Mom and I sat at our kitchen table, and she studied me from over her coffee. My gaze shot to the stove, but Mimi had already returned to her laundry room window.

"I know the sound of your bedroom window opening," she continued.

"Only because you snuck out of it so many times." On the sill, carved into the old wood, was Mom's name. Beside it was a clumsy heart and my father's name.

"And now you've snuck in," she said, amused. "Tell me, was it your first time? You were super loud."

"I fell inside, to be brutally honest." I'd landed on my elbow.

"Amateur mistake."

"And *I* see your hands are covered in paint." White and blue splotches stained her fingers. "Something new, or are you actually going to finish the wall?"

She hissed as if I'd burned her, but her eyes were lit with

humor. "You're grumpy when you're guilty, and here I didn't even ask what you did."

"Keep your voice down," I insisted. I took a fortifying sip of coffee.

"I'm sorry, but aren't I the one you should be hiding this from?" She leaned back in the chair and cocked her head to the side.

"You're the one who made it so that window never locks."

"You're welcome. Tell me where you were and I won't tell Mimi."

"Tell Mimi what?" my abuela asked as she returned to the room carrying a box of mason jars. She set them on the counter and explained, "Jellies. Strawberry, I think. They will go good with pan tostado."

"Are you bartering your services now?" Mom asked. "What's next? A cow?"

"Tell Mimi what?" she asked again stubbornly. Her suspicious gaze jumped between Mom and me. I felt like a surreptitious accomplice to some unknown crime.

"About your granddaughter's activities," Mom said lazily. I shot her a death glare.

Mimi crossed her arms.

I was going to throw up my coffee and morning pastelito. Mom had picked them up from the bodega this morning in some bid to soften me up before killing me.

"She found a new officiant for Clara and Jonas."

I relaxed so quickly I nearly dropped my coffee mug.

"He's very earthy and hippie," Mom went on about the news I'd told her earlier. "But bilingual. Cuban, right, Rosa?"

He wasn't actually. I bit into guava and cheese.

"Well, that's something." Mimi kissed the top of my head and returned to her window.

Once she was gone, I glared at Mom. "Are you trying to kill me?"

"Just keeping you on your toes." Her grin was devilish. She took a big bite of her pastelito, smiling at me as she ate it. "My baby girl is a little sneaky. Is it wrong to be proud?"

Being sneaky was exhausting. I was an anxious mess over staying out late on the docks, and my mother was smiling like I'd made honor roll. "It's definitely twisted."

"It's fun not to be the wild teenager in this house anymore."

I raised a disbelieving brow, and Mom's smile faltered. "It's just nice to see a little of me in you sometimes, too."

❖

Later that afternoon, I headed to my high school. It was weird to not have to *be* here anymore. Everyone was here. Ana was probably fighting someone in the band room, and I bet Mike was sketching out design plans for his boat instead of the assigned work. For a couple more weeks, they belonged. But no one was saving me a seat except for

Ms. Francis, the guidance counselor, whom I'd made an appointment with to discuss my suddenly no-longer-concrete plans in the face of my looming deadline.

"I have to say, Rosa, I'm very touched you came to me about this instead of Malcolm. All my dual-enrollment kids go to Malcolm." I liked Ms. Francis. Funny and honest, for an adult, she was a white woman somewhere in her thirties with curly red hair she always wore in a messy topknot. She walked Flotsam and Jetsam, her two Dobermans, through town most afternoons, and they were suspicious of everyone. I'd been meeting with Ms. Francis a lot over the years, and our relationship was now an easy, comfortable one. She knew about study abroad from the jump, and I knew she was ready to settle down, though she was having a tough time finding someone her dogs liked.

Ms. Francis leaned back in her desk chair. The Spice Girls played on her radio. "So, your study-abroad program is on ice. Is it just for the upcoming semester?"

"Maybe. According to the e-mail I got, they're monitoring national policies, but with the current administration . . ." I stopped and shrugged. "There are other schools with programs at the University of Havana, but not only is there not enough time to apply, but they're probably going to get canceled too. I can't take that chance, especially when it means losing scholarships."

She clicked her pen and turned to a blank piece of paper in the notebook in front of her. "Well, whenever *someone*

I know—I won't name names—needs to make a big decision, they make a highly detailed pros and cons list and then draws all over it."

I smirked. "But Havana *can't* be on my list. It's no longer an option at this juncture."

"Is Charleston still on your list?" When I hesitated, Ms. Francis sat up. "Instead of focusing on the Where, give some thought to all the Whys."

I wanted specific, concrete advice, not an essay topic. "Honestly, I'd rather just think about Port Coral right now."

She tapped her pen and considered me. "So you're helping take care of home before you leave?"

Her implication hit me weird. "It's not like I'm leaving forever. This will still be . . . I'll still live here, too."

"College is a moment, Rosa. An important one, of course, but it's not about the destination, it's about—"

"I swear, if you're about to say *journey*," I interrupted.

"—exploration," she finished with a sharp, teasing look. "You're fixated on place because Havana was your answer for a very long time, for very important reasons, but it wasn't ever about Charleston. It was about Charleston's connection." Her pen was still tapping. My pulse picked up as I watched. "This moment of indecision is ripe with the opportunity for a fresh perspective. Picking a school isn't going to answer all your questions, because if it does, you need to ask better ones. Demand more of your possibilities." Her phone buzzed with an alarm, and her pen came to an abrupt stop. "Dang, time for my next appointment."

I still didn't know what to do. "I need to secure my spot by May first."

"Your spot at Charleston?"

"I don't know anymore." I picked up my bag. She stepped past me to open her door.

"Maybe I'll pick one of the other schools that accepted me," I said and slipped my backpack straps over my shoulders. "But that's terrifying to consider this late in the game."

She huffed a laugh. "You're so young. I promise you it is not late in the game, Rosa."

I hated when adults said that. High school was all fun and games until they threw huge deadlines and choices at us that would decide the direction—and debt—of the rest of our lives. "But what if I stayed in-state? I could save money and—"

With a small, frustrated huff, she popped some gum in her mouth. "It's two years, Rosa. I won't even tell you where I got my undergrad—"

"It's right there on the diploma on your wall. You went to Nebraska."

"You are one of the most tenacious students I've ever had walk into my office. You're determined, but sometimes that single-mindedness can narrow your focus too much. You don't know what you want for a reason. Figure out the reason, and I bet you'll figure out what you want. You have a couple of weeks to think on this, and I'm here if you need me, but go for now, because Chris Miller's father is on his way."

Chris's dad was a divorced veterinarian whom Ms. Francis had her eye on since the beginning of the school year. Apparently Flotsam and Jetsam didn't mind him. I wished her luck and left.

Outside, PE was in full swing. The noise soared and clattered before rushing past. Laughs rang out, and a whistle blew.

"Rosa!" Benny walked over, hands in his pockets. He fell in step beside me. "What are you doing here? Getting up to some more brujería?"

"Meeting with Ms. Francis."

"You in trouble? You're stirring up a lot of chisme lately."

"Not everyone goes to their guidance counselor because they're in trouble. And what chisme?" He shot me his bright, charismatic grin, and I rolled my eyes. "Forget it." I noted he wasn't in gym clothes. "No mile for you?"

"This knee gets me out of everything now." The words were teasing. The tone was not.

"Like soccer?"

"We're not talking about soccer."

I sighed. He was so stubborn. "You are such a Taurus."

"Not talking about that either—we're talking about you and your old-man-and-the-sea boyfriend."

"*What?* Your family is the worst. He's not my boyfriend,"

I shot back even though my lungs did a weird, concerning squeeze. "Also, he's not an old man."

"That's not what I hear."

"Because you don't listen."

"Perhaps, but is it true that he has a boat?"

"Why?" I asked, suspicious, before the obvious reason for him asking hit me. "Oh my god, first of all, I know my own curse, and secondly, it doesn't matter because he's *not* my boyfriend."

"This isn't about that." Benny lowered his voice, and his eyes darted around the open field. "I think I know where the Golden Turtle is."

I was starving, and if I hurried, I could make lunch before Mr. Peña switched to dinner and I missed out on the croquetas. "The wha— Are you seriously still on this? Benny, you have got to stop. We are not going to find lost treasure in Port Coral."

"I found the map today."

"Whose map?"

"*The* map. Every year there was a map, a way to start the quest. But no one ever found the last one, thus never found the turtle, and the mapmakers never confessed."

"And you found this long-lost map?"

"I've been doing independent study during second period, which apparently means cleaning out old storage rooms. Anyway, today, I got to some yearbooks from the early 2000s. I looked up our parents, and there in a collage was this graffiti map of our town. And what do I see on it? A freaking golden turtle."

"And no one noticed this whole time?"

"It was a yearbook. No one looks at theirs after graduation. And it was a mess of a map. Busy as hell. The aesthetic back then was ridiculous."

"Wait. What does this have to do with Alex having a boat?" I asked.

"Because it's on a barrier island."

I stopped walking. I couldn't go on a barrier island. Then again, a week ago I thought I couldn't go to the marina.

"We can become legends in this town." Benny flashed me a grin. "We just need you to ask your old-man boyfriend to take us."

❖

I hustled across town, kicking up pink-and-white petals in my rush, before dashing into el Mercado. Alex didn't have a phone, which meant I had to go to the marina and try to flag him down from outside his boat or something. I needed food first.

There were still a few croquetas behind the glass counter. Farther down the counter were the new desserts, and there were pastelitos again. Jackpot. The air was cinnamon-sweet, so the baked goods must have just arrived. I looked for Mr. Peña, but someone else was behind the counter dropping off boxes of cookies. Afternoon light sifted in from the window behind him, making the blue waves across his arm shimmer, and revealing the flour dusting his gray shirt.

"You're the baker?"

Alex froze. He set down the last box and turned. "Rosa?"

I opened my hands to encompass all the baked goods between us. "You baked this?" He nodded. "Why didn't you tell me?"

He looked confused. "You didn't ask."

"If I baked all of this, I would tell everyone. Any and every conversation I had would start with, 'Have you heard the good word of dulce de leche?' Oh my god." I covered my heated face. "You make the dulce de leche." I groaned into my hands.

"Is that a good thing?"

"Yes," I said without lowering my hands.

Mr. Peña came in from the kitchen. He gave me a look and gruffly told me, "I have three left." He scooped the last croquetas into a small paper bag for me. Alex and I were still standing there as Mr. Peña began setting out the rice for dinner. I looked at Alex and asked, "Do you have a minute?"

He slipped car keys out of his pocket. "Sure. I just have to drop the truck back off at the marina."

I followed him out of the bodega. It was a small blessing that no one was in the break room to see us as we headed to the parking lot. Was he smiling? The afternoon sun was blindingly bright at the moment, so maybe he was just squinting. I had to stop staring at his lips. I hurried to keep up with his longer stride. At the old blue truck we stopped, and I gripped the straps of my backpack. In a rush, I said, "There's this local legend from forever ago, when a class hid a—"

"Golden Turtle."

I stopped, relieved. "You know about it?"

"I grew up here, too, Rosa." He cocked his head.

"My friend found the map." I checked around us and leaned closer. He met me halfway, and I was momentarily distracted by the smell of sugar on his warm brown skin. I leaned in even closer and whispered, "It's on a barrier island."

"Yeah? I drew fishing maps for the area years ago and know the islands around here well."

"Good! That's good. Because I was going to ask if you'd take us out there."

"Really? You're ready?" The question was simple, but huge. He understood what I was asking was bigger than our town's legends. It was bigger than me snooping around the docks at night looking for some marker of my father's life. Rosa Santos was asking to get on a boat and leave this shore.

I wasn't ready. But I wanted to try.

15

"Rosa, you can't wear two life jackets," Ana insisted.

I stopped trying to clasp the second one. "Fine."

Instead of Alex's sailboat, we boarded a pontoon his parents chartered out. He tried to explain how complicated sailing was in an effort to reassure me that this would be an easy trip, but it did nothing to calm my nerves. The pontoon was basically a bunch of couches in a floating bathtub. Alex sat behind the wheel as we slowly made our way out of the marina.

"The Gulf isn't really the ocean," he explained for my benefit.

"Semantics," I said, and gripped the edge of the small table bolted into the floor in front of me. "It is an ocean basin, connected to the Caribbean Sea and Atlantic."

"According to your map, we'll be there in a few minutes."

"It's not my map." I hadn't given myself enough time to think about this. As soon as Alex agreed, I texted Ana, Benny, and Mike to meet us at the dock if they wanted the infamous turtle. I even included a cute little turtle emoji. I was orchestrating this wild quest, all because I had an ill-thought-out crush. We were doomed.

Benny looked comfortable with his arms stretched across the back of his chair. He grinned as he looked at the open water ahead of us.

"What's in your bag?" I asked him. This was all his idea, but he'd been last to arrive at the docks.

"Bottle rockets. If you're going to win, win big." He patted the bag next to mine. "And we can use them for flares if we get lost."

Alex turned the wheel by small degrees. "We're not going to get lost." He glanced at me and offered me an encouraging nod. We were surrounded by water and a deep orange sky, but behind us, Port Coral was alive with the lights along the boardwalk. I watched it become smaller. It looked like a postcard. A perfect snapshot of home.

"It's something, isn't it?"

I looked over my shoulder to see Alex smiling at me.

"I've never seen it from this angle," I said, awed. This sleepy harbor was just as welcoming as Mimi's house, as soft and warm as a guava pastelito. It wasn't haunted and gloomy. It was alive and so worth saving.

"Just a little farther," Alex assured me.

"I can't believe the map was in the yearbook the whole time," Ana said. She flipped through, laughing at the older pictures with Mike. "That's evil."

"I'm not surprised," Mike said. "Check all the heavy eye-liner they're wearing."

"Let me see." I was too nervous to get up while the boat was in motion, so Ana brought the yearbook to me. I opened it to the map page again and dragged my finger across the bubble-gum-bright image. There was our town square on the map, the grass basil green and surrounded by familiar buildings in sandy shades of brown and coral pink. Just west of it was my street, the houses too small to distinguish, but in front of Mimi's was a splash of green dotted with yellow: her lemon trees. "It was probably a sneaky-as-hell editor who wanted to watch the world burn."

"Smart but dangerously subtle," Alex said.

"But the mystery of it. It's the sort of mess I would have made if anyone left me in charge of the yearbook." I'd been editor in middle school and thought I would be again, but high school gave way to college too fast to stick around and play pretend.

I glanced up and my gaze caught Alex's. He jutted his chin toward the map. "What do you see?"

The question startled a laugh from me. "You just reminded me of my mother."

Alex looked surprised. Benny frowned and jerked his head in an *Abort, you're being awkward* way.

"No, it's just my mom and I traveled a lot when I was younger, to really ordinary places, and she'd always ask, 'Where are we, Rosa?' and that was my cue to pretend that bit of sky was actually California or that orchard a vineyard in Italy. Like the sea right in front of us was Cuba."

Alex looked at me thoughtfully. "Do you want to go to those places?"

"Of course."

He turned the wheel a little, and old memories stirred. Windows open, my hair flying, another map on my lap. Mom singing and tapping along to an old country song on the radio. Ana took the yearbook to tell Benny something I couldn't hear over the engine and wind. There were so many places I wanted to go, and sitting here with my friends was the first moment in a long time where I felt capable of going anywhere.

"We're here," Alex announced.

The engine cut off and the boat coasted to a stop. I shot to my feet. The shocking realization that I had crossed a small body of water and was now on an island was over-shadowed by the sight of other parked boats and several dots of lights bouncing around the island.

"Benny!" I shouted.

"Okay, so I wasn't the only one in that storage room, and it turns out I'm pretty loud when I talk."

We scrambled off the boat. "God, my family is the worst," Ana announced as she jumped over the side.

"Never tell a Cuban a secret," I agreed, steps behind her.

"Hey, we're the only ones with the yearbook." Benny turned on his phone's flashlight, and we all followed suit. It wasn't fully dark yet, but it was close, and though the unin-habited island wasn't big, it was overgrown. "Give me the yearbook, Rosa."

We huddled around it. I could hear voices from the other groups. So far, no one was screaming about snakes or gators. And no one was shouting in victory. I pointed at the turtle. "According to this very funky compass rose, it's on the northwest corner." I looked up from the map. "Which way is northwest?"

Alex took the lead. "Be careful." He scanned the ground. It was all dirt, fallen palm fronds, and scattered shells.

"According to old pictures, the turtle is the size of a football." I hurried forward and bumped into Alex's back. "Sorry."

"It's okay." He slowed his stride to meet mine. I wanted to move closer so badly it was like fighting a magnet.

"What do we get if we find this thing?" Mike asked. He kicked over a log. "Holy shit, there's, like, a city of bugs under this thing." He squatted to investigate with a stick.

"We get to be the ones who found the Golden Turtle," Benny said. "That's huge. Rosa?"

"What?" I said without looking back. I was trying to walk while focusing my peripheral gaze on Alex again.

"My dad said the winner got free pizza at Bonito's," Mike said, and turned his flashlight just enough to quickly blind Ana. She lunged for him as he darted away, laughing.

"Rosa!" Benny shouted.

"What?!" I stopped and looked back at Benny. The other voices were getting closer.

"We're doing this to find something that's been lost almost as long as we've been alive," Benny said, sounding serious. This mattered to him. He opened his hand for the yearbook, and I gave it to him. We headed northwest by the light of Mike's flashlight in search of treasure.

❖

After a half hour, we still hadn't found it.

It probably didn't help our cause that Benny was the only one really looking. Alex left to watch after the boat, Mike was looking for sticks to whittle, and Ana and I walked together, kicking aside leaves and muck.

"Your new boyfriend is super hot," she said.

I shushed her. "He's too much. I look at him and I want to just, like, move closer. It's making me all clumsy and sweaty."

"The height difference is very tol and smol. You could climb him or something."

"Right? I'll build a nest up on his shoulders where I can bring him small trinkets. I was *months* deep on the viejitos' Insta searching for any crumb of information about him, but there was nothing, and now to find out he bakes, too?"

"Lethal."

"I'm going to fall too hard. This is level-five crushing.

I mean, we have a past. We had lunch together for an entire semester, reading and never speaking. I have no idea what to do with that."

Ana laughed. "Silently reading beside you? God, that's, like, your ultimate romance. And with the way he was watching you on the boat, I think he'd be up for that nest."

I stumbled over a huge rock. "He was looking at me? Describe his face."

"Hey, look, it's Benny," a voice shouted from the dark trees.

Benny shoved the yearbook back at me and muttered a curse. "There goes our element of surprise."

"We lost that as soon as you found the map, big mouth," Mike pointed out.

The light of my cell phone shone on a corner of the rock that I'd tripped over. There was something very curiously round and smooth about it. I bent to brush away the dead foliage.

A golden shell came into view. Holy crap. Benny was right.

"Benny!" I whisper-screamed.

He whipped his head around and met my gaze meaningfully.

"I caught the oiled-up pig," I told him.

He grinned. "Lucky, now you can marry a girl from your village." He headed toward the voices with an easy walk, and cracking jokes I couldn't hear past my racing thoughts.

I bent quickly and shoved away the rest of the dead leaves.

Mike and Ana huddled too closely around me. "Be cool, you guys," I hissed. "Look natural."

They immediately dispersed. Mike sang, "Look at the stars, Ana. Look how they shine for you."

"You're damn right they do," she said.

There it was. The Golden Turtle. Rustier than the pictures, but it was unmistakable. I picked it up and realized it was bigger than a football.

Ana bumped into my side. "Damn, we actually did it." Her awe turned cutthroat. "How the hell are we supposed to get that back to the boat without being seen?"

"Why can't we be seen?"

Mike huddled beside us. "Because this is an island of mice, and you got the cheese."

I whipped off my backpack.

"It's not going to fit," Mike whispered.

It would. Everything did when I needed it to, and sure enough, even with my laptop and books in there, I was able to fit the statue. I zipped it closed and had the bag on my back again just as Benny came over with his group.

"Hey, assholes." He was smiling and looking only at me. I smiled back. "What, already bored?" he asked.

"Extremely," Ana told him. "Plus, our mothers would kill us for being out here, trying to get murdered."

"Too many podcasts," I told her in a singsong voice.

"We're out," Mike decided.

"Fine," Benny said, his voice dripping in disappointment. "Have fun searching," he told the others and followed our casual stroll back to the boat.

Alex got to his feet when he saw us coming. When we started running, he cranked the boat. As soon as we boarded and I was back in my life vest, Alex pushed the throttle and pointed us toward open water. We screamed in victory. Somewhere on the island, curses rang out. By flashlight, we took pictures with the statue to immediately post our proof.

"I can't believe we found it." Ana held it in her hands, her hair flying in the wind.

Benny sat back and crossed his feet, a content and cocky grin on his lips.

"You know what this means," Ana shouted over the roar of the boat and wind. "We'll be the ones to hide it again before graduation."

"You know what else this means?" Mike asked. "Free pizza."

❖

Back at the marina, everyone headed toward the square, hoisting our treasure. I lingered with Alex as he settled his boat. "Are you coming?" I asked him. "Mr. Bonito can be a little heavy with the sauce sometimes, but the best pizza is the free kind." Behind him the sky was midnight blue and glittered with stars. His dark hair danced softly in a restless breeze.

Alex was the sea, and I wanted to close my eyes and jump.

"I've still got stuff to take care of, but thanks." He tried to calm his windswept hair. "Enjoy the victory."

"Couldn't have done it without you." I slipped my thumbs beneath the straps of my backpack and looked up at him. "I mean that. All of this. Going out there and finding it, but also just *going* out there. I can't believe I did that, but it was . . ."

He waited.

"Incredible." My hair was a mess, and my lungs burned from the rush of cold sea air, but I couldn't stop smiling.

Alex looked pleased. "I've got some news."

"What is it?" I didn't mean to whisper the question, but he stepped closer. And glanced at my lips. I tried to remember how to talk.

He reached into his pocket and slipped out a phone. "I got a new one."

"Can I have your phone number now?"

There was a striking moment of silence that nearly killed me before he laughed suddenly. The deep, honest sound was a wash of relief that teased an equally bright smile from me. He climbed back onto the boat and from some unknown cabinet fished out a slip of paper and pencil. As he scribbled something on it he said, "So, not only do you deliver bread by bicycle and save seaside towns, but you have an impossible backpack that can hold anything."

In my back pocket, my phone vibrated, once, twice, and then again and again—my friends, ready to celebrate, no doubt. I ignored it as I did a quick half turn to show off my beloved bag.

"Your story is definitely an interesting one." He stepped off the boat again.

Oh, how I wanted it to be. "I'm still figuring it out, to be honest."

"Well, in tonight's chapter, you took a boat by moonlight and found a pirate's lost treasure."

A startling whine sang out, and the sky exploded in yellow sparks. Three more bottle rockets sailed above us as Benny broke into his stash. But I couldn't look away from Alex's warm gaze.

I wanted more. So much more.

Ana screamed my name, and Alex looked past me. His chest rose and fell. He offered me a small but gallant bow of farewell before handing me the piece of paper. "My number," he said. I clutched it in my hand.

"Rosa!" Ana shouted from the dock.

"¡No me grites!" I screamed, turning toward her, the fireworks, and the oldest pizza spot in town.

16

We emerged from our victory meal, phones bursting with notifications. Outside, a car waited. Three girls, all on the dance team, leaned out the open windows and smiled at Benny. He glanced back at us with a bright smile. "Can I have the turtle tonight?"

I guess the star soccer player is back.

"No," Ana said as I asked, "What are you going to do with it?"

"This old guy has been lost for a long time, Rosa. He deserves to celebrate."

"I think you're the one who's been waiting to celebrate," I said.

A song's deep bass rolled out from the waiting car. They were growing impatient for their hero. "I'll keep an eye on it," Benny told me, grinning.

"Yeah, I bet," I said. "Just don't lose it or be gross."

"Wise words, but my chariot awaits." He climbed into the car.

"You're not going with them?" I asked Mike once they left.

He slipped a toothpick in his mouth and shrugged. "It's been a long night, and we ran out of bottle rockets."

We followed the winding sidewalks back to our neighborhood. The houses that lined this street were mostly one story, squat, and made of concrete, but painted in bright shades that complemented their well-tended gardens. Nights were growing warmer now, and the evening air whispered to us in sweet-tart breezes that rustled the many citrus trees on the block.

"Do you think he's going to lose the turtle?" I asked Ana.

She twisted her curls up into a careful knot before checking her phone. "Nah," she said. "I think he's going to straight-up trade it away." She slipped her phone into her back pocket.

An electric sound screeched from the house in front of us. We stopped walking. The garage door stood open, and inside someone was kneeled in front of an amp. He looked over his shoulder and noticed us. "Ana!" he called, smiling. I recognized Tyler Moon, the lead singer of the Electric, from school. Tyler was short, spry, and blinded you with his shiny blond hair and megawatt smile. He had been a senior when I'd started dual enrollment.

"Band practice this late?" I asked Ana.

"Hey, Ana!" Tyler called. "You gotta hear this."

Ana peeled away from us and headed up the driveway.

"Don't forget your curfew," I called, and she hissed, "Okay, *Mom*."

I blew her a kiss and then Mike and I continued on our way. "Hey, congrats for getting on the boat." He raised his hand for a high five. "Big deal for a Santos, yeah?"

I slapped my hand against his. "I returned in one piece and even found a treasure."

Mike laughed. "Hopefully it doesn't belong to the dance team come morning." He waved good-bye and I walked the last few feet home. Across the street, Malcolm's car pulled into his driveway. I headed his way.

"Long day at the office?" I asked.

He straightened and offered me a tired smile as he loosened his tie. "Not every student is as motivated and organized as you."

"Ah, you just say that because I'm your favorite." Malcolm was very cool and scholarly but was a total mother hen. He helped me through all the new rules and requirements that popped up when I decided to pursue dual enrollment. And reminded me I was capable when it got overwhelming.

"How's everything going?" He crossed his arms and leaned his hip against his car.

"Good," I said, meaning it.

Malcolm studied me like he might a disorganized bookshelf. "Just checking in. I heard about study abroad, so I was wondering how you were."

"Oh, right. Of course I'm super bummed. I meant to tell

you about it all but got sort of distracted by all this festival and wedding stuff."

"That can be a good thing. Are you still planning on Charleston?"

"I'm not sure. I'm taking a moment to evaluate all of my options." I crossed my arms and shrugged. "But I'm good. Super good."

"Right," he said, sounding like he didn't believe it but didn't intend to press. "Well, I saw your mom by her mural earlier. She looked a little stressed-out."

"That's how she always looks."

"Is she still here?"

He didn't mean anything by it. I knew this. Malcolm was someone who always checked in after Mom left, and distracted me with new books when I was a kid, and new books with bonus stationery now that I was older, but the *still* in that question stung. "Yeah, she's home. We should all do dinner tomorrow or something."

"Sounds like a plan. Have a good night, Rosa."

"You too. Hopefully Penny lets you guys sleep."

His laugh sounded a little delirious as he headed up his front walk.

I crossed the street. Our porch light flickered, and I made a mental note as I opened the front door to buy bulbs. In the living room my mother and grandmother stood at odds, their faces tight, and last sharp words were swallowed by my arrival.

Mom's bags were at her feet.

"What's going on?"

"Your mother is leaving," Mimi announced. My face still burned from the cold, the same face all over social media right now holding up a long-lost treasure while wearing a very bright life jacket. An ache gnawed inside me where possibility had just bloomed. Mimi began begging the saints and ancestors in Spanish for patience.

"I'll be back soon," Mom said, sounding anxious. Those were always her first words. It was a promise and a curse.

"Why tonight?" I asked, hating the shake in my voice. "Why does it have to be *right* now? What about your mural?" *What about me?*

"There's this painting I sold and I need to go and—" Her face tightened, distracted by Mimi still wailing about the darkness my mother carried inside. "I got an order, and I need to—" Mom tried to focus on me, but her breaths rumbled like thunder. "Enough!" Mom finally burst out and whipped around to Mimi. "I am trying my best. And I'm sorry that it's so disappointing."

"What are you looking for, mija?" Mimi implored. "And why isn't it here? Why is this not enough for you?"

Mom froze, shocked and angry. Her chest rose and fell. This fight was building into something too big. "Because it was never enough for you."

Mimi blinked. "How can you say that to me?"

Mom's head fell back, a bitter laugh escaping her. Her

dark hair was wild and loose, her eyes bright with unraveling emotion. "Your story is a tragedy, but somehow in mine, I'm the villain," she snapped. "We *both* lost, Mom. I'm trying. I left Rosa in the place she loved that never loved me back."

"You're not leaving because of a painting." I tugged my backpack off and dropped it at my feet. "At this point I deserve better than that. We have breakfast, we laugh and make plans, and I stupidly think, 'Hey, maybe this time, we've figured this out,' but you were already gone, weren't you? Were you already packed?"

Her eyes watered. She said nothing.

We made no sense. Love wasn't supposed to be like this. I looked at Mimi. "You tell me, then. Why does she leave? Why do you refuse to talk about Cuba? Why are we like this?"

Mimi's eyes closed. One hand went to her brow, the other to the saint medal she always wore. Anger over hurting her swept through me. This is what happened when Mom came home. I became an accomplice to this.

"Tell her what you said to me," Mom said to Mimi, her voice rough.

Mimi stilled. Her eyes opened and narrowed on Mom.

"Everyone remembers me screaming at the docks for him, but tell her what happened right before that."

"You understand nothing," Mimi said, quiet. "You run and believe it's only you who has been hurt."

"Tell her that my love killed him," Mom continued, loud and relentless. "I loved him too much, so the sea took him. When this whole town cried for the lost boy at sea, you looked at your own daughter and her growing middle and said it was the curse. That it was *me*."

The last word rang like the toll of a bell that stirred our ghosts. The room grew colder.

"You don't know what it's like to return. To bite my tongue and live with looks like I'm bad luck walking. To hear him around every corner. I crawl out of my skin, but I come back for my daughter, because after everything, this is the place she loves. That's *my* curse, not your stupid sea."

Where Mom was unraveling, Mimi was throwing sparks. I'd seen her and Mom fight, but never like this. "I understand," Mimi whispered.

"You don't, if—"

My abuela snapped. "I climbed out of that broken boat with you in my arms knowing every step I took was a step away from him." The words were rough with rust, but Mimi dug them up with gritted teeth. "I watched him sink. I watched him drown knowing there was nothing I could do. I pulled myself out of the sea and stepped onto land for you. I bit my tongue over and over as I learned a language for us, and every time I looked out at the sea I mourned him, and then I watched it happen again to you, and I stayed. For you." She looked at me. "And for her. I understand, but yet I am *your* villain, Liliana."

149

"You pushed me away," Mom whispered.

"And what are you doing to her right now?" Mimi shot back.

Their gazes turned to me at once. It was too much. I stood at the crossroads of all their pain and love, and I couldn't carry it all.

"I keep trying to fix this." I laughed, edgy and vulnerable. "Because maybe then Mom will come home and her mother will tell her she loves her and maybe, maybe, maybe."

"Rosa—" Mom started.

"No," I interrupted. "It's my turn. Because in a few minutes you're going to walk out that door and Mimi is going to disappear into her room and I'll be left alone." I gestured to the three of us, and the triangle we made. "Something is broken here. It is sad and tired, and we keep breaking it more."

I bent and opened my backpack. I slipped Mimi's notebook out and handed it back to her. "I was looking for ways to cleanse myself of bad energy. I burned one of your roots and threw pennies into the sea. No one tells me anything, so I tried to find it myself."

Mimi took the notebook. "No one tells you anything? Okay. Come with me." She turned and went to her garden room. I followed and watched my usually calm abuela shove bowls and mortars and pestles from her table and spill a bowlful of dirt. She lit a candle and slammed it into the center of the dirt. I watched, fascinated and confused. I wasn't sure what she was doing, because I hardly ever saw Mimi do this kind of magic.

"How many pennies did you throw?"

"What?"

In a flash of motion, she snatched up the candle, turned it upside down, and extinguished it in the dirt. I started at the impact.

"How many?" she asked again, louder.

"Seven," I blurted. "I got them from your pile."

"Bueno," she said, relieved.

Mom stood in the doorway. "I act like a borracha when I'm sad, but you're acting como una bruja."

"Y dicendo verdades," Mimi returned. They were mirrors of each other. Mimi, alone in a new land, had buried all of her pain, and from it an angry daughter had grown.

"Who's Nela?" I asked suddenly.

Shadows curled and warnings whispered along my skin. The surprise in Mimi's vulnerable gaze broke my heart. "Why do you ask me all of these questions?"

"Because you're still not telling me anything."

"I teach you *everything*, but you are impatient. It is you who tells me nothing." Before I could argue, she snapped, "You search for all my secrets while you keep so many. College, Havana, y qué más? ¿Tienes novio?"

"What? No, I don't have a boyfriend." Icy panic cracked in my chest.

Mom barked a bitter laugh. "What's the point of romance when we have to live with your curse?"

"¡No es mío!" Mimi shot back, her voice breaking. "It is not *my* curse. I died on that boat, too." Mimi stepped back and did something she never did in the midst of a ritual: She blew out the candle instead of letting it burn down.

She passed me and I tried to reach for her, but she continued to her bedroom. Her door closed softly. It was worse than it slamming shut.

"Rosa," Mom said.

"Just go." I didn't turn around. She hesitated, but she walked away from me like always. The house fell quiet. My mother was gone, and so was Mimi, but our ghosts remained.

17

Outside my bedroom window, past angry stone-gray clouds, the sun was missing. Swallowed by the impending storm. I was sure of it.

In the kitchen, Mimi stood at the stove, her back to me. We said nothing to each other, both too battered for fresh words. Her laundry room window stayed closed as she made a breakfast flavored and seasoned by her frustration. She made it every time my mother left, salting it with tears, heartbroken regrets, and angry prayers. My laptop whistled with news of the return of my Wi-Fi, but I gently closed it. I didn't want the rest of the world today. I wanted an ugly daisy blanket and the consuming quiet that always crept into the space left by my mother.

My first lost love.

Maybe this was what the memory of home felt like for Mimi: the ache, loss, and stubborn love. Desperate to keep the soft memories, even as you counted new scars and mourned all the choices you never got to make.

I settled into the chair and lit the candle on my window-sill. There were three acorns in the grooves of my parents' carved names. I pulled the yellow blanket around me, and like a lighthouse, I tracked the storm and kept watch over my harbor.

18

The rain eased, and the next morning revealed a low fog that wove a hazy cocoon through town. Mimi offered to make me a café con leche and prepared it like when I was younger: bringing the milk to a gentle boil and mixing it with the sweet coffee before pouring it from one mug to the other, back and forth, to create the froth. When she was done, she slid it across the counter. I didn't ask her about Nela, and she didn't tell me I couldn't know. The conversation went up on the shelf like one more ghost to never talk about.

I packed my bag and prepared to head down to the Starfish. Alex had sent a text yesterday asking to go over the menu for the wedding. I had no business having a crush on him. I needed to focus on my next step. Acting like my mother would not break this cursed cycle. I needed to finish coordinating this wedding with Alex, and then the festival would save the harbor, and I'd be on my way out of here. Just like I planned. I slipped on my shoes, checked my lipstick in the mirror above my altar, and popped a strawberry candy. Life continued like always.

On my way to the boardwalk, I avoided the fire station, walked right past the bookshop without pausing to worry about broken ankles and angry seas. I headed down the stairs, all the way to the kitchen. No stumbling steps, clumsy tripping, or anxious reflections.

So maybe it wasn't *totally* like always.

Inside, the restaurant was empty. It was early, but warm sugar was heavy in the air.

"Alex?"

The door behind the bar opened, and Alex leaned out. He spotted me and smiled. "Come on back."

I followed and found a confectionary fantasy in the kitchen. The room smelled of citrus, bananas, and cinnamon, and every counter was covered with cakes and flaky pastries. Somewhere a radio played a blues song that sounded rough with age like one of Mimi's records. I looked at Alex, shocked. "Is *all* of this for the wedding?" The overachiever in me was in awe. The rest of me wanted one of everything.

"Of course not." He lifted a tray of various small delicate slices of cakes. "These are. Clara liked them all and asked for your opinion. The rest of this is just what I bake for the Starfish and el Mercado." I couldn't stop staring at him. He shrugged and set the tray down like he'd simply shown me his homework. "Everybody has to work, and this pays the bills for now."

"It's like hearing Mary Berry say her cherry cake is just a hobby."

"Who?"

A man I didn't know walked into the room. He looked like Alex but older, shorter, and with a softer, more open face. "He doesn't watch a lot of TV," he said, good-naturedly. He came forward and shook my hand. "I'm his older brother, Carlos. It's nice to officially meet you, Rosa. You two are the big story of the docks. Alex talks to nobody, but here he is, all Chatty Cathy with you, sneaking out pontoon boats like he's fifteen and got a secret hot date."

"Oh, it wasn't anything like that," I hurried to say.

Alex's expression shuttered. The return of the surly fisherman. Or baker, rather.

Carlos's grin got bigger. "Yeah, well, it's a good move. It's how I got my wife. Come to think of it, it's how our sister got hers, too." Carlos smacked Alex's shoulder. "Like a big, silent tree, this kid. Listen, I've got a couple calls I need to make, but we're running late." He handed Alex some paperwork, and they both bent their heads over the order forms. I drifted away to peek in on all of the various ingredients scattered around the kitchen. Strawberries and lemons. Fresh cream. Dark chocolate shavings. I wondered how long until his mother came in and told him to clean up his mess. Was she the type? Mine wasn't, but everyone always had funny stories about their Latina moms dragging them out of bed on Saturday mornings because no one helped them. Whenever I tried to join in and tell stories about mine, I inspired such sad looks.

Your mother leaves?

Yes, but she always comes back.

Poor baby Rosa.

I plucked a strawberry from the basket and bit into it. Juicy red sweetness rolled over my tongue. I snuck a glance back and found Alex—now alone—watching me. "Sorry," I said, embarrassed. "They looked delicious."

"That's a good thing," he said. He continued to study me. "You're sad today."

The last time he'd seen me I was celebrating finding the Golden Turtle.

I moved around the counter and felt his gaze follow me. "A little." I hated what I had to say next and the reaction it always inspired. I didn't want him to look at me like some lost kid. I was frustrated and tired, and wanted to complain and possibly cry, but I also wanted to defend my mother before anyone else could say a word about her.

"My mom left yesterday."

"Why?"

It was always left to me to answer that question. "Because this town is stuck in a time loop for her, and she becomes seventeen and heartbroken all over again."

I watched Alex's gaze soften as a hint of golden sunlight sifted into the room, and around us, sugar sparkled and caramel bubbled. He slid the tray of wedding cake samples closer to me.

In the dream-lit kitchen, I dipped a fork into the yellow one and took a bite. Sharp as a sudden memory, my eyes closed to capture the flavors. Gently tart, creamy lemon burst like fireworks, and I rushed to offer a bite to Alex before I finished the whole thing. Focused on me and my reaction, he dipped his head and took the bite. The room grew warmer. Alex swallowed, still staring at me.

I covered my mouth and worriedly asked, "What?"

"I just . . ." He shook his head like he was clearing it. "You make me remember things."

That sounded both gentle and powerful. I liked it. "Tell me yours and I'll tell you mine."

He leaned into the table between us and picked up the fork. He cut the corner off the chocolate cake. "Growing up, I spent every afternoon and summer at Tía Victoria's. It was always so damn hot in that house. One window A/C, box fans everywhere, none of it able to cut through the heat, and still she was always cooking chiles, making my eyes sweat, too."

"I reminded you of roasting chiles?" I teased. "If you call me spicy, I'm out of here."

He finished the bite with a smile. "She's the one who taught me how to do this." He gestured to the desserts around us. "I was kind of a hyper kid. Surprising, I know. But to get me out of her hair, she taught me to make arroz con leche, then sopaipilla. Pan dulces were my favorite."

I relaxed, melting against the counter, as the deep timbre of his voice—he smoothly rolled his *r*'s *and* had a soft, Southern flow—transported me to a too-hot Texas kitchen where a little scowling Alejandro leaned over a mixing bowl with determined focus.

"Seeing you enjoy something I made reminded me of the first time I baked something that tasted really good," he admitted. He slid the tray of cakes even closer to me with a small but insistent nudge. "Now, what was your memory?"

I picked up the fork. "To celebrate my last day of fifth grade, Mimi made this ice cream with lemons she let me pick off her tree. That was a big deal, because my abuela does not play when it comes to her trees. The three of us sat on the front porch to eat the ice cream, and it was the best thing I'd ever had." I finished the cake with a soft sigh. "Mom left later that summer. I don't eat many lemon desserts anymore, but they're still my favorite."

"There's a hundred things I want to bake you now."

I laughed, the sound loud and loosening the knot in my chest I'd been carrying for the last two days. We finished the rest of the samples, and it was tough, but for Clara I picked the hummingbird cake with the fluffiest cream-cheese frosting I'd ever had in my life. At the door, Alex handed me a small bakery box.

"You have to stop feeding me," I said, even as I took it. "What's inside?"

He tapped the top of the box. "With the leftover cheese-cake, I made a few dulce de leche bars." I brought the box to my chest, protectively, and he leaned in the doorway with a smile that warmed his eyes. "It's nice to remember how much I like doing this."

"Feeding me?"

"Baking." He laughed and returned to his kingdom of caramel and chocolate.

I left with my box and had no intention of being patient. Maybe I didn't have time for doomed crushes, but there was time for desserts, right? Back outside, a blazing morning sun burned off the last of the gray.

19

A heat wave found us, and after eating Alex's cakes, I felt responsible.

I woke Saturday morning, flushed and still tired, my sheets kicked off the bed and the fan spinning slowly. I rolled over, reached for my phone, and had way too many notifications for this early in the morning.

I scrambled up to sitting. It wasn't early. It was ten thirty a.m. The day was practically half-over.

Ana—who was notoriously late to things—had already sent several texts that grew in annoyance. Everyone was meeting in the square to work on festival prep, and I was *so* late. I jumped out of bed, dressed quickly, and raced to the square, kicking up my skateboard and running across the grass.

I stopped beside Ana, who took in my outfit with a look of surprise. There hadn't been enough time to wash my hair, so I pinned it back and covered it with a red kerchief. Nothing was ironed, and it was too hot for my cardigan, so

I'd thrown on my gardening clothes. The jeans were worn, with stubborn grass stains, and the fitted shirt was a little too tight around my bust, but it was dark enough to hide my sweat.

"What?" I asked.

"You look ready to flex and tell us we can do it." Ana fanned herself with a piece of paper. The cool spring breezes had turned too warm, and humidity was settling over everything. Somewhere up there the lid had been dropped over the boiling pot, us still inside, simmering like soup.

Mrs. Peña was in commander mode, armed with pens in her hair and the clipboard in her hand. There was no poster board behind her this time but instead a stage with lots of people walking around with boxes and cords. Right beside her stood Mr. Peña, stoic and silent, his arms crossed. He shot dark looks to anyone not listening to his wife.

Mrs. Peña smacked the clipboard in her hand. "Vendor applications are due today, people. Make sure they're in my hands. We've got one week, okay? Una semana." She shot a death glare at the viejitos and their phones. "Where are we on the wedding, Rosa?"

I counted off my tasks on my fingers. "Oscar is finishing the arch, I will be roaming the neighborhood taking any and all flower donations from local gardens—"

"Stay away from my yard," Gladys interrupted.

"—and a local orange grove heard about what we're

163

doing, and they're giving us cases of their sparkling grapefruit wine for free." I spotted Mimi across the square. She shot toward me like an angry missile. "I will not be drinking it, of course, but what a steal."

"¿Qué pasó?" She stopped in front of me, her eyes wide and hand over her heart.

"Nothing happened. I got a good deal."

"Pero mira tu ropa." She waved a hand in front of me and my clothes. "Did the iron break?" She reached out to pluck all the nonexistent lint from my shirt and tsked at the tighter fit.

I pushed at her hands. She was carrying a basket of shells, a bushel of lavender and rosemary, and a takeout bag from Beta & Eggs. "Wait, what were you doing?" There had been a thoughtful, quieter energy to Mimi since Mom left. Last night when I'd gotten home from work, my abuela—who never went out past the six o'clock noticias—was also just returning from somewhere. When I asked where she'd been, she said, "I needed an answer." And, story of my life, she didn't tell me from who or if she got it.

"Mimi will be setting up her own area for the festival." Mrs. Peña's smile grew strained. "She told me only an hour ago."

"Really?" I looked at Mimi. "You're just full of surprises lately."

"And to make it even more exciting, she won't tell us what it is or if she needs anything. But I'm sure it will be great." Mrs. Peña turned to Mimi for confirmation. "It'll be great, right?"

"Claro que sí," Mimi declared with easy confidence. "Carne con papas for dinner," she said to me, her voice soft, before walking away. I didn't know what was going on with her, but who was I to say no to my favorite dinner?

Ana waved at her mom. "I'm out. The guys are here." Tyler and Lamont headed toward the stage. "See you later," she told me, and took off toward them.

Mrs. Peña glanced at her clipboard again. The group around her had dwindled as she handed out tasks. Electric drills whined, and I spotted Oscar and Mike together on the east side of the square working on tables and what looked to be a very elaborate platform. The Golden Turtle sat proudly atop it. I was surprised Benny wasn't hovering around his treasure.

"Shoot, where's Benny?" Mrs. Peña asked, as if hearing my thoughts. She looked around her but didn't spot her son.

"He went to the soccer game," Junior answered.

The festival commander shifted instantly to worried mother. "Is that okay, you think?" She glanced at her husband, who nodded. She didn't look reassured, though. Hoping to alleviate some of her concerns, I stepped forward.

"I'll take whatever task is left."

"We need these flyers and coupons to be taken to a few neighboring towns to stir up more advertisement, but you don't have a car, Rosa."

From behind me, a now familiar voice said, "I do."

I shot around and Alex slid me a soft smile. His hands were loosely tucked into his pockets, and the sea on his arms was vividly blue on this sunny day.

"Perfect," Mrs. Peña said. "Thank you, Alex."

Mrs. Peña handed me a stack of papers and a list of the places where we needed to deliver them.

This was fine. This wasn't about having one-on-one time with Alex, who I had decided I didn't have the time or emotional capacity to indulge in a crush on right now. This was about the festival, and after mostly working on wedding tasks, it was nice to do something for Spring Fest, too. "Time to get down to business," I reminded myself as we walked together to the marina parking lot.

"What?" He leaned closer.

"Nothing. Just reading the map."

Alex opened the passenger door for me, and I slipped inside. As he walked around to the driver's side, I mumbled a prayer for cool confidence. I'd take help from any saint listening. His rope sat in an intricate knot in the middle of his truck's console.

He got in, started the engine, and the radio kicked on, in the middle of "Candela" by Buena Vista Social Club. My eyes widened at the sound of the old Cuban band in Alex's truck. It felt like a good omen, but Alex looked pained with embarrassment. Without a word, he shifted the gear stick and backed out of the parking spot.

We rode in awkward silence for a moment. He shook his head with a self-deprecating laugh. "A guy starts talking to a Cuban girl, and suddenly he's listening to Buena Vista Social Club."

I had no idea what to say. Sure, there had been desserts, lost treasures, my erratic heart rate, wedding planning, and the fact that now every song reminded me of him, but when had my secret crush blossomed into *talking*? Oh god. Did he like me back?

He shifted gears as he merged onto the interstate.

We hit the nearby popular tourist stops along the interstate. The first one had an outlet mall and antique shops along with huge bold signs that advertised the interesting, very Florida combination of gator meat, boiled peanuts, and orchids. I talked up the beauty of Port Coral with the flyers and enticed with the coupons. I must have been a very convincing ambassador, because they placed our offerings in plain sight near their registers. When I walked out of the citrus grove's gift shop, Alex was waiting for me by his truck. At my approach, he coyly offered me a tangerine lollipop.

"Did you steal this?"

He laughed, surprised. "Of course not." He unwrapped the other one and popped it into his mouth. I did the same. Something about both of us eating the same candy, at the same time, felt like flirting. Probably because of all the eye contact.

"What are you thinking about?" I asked, squinting a little against the sun.

"Making a honey tangerine marmalade."

"And do what with it?"

The sweetly tart candy gently clicked against his teeth as he gave my question some thought. "Bake rolls with lots of butter."

I was enthralled.

"Serve the marmalade while they're still warm."

I closed my eyes on a groan. Alex laughed and went to open my door.

Our last stop was farthest away, but the exit was the first major one headed toward Port Coral with a visitor's center, so it was important that we brought them word, too. There was less development out this way, thankfully, leaving it green and alive. The bottoms of ancient cypress trees spread out like knobby knees that dug into swampland. Watching the land turn wild, even for a brief moment, made me realize I hadn't left Port Coral in years.

"Where are we today?" Alex asked as he shifted gears. He remembered my story about road trips and my mother's eternal question.

Amused, I told him, "An underwater forest."

"What?"

I laughed at his alarm. "We're near one. Not far from Gulf Shores, Alabama, there's an underwater forest with cypress trees from an ice age, like, sixty thousand years ago." I gazed out the window. I had fallen into the information by way of a project for an ecology class but had continued researching to feed my own curiosity. "They discovered it after a category-five hurricane stirred up the waters. The Gulf is pretty much all sand, but there right at the edge is a preserved, ancient forest that shows the paths of long-ago rivers and valleys." Outside my window, bald cypress gave way again to more manicured groves. The farms here had struggled from citrus greening, a terrible, incurable disease that ate through the trees.

"Did you come by this affinity for plants from your abuela?"

"It's hard to imagine it wasn't an inherited thing, but I'm more interested in what we can do for them, and people like Mimi who know the old ways to heal with them. When I think about Cuba, yeah, it's about me and my family, but it's also bigger than us. It's about the island's incredible biodiversity and its future. I want it to survive and thrive." I pointed to the grove just beyond us. "And I want those oranges to come back next season." I turned to face Alex. He had a relaxed hand on the wheel, and the bright sunlight nearly made him glow. Something significant was coming together in my mind, unfolding and getting bigger, like when I saw the photo of President Obama laughing in Old Havana with his daughter Malia. "I want the harbor to survive for another hundred years."

His eyes ahead, Alex nodded. "Me too. I really hope this

works out." He started to ask something but turned back to the road instead. His hand tapped against the gear shift. He reached for his rope and then dropped it. I watched him hesitate until finally: "Any update on the big college decision?"

I went from calculating hundreds of years to being faced with only days. "I don't—" I began, but stopped because smoke was rolling out from beneath the hood of the truck. Alex cursed under his breath. He pulled over.

"What happened?" I asked.

"It overheated. It got way too hot too fast today, and my temperature gauge is broken." He shifted to park and turned it off. He muttered another curse. "I've got coolant, but I have to wait a couple minutes for it to cool off enough for me to open the hood. I can run the heater to divert some of the heat." He dragged his hands through his hair. "I'm sorry about this."

"It's fine. We'll take a break to enjoy the scenery." I was starving, starting to sweat, and my blood sugar was taking a dive. I wished I had another tangerine lollipop.

"Let's get out before we cook in here." He climbed out and I followed. With no buildings for miles, we must have been in the back of someone's orange grove where the trees ended just a few feet past the interstate.

"You want an orange?" I asked.

"You worried I stole the candy, but now you're offering pilfered citrus."

"Pilfered, huh? I like that. Come on, it's one orange.

Maybe two, from an entire grove. There's already a bunch on the ground."

"I'll stay here, but thanks anyway, Eve."

I barked a laugh and considered the distance. "I'm going for it," I decided. The tall weeds along the highway skimmed my ankles and knees. Who was lucky to be wearing her gardening jeans and sneakers now? I took a bigger step to avoid what looked to be the remnants of a blown tire. But when my foot landed, the ground gave way with a burp, and I fell forward onto my knees. The whole perimeter around the grove was a swampy mess, hidden by the weedy grass, and now my legs and hands were covered in muck. I leaned up and looked over my shoulder, but Alex had missed my fall as he leaned inside the driver's side of the truck.

"All for an orange," I muttered. I tried to stand, but the mud didn't make it easy. I finally made it to my feet, only to look over and see a gator.

The tiny, angry dinosaur watched me from a few feet away, its stillness an implied threat. There was something unnervingly ancient about alligators, which was why you didn't step into any grassy area in Florida, oranges or not.

"Alex," I called carefully. My legs twitched, and I swore I could see the gator noting it. I was going to throw up my candy.

"What's the matter?" Alex's voice was coming closer.

"Gator," I choked out. I heard him stop.

"Where?"

I couldn't move. I jerked my chin a little in the direction of it, but otherwise stayed frozen. I was a melting block of ice on the hottest day of the year.

"Listen, it's very small, and probably more scared of you than you are of it," he said.

I wanted to roll my eyes. People always said that. Those people were really underestimating how scared I could get.

"Just walk back to me."

Above us a group of sand cranes swept by, screaming their little hearts out. It was like a fire alarm. I turned around and started to book it back to the truck.

Unfortunately, Alex was right behind me, and I might have been small, but my momentum and desire to live were mighty. I took him down like a chopped tree. He fell back into the mud with a grunt, and I landed sprawled on top of him.

"I'm so sorry!"

He let his head fall back into the dirt and huffed a laugh. "We keep meeting like this."

I jerked up to check behind us for a hungry gator, but it was gone. The relief was instantaneous, and my bones melted. I smiled down at Alex. "It's gone."

"It was a very tiny gator, Rosa. It might have actually been a lizard."

"Perhaps, but I'm also pretty tiny. Who knows who might've won."

"My money's on the tiny linebacker." His voice grew

quiet. "I'm not complaining, but we're still on the side of the highway." I'd been watching his mouth, so it took a second for the words to make sense. I jumped up and let him get to his feet. Thanks to the fall—and me landing on top of him—he was now covered in mud.

I tried brushing the dirt from his shirt, but it was only making a bigger mess. I met Alex's patient gaze, and memories of warm sugar and burnt caramel swept through me. He carefully took my face in his hands. His thumbs gently swiped dirt from my cheeks.

"I didn't get the orange," I whispered.

He smiled and ducked his head. He captured my lips in a kiss that already tasted bittersweet. *He's a boy with a boat, and you're leaving. And he knows it.*

My hands tightened around his wrists; to hold him in place or keep myself from falling, I didn't know. Maybe both, as Alex offered me soft, biting kisses that felt like questions. This language was new, but I followed his slow, careful steps. When he stopped for a breath, I stretched up on my toes and caught his lips in a deeper kiss, too feverish for useless things like air. His hands slid down my sides and he wrapped his arms around me. Held by the welcoming blue waves of his ocean, I pressed my wildly beating heart against his. I was going to succumb to heatstroke, but I didn't care. He tasted of tangerine, and I couldn't remember the taste of my once-favorite strawberry candies. Spring had hurried into summer because of a kiss.

A blaring horn finally tore us apart. A semitruck flew past. Alex appeared as dazed as I felt. I smiled. *I'd* done that.

"Keep looking at me like that and we'll never get out of here." He chuckled and offered his hand as he helped me back to the truck. He opened the hood, the engine finally having cooled off. Once we were back in the truck, neither of us said a word, but I couldn't stop myself from checking the secret smile that danced around his lips.

Outside our last stop, we kicked the mud from our shoes as best we could. Everyone watched us walk to the visitor's center counter. The older woman's brows shot up to her hairline. I hurriedly told her all about Port Coral. She stood silent, her curious, worried gaze taking in Alex and me. When I asked her to please keep us in mind when speaking to tourists this week, she looked from us to the papers in her hand, then back to us again. Alex politely kept his hands behind his back. I'd lost my kerchief. We looked like swamp people.

"What sort of festival is this?" she asked, her Southern accent pronounced.

"A really awesome one," I told her breathlessly.

20

"Why did the gator cross the road?" Ana asked the next day. I ignored her, but she was way too amused to let the joke go. Seated behind her drum set, she asked again.

I sighed. The oscillating fan barely reached me from my perch on the couch in their garage. Benny and Mike were blocking most of the cooler air. "I don't know, Ana. Why did the gator cross the road?" I finally indulged her.

"To steal an orange!" The drums went *ba-dum-tss*, and Ana cracked up.

Benny put down his soda. "I don't get it."

"She's making fun of what happened to me yesterday."

"No, I get that. But the joke sucks."

"I Icy." Ana pointed her stick at him. We never told her how much she looked like her mother threatening us with a wooden spoon when she did that, because then she might actually swing it.

"Where's your boyfriend?" Benny asked me. "He return to the sea?"

175

"Give me your drumstick," I said to Ana.

"Sure but tell me about the kiss again first," she returned.

I glanced at the guys, who both suddenly had something else to look at. "Yes, fellas, you missed your chance. Your girl Rosa is out here getting kissed by cute boys with man-beards and baked goods."

When Alex and I got back to town yesterday, I was scheduled to work at the bodega. He offered to walk me back, because he was a gentleman, but I turned him down to save him from sarcastic Cubans and their chisme. I had no idea what we were doing, but it was hard to see reason after being kissed so well by a hot baker. I was living in the very sweet moment.

"What else are we supposed to talk about with that glazed look in your eyes? You look high," Ana complained. She was practicing for her upcoming gig and hit a cymbal in a dramatic finish.

Pained, Benny muttered, "I miss the bongos."

"Forget them. Now that I'm in the Electric I can officially tell Mom and Dad I quit jazz band." Ana let her accent drop an octave and become super Cuban. "Band is okay if it gets you a scholarship para una universidad you don't even want to go to."

"And tell me again why you don't want to go to college?" Mike asked.

"It's a waste of money and my time. I'll take a few classes, whatever, but I'm not packing everything up to go hang out with nerds and hipsters. No offense, Rosa."

"Wait, which one am I?"

"I'd rather work and play my drums and figure the rest out on my own time and dime. And it's not like I'm totally against higher education, I saved the application to Port Coral Community on my phone." She pointed at her brother. "Don't you dare tell Mom and Dad. They think I already applied to state schools like everybody else."

Benny finished the rest of his soda and shook the empty can. "That's your business. But don't come crying to me when all your friends are gone." He looked around the garage. "All two of them."

"Mike might not be leaving me," Ana pointed out.

"What?" I asked. "Since when? You got into Florida!"

Mike raised a hand to halt me. "I don't know yet. I really like this apprenticeship deal and Port Coral Community is right there, so I have a reason to stay."

"I do, too, now." Ana played a quick beat. "Tyler mentioned doing a small tour this summer to hit up all the tourist spots."

Ana planned out her dream tour for us, but I couldn't stop thinking about yesterday. The brief road trip with Alex had been about more than really good kisses. My ideas for the next two years of college had unfurled at the sight of those orange groves and cypress trees. Four universities had accepted me as a Latin American Studies major. Those schools also offered minors in environmental sciences and sustainability studies. It wasn't a straight shot to Havana anymore, but with only days left, I'd done the wildest thing so far: I'd made a brand-new list in my journal.

"Is that Mimi?" Ana asked suddenly. "Where's she headed in such a hurry?"

My abuela was hustling down the street carrying three bags. Mimi had been acting so weird since Mom left. She was spending less time at her window, instead disappearing for long spells. I'd think she was avoiding me except whenever we were home together, she hovered or insisted I help her in the garden.

"I don't know," I said, and jumped off the couch. "But I'll see you guys later."

I hit the sidewalk and followed at a careful distance. I couldn't ask her directly. That would only earn me an expertly applied guilt trip—or worse, a different, but no less intrusive question in return. If I was going to figure out what was going on with her, I had to do it in stealth mode. Yet another secret. All three Santos women were collecting a lot of them lately.

"Hey, Rosa!" Ms. Francis walked up to me with Flotsam and Jetsam. Her dogs didn't even bother sniffing me but watched for any sudden moves. "How's the big college debate coming?"

"Oh, right, yeah. It's happening." I checked over her shoulder to make sure I hadn't lost sight of Mimi.

"Great, did you pick?"

"Pick what?"

"A college?"

"Oh god, no. Hey, I have to go, so I'll see you later, okay?" I waved and rushed down the road to catch up just as Mimi stopped. I dove into the yard beside me.

Gladys sat up on her front porch. "Rosa Santos, you better not be stealing my flowers!"

I waved my hands, begging for silence.

"I know you ain't telling me to be quiet in my own yard."

"Where is she going?" I murmured as I checked around the gardenia bush. Mimi looked one way, then the other, before continuing down the street again. I hurried after her. My steps scattered fallen magnolia leaves, the air soft and sweet with the flowers' perfume. Up ahead, a crowd was gathered in the square. It was late afternoon, so foot traffic near the bodega or diner was to be expected, but everyone was staring up at the brand-new, exceptionally tall white tent suddenly taking up a whole corner of the grassy square. Mimi marched past everyone and slipped inside. No one questioned her and no one followed. *What in the world?*

I walked up to the white wall and noticed the many signs around it.

DO NOT OPEN OR ELSE.

How secretive and threatening. I, of course, immediately wanted to know what was happening in there. Papá

El rolled over to me with his Popsicle cart. His flavors today were watermelon, mango, and arroz con leche. "It showed up last night," he said, sounding as confused as I felt. "Everyone is too afraid to see what's inside. The signs are very convincing."

"Mimi just went in there."

"Then I'm definitely listening to the signs."

I went to find Mrs. Peña to investigate.

"Mimi," she complained as she straightened from stocking soup cans. "We wake up and it's there. She calls and tells me not to look at it, touch it, or worry about it." Her hands dropped to her hips. "How am I supposed to not worry about it? The festival is in less than a week, and your abuela is out there putting up secret tents with who knows what inside. Has she told you anything?"

"No." Mrs. Peña didn't look like she believed me. "I swear. But I did see a note in our calendar about the upcoming full moon."

"Por Dios." Mrs. Peña pinched the bridge of her nose before returning to the soups.

Back outside, I slipped my sunglasses on and faced the tent. It was both a riddle and a temptation. I could just march inside, signs or not. Rip the fabric aside and find some answers. I needed less mystery in my life right now. But Mimi had called me impatient. And it was the first time someone had ever said that to me. I was the tiny late bloomer who read big books. Impatient? I was all about patience and faith.

Right?

Well, here was a test. I passed those all the time, so I planned to ace this one, too. "Fine. Have your tent, Mimi."

I turned to head down the boardwalk. I could check on Clara. Her mother was arriving soon and she'd want to go over the final details. Several feet ahead of me, the door to the barber shop opened and Alex stepped outside. He stopped, his gaze out toward the sea. My steps slowed. Here was another little test. If he turned for the marina, I wouldn't chase or bump into him. I had a list of things to do, and I needed time to think about this crush business now that we'd leveled up into really good kissing.

He turned my way, and smiled. I was right; it was lethal. We met each other halfway.

"Hey," he said.

"Hey, yourself," I returned. "Nice 'do." He slid a hand over the shorter sides. Because I really wanted to do the same, I shoved my hands in my pockets.

"I hear that tent is Mimi's." He jutted his chin toward the square.

I glanced over my shoulder. "I hear the same things, but don't ask me for details. The women in my family are notorious for not telling each other anything." I had received a new message from Mom this morning. A picture of her painting featuring a moonlit street I knew from memory. The view of a gray sky from an airplane window. A bodega cat reigning over bags of rice. I used to search the pictures for some kind of coded message, but now I understood them for what they were: moments my mother missed me.

"I have something I want to show you," Alex said. His hands dove into his pockets, too, and he leaned forward a little on his toes. And then shifted back. "It's important, I think."

"Sure," I said, both curious and a little worried. It wasn't that I didn't like surprises, I just didn't enjoy feeling unprepared.

"It's on my boat." He turned quickly as if to make sure it was still there.

"Of course it is," I murmured and motioned for him to lead the way as we headed down the boardwalk to the marina. The days were still so warm, but the heat was somehow softer here. My hair danced in a wilder gust and the ground grew unsteady as we reached the docks. I was nervous and off-kilter, but my fears were also making room for a thoughtful sort of wonder. At his boat, he offered me a hand to cross over just as an older man approached us from farther down the docks. Alex's hand hesitated.

I steeled myself. The man gave me a short, sweeping look before focusing on Alex. "I had you scheduled to do the chartered sunrise fishing trip this morning."

"Carlos did it," Alex replied, his tone stiff. "I had stuff to do in the kitchen."

"Right, the baking. Well, Carlos has a wife and baby on

the way any day, so he doesn't need to be out right now. Plus, you're the sailor."

My passive-aggressive alarm sounded when he said *sailor*.

"Hi," I said, and offered my hand to cut through the tension. "I'm Rosa."

We shook. "Javier," he said.

"My dad." Alex sighed.

"Oh!" I was still shaking his hand as I processed their similarities. Javier was shorter and stockier than Alex, but he had the same dark eyes and beard. The same frown line between his brows. I dropped his hand and tried a friendly smile. "Alex has been a big help with the festival and saving Jonas and Clara's wedding."

"Well, he told me he was coming back home to help with the marina, but I haven't seen him much, so at least he's busy."

"The festival is ultimately about saving—"

"The harbor," he interrupted, nodding. "Right. Let's just hope all of this . . . works." He paused as my alarm rang again. He was good at this, nearly Mimi-level skilled. "You're still ready for the regatta, right?"

"Of course, Dad. I said I'm going to do it."

"Just making sure. I want to see the sailor in action before the big trip." The phone in his hand sounded, and he answered, "Port Coral Marina." As he listened to the caller he nodded at us in farewell before heading past. Fathers were strange creatures.

"Big trip?" I asked.

Alex rubbed his brow. He offered me his hand again and helped me navigate that tiny bit of space between dock and boat. I grabbed the side for support as he smoothly crossed over and headed down the steps to the door. He lowered his head and walked inside. Was I meant to follow? I hurried after him and found myself in a small kitchen with a single bowl in the sink. Beside me was a corner bench and table piled with books. Luna was asleep beside them. It smelled like oil, cinnamon, and the sea. Alex headed toward a room in the back, presumably his bedroom.

I pressed my hand against my middle to stay all the butterflies. I was way too on edge right now to be thinking about other people's beds.

After a moment, Alex returned with a rolled-up piece of paper. He pushed the books aside—much to Luna's annoyance—and spread the paper out on the table, revealing a map. Not an abstract drawing or graffiti art interpretation, but a functional map with notations all across it. There was a very definitive line that wove through the blue. This wasn't a trip to a barrier island. Alex was going to sail across the sea.

"I've been planning it forever, but it's taken time to prepare everything I need and save the money for it." He smoothed a crease in the paper. "I want to be out there for a little while."

I traced the lines that felt warm to the touch. The sea outside sang for him.

"What do you think?" he asked, a nervous edge in his voice. I looked at the map, and my tiny little heartbreak swiped against a hollow place inside me. This wasn't just some crush on a boy with a man-beard who baked the most dreamy desserts. I'd been in a confectioner's sugar haze. Alex was a sailor. With a boat. And he was bound for the sea.

"When do you leave?"

"Next month. The goal is to spend the summer sailing." The admission wormed its way between us, taking up too much air in the small space. "Hopefully everything goes well, and when I get back, the university's team will be here to start work. So, if I'm ever going to do this, I've got to do it now."

"That makes sense." I stepped back from the table with a sinking heart. "Wow. A whole summer out on the water . . ." I trailed off as my throat grew tight. I waved a hand above his map but didn't touch it. This map was proof that there was no next step for us. Our expiration date was written in his notes charting distance and dangers. *Don't Date Rosa Santos* ought to be written in a very threatening shade of red over the whole thing.

"I wanted to tell you because—"

"You're leaving," I said, trying to keep my voice light. It broke at the end, though. I inhaled sharply. "And so am I, so these are important things to know, of course. Despite all the . . ." I touched my finger to my lips.

"I know," he said. "We're both leaving. But maybe we

have dinner first?" He shrugged, an attempt at lightness, but his eyes gave him away. This was important to him. *I* was important to him.

"You're trying to feed me again," I teased in a whisper. This was such a disaster. I liked him so much. Too much. I'd always sworn I wouldn't become my mother, and yet, despite all of my effort, I was standing on a boat, at this dock, giving my treacherous, dangerous heart away.

"We already sat near each other for a whole semester eating alone," he said. "This time we'll just sit at the same table. Give me one date, Rosa."

"Okay," I said. My foolish heart.

21

With only two days until the festival and wedding, I didn't have time to obsess over my first real dinner date. I flew on my skateboard to Clara's bookshop and finally got to meet her mother. The three of us made final decisions on the location everyone would get ready at before the ceremony so I knew where flowers, makeup, and dresses needed to be. Next I dashed off to Oscar's to check that the arch and my secret order were ready to go.

Outside I checked my mother's mural and found she hadn't left it completely blank. There was a sketch of someone, but Mom had yet to color them in or give them any real, defined shape. It looked like a ghost. Her goth contribution to the town. My mother returned home to get trashed and paint ghosts.

"And yet I'm the one they keep blogging about," I muttered. Alex was meeting me after work, so I rushed home, hurried into my room, and stopped in front of my closet. The yellow dress spoke to me. So did the red skirt, but I needed to be low-key about this date, so maybe red wasn't the way to go. The sleeveless green had such a great silhouette and made me feel very earthy and chill. And the latter was eluding me. I slid aside one dress after another, every squeak of a discarded hanger louder than the one before until finally this tiny feeling of indecision uncorked all the frazzled tiki-tiki I'd been bottling up lately. My nerves made my knees give and I dropped to a clumsy seat on the floor. I pressed my hand to my chest as I tried to deepen my breaths and studied my altar right in front of me.

My abuelo was leaning back against a palm tree, his arms crossed over his chest. He looked stoic and strong. In the other picture, my father sat on top of a picnic table, a fishing pole beside him. His smile burned brightly for whoever was behind the camera. "I should talk to you both more," I said. These were more than photos. They were here to be remembered. The sight of dust on the pictures filled me with panicky guilt, but it also gave me something to do. A way to fix *something*.

I grabbed my toolbox. Plastic and riotously pink, the makeup box was a forgotten artifact from when this room was still my mother's. It held candles, bottled dried herbs, Florida Water, and other witchy odds and ends. I poured some Florida Water into my palm before running the perfume over my neck and collarbone. The sweet citrus scent settled over me in a soothing wave as I lit sage incense and waved the stick around me. I grabbed a kerchief and cleaned the whole table of dust, then wiped it down with more Florida Water. I put the photos back up and lit a candle. I sat before my ghosts again. "I could really use some help with college. Can you see the future? Yeah, it probably doesn't work like that. But maybe you can get together with my other ancestors and let me know what you think? Some clarity on this would really help."

I unwrapped a strawberry candy, popped it into my mouth, and shuffled my tarot cards. I cut the deck and set out three cards in a simple spread. I glanced at the pictures on my altar again. My hand stalled above the first card.

"Rosa!"

My bedroom door shook with Mimi's shout. My hand drew back guiltily. "What?" I called.

"¡No me grites!" Mimi shouted back. I rolled my eyes, but shot to my feet when her shuffling steps drew closer. I ran to my door and opened it just wide enough to peer out. She stopped in front of me.

"What's up?" I leaned against the doorframe.

"I thought you were at work." Her hair was curled and her housedress was turquoise today. In her hand she held a hanger with my freshly ironed daisy-yellow skirt. She smelled of her favorite face powder and the homemade herbal cream she used for her arthritis.

"That's in an hour. I was running wedding errands this morning."

Mimi tried to lean around me, but we were both five

foot nothing and I blocked her with a swift, smooth slide. She handed me the skirt, and I clutched it against my chest. We stood there for a beat, facing each other with a half-closed door between us.

"What are you doing today?" I asked in a rush. The skirt was wrinkling in my death grip.

"I'll be in the garden," she said and then pointed behind me. "Clean that up."

I glanced over my shoulder. In my haste to beat Mimi to my door, I had knocked over the rest of my cards and bottle of Florida Water. The perfume smell was potent. "Oh, no, no!" I guiltily looked back at Mimi, but she was gone.

I stared at the pictures. "My bad."

❖

Fifteen minutes later, I stood at the threshold of Mimi's garden room. "Mimi!" I called for the third time. The earthy scent of watered soil and sweet floral was strong today.

"¡Aquí!" she returned from somewhere near the mugwort and yarrow.

I stopped beside the mugwort. The herbal, almost-sage scent was heavy, but no Mimi.

"I'm right here," she called, very obviously not *here*. I turned on my foot and followed the music of her bracelets. On the east side of her garden I found limes, an umbrella plant, and bananas, but no abuela.

"Mimi, seriously!"

She popped up on my left.

"Jesus!"

She flashed me a scowl and spritzed me with her peppermint water. "¿Qué pasó?"

"Nothing happened." Well, lots of stuff had recently happened, but I didn't know how to tell her about any of it, and it was killing me. I wanted to ask her about college, but after the Big Fight, I was afraid to test those waters again. I also wanted to tell her about my upcoming date but didn't know how since it meant telling her about Alex. "I just wanted to talk to you before I left for work. What's going on with the tent, Mimi? Everyone at the bodega thinks I know what you're doing."

"Tell them you don't. That is the truth."

"But why won't you just tell me?"

"Because you will see." She gathered herself and set her spray bottle down. "I want to tell you everything, mi niña, and I will. You'll see."

"See what?" I asked, exasperated.

"Everything." She grabbed my face in her gentle peppermint hands and laid a soft kiss on my forehead. "I wish I could show you my home, *our* home, but I will try."

"I could go to Cuba now," I whispered and grabbed her hands. The confession was huge.

Her eyes turned sad. "And I cannot." She brushed my hair back and looked at me like I was seven years old again and begging to never leave Port Coral. What must it have cost her to stand between Mom and me? Mimi, my home, my haven. My island. I just wanted her to understand how much I loved her. If I could reconnect us to our roots, maybe then we might grow something new in the mess we'd made.

She gave me another kiss and disappeared into her wild garden. The wind chimes played a soft song, and I wished for the words—in either of our languages—that would make all of this easier.

I tried to conjure Mom's voice quietly promising me by moonlight that I'd find my magical seashell. *It'll take you wherever you need to go*, she'd whisper against my temple, sealing the wish with a kiss before I drifted to sleep. And I still believed in that one impossible day. It reminded me so much of my eternal optimism about Cuba.

And my family.

My shift at the bodega ended at six, when Alex would meet me for our big date. In the back room, I hung my green dress in my locker, then tied on my apron and checked the daily schedule.

"You're at the deli counter," Ana said from behind me. She popped her gum and grinned. "Nervous?"

"Working with your dad isn't that bad."

"No! About your date, you weirdo."

I tried to shush her, but Benny swept over to us with a broom and dustpan. "Too late. She already told everybody."

Ana gave me her most wide-eyed innocent look. "It was an accident, I swear."

Benny went to sweep my feet, but I shot him a death glare. It was an old superstition that having your feet swept meant you'd marry an old man. I went inside, and Junior came around the corner with a cart of bananas and avocados. "Hey, Rosa, excited for your big date?"

I kept walking. "I'm going to kill all of you."

When I got behind the deli counter it was a relief to be faced with Mr. Peña's silence.

For the entirety of my shift, everyone was on Rosa's Got a Date watch. They hovered around the deli and outside the window, annoying Mr. Peña and ratcheting up my nerves.

"It's not that big of a deal," I said as I leaned against the wall with Ana before I clocked out.

"Rosa," she said simply.

"I know, I know." I kicked back at the brick wall. "I like him so much when I know I shouldn't, so this feels like I'm tempting something."

"Yeah, you're tempting a sailor who dropped out of college."

"I meant fate. I'm doing exactly what my mom did."

"Stop worrying about your mom. You have a crush, and that's fine. You got three days, mermaid. Go wild. You're not changing your plans because of him; you're enjoying the moment. Just don't fall in love and start paying his phone bill and you'll be fine."

"What?"

"I don't know, that's where Paula tells me it always goes wrong. Speaking of, here she comes."

Paula hurried up to us with bright eyes. She whispered, "Your date's here."

I jumped away from the wall and glanced around the corner. Alex was waiting just beyond the tables. He'd put on a white button-up with the sleeves rolled to his elbows.

Blue ink cascaded over his bare forearms, and I could almost hear the waves lapping his skin. He wore a dark blue tie.

This was my date-with-the-Head-Boy-of-Ravenclaw fantasy come to life.

Alex noticed our trio and headed our way. Paula let go of a long breath.

"What's with the tie?" Ana asked. "He looks like a nerd."

Paula made a low noise. "He looks like a slow jam that wants to do my taxes."

It was a familiar feeling to stand beside Paula and spot a cute guy coming over to flirt with her. Not me. Never the eternal baby sister.

Alex stopped in front of us. "Ready?" he asked me.

"Yeah, just give me one second." I rushed into the break room with Paula on my heels. Once we were out of sight, she gaped at me and smacked my shoulder proudly. I shook my hands and squeaked. Paula whipped me around and helped me get my apron off. I grabbed my dress from my locker and changed in the bathroom.

Before I knew what was happening, Paula was in the bathroom with a bottle of perfume she sprayed down my cleavage. Then she grabbed my shoulders and said, "Scoop him up and throw some sprinkles on that. Drizzle the caramel. You get me? Doodle his name in that little journal of yours. Doodle it hard."

"Is that a euphemism?" I asked, confused, but suddenly wanting ice cream.

"Somehow you got this," she said, awe in her voice. "So go get it."

Outside, Alex was waiting for me with his hands in his pockets. He smiled as I moved past curious viejitos with their phones out. Whether they were going to call Mimi or post about us, I didn't know, but tonight I was a mermaid, and I was going for it.

❖

We reached the marina, but instead of heading down to the docks, he led me to the restaurant. The dining room was empty.

"Is it closed?" I asked.

"It is tonight." There was a table set beneath the low lights. A bouquet of pink roses and red tulips sat upon it with two covered plates. I couldn't believe the level of romance unfolding right before my eyes. He held out a chair for me. It was another postcard moment.

"Holy crap, are you kidding me right now?"

We sat down. As he went to uncover our plates, Alex nearly knocked over one of the candles, and the metal cover clattered against the plate in his rush to save the candle.

"I'm a little nervous," he admitted with a half smile.

We both relaxed as the rich scent of garlic and butter floated over us. He set the cover aside, revealing linguini with scallops and fresh garlic bread. My stomach rumbled.

"Did you make all this?"

He ran his hand down his tie. "I baked the bread and got the scallops and thought—"

The kitchen door flew open, and light and commotion poured out.

Alex shot back to his feet. "Oh no." He closed his eyes, pained. "I can't believe this."

"What's happening?" I sprang to my feet. If this was a quick escape situation, a girl needed to be ready.

He sighed. "My family."

"Alejandro!" Mrs. Aquino came to him with her arms wide open. "What a surprise."

"I told you I was making dinner tonight, Mom. A private dinner."

She abruptly shouted, "Javier!" and then smiled at me. "My husband is in the kitchen. Oh, and here come all my children. Well, they're not all mine, but just about."

"Everyone is here?" Alex demanded. More family entered the room. Two women—one blond, one brunette—and Carlos, who held a very pregnant woman's hand. Two kids flew in behind them, their voices raised as they argued over a phone. Everyone was generous with their affection for Mrs. Aquino before zeroing in on me.

"This is Rosa," Mrs. Aquino announced. "Alex's friend."

Everyone in the room heard the inflection. I was sure even Paula and Ana caught it back at the bodega.

"This is my daughter, Emily, and her wife, Fiona." Mrs.

Aquino introduced me to the pretty white blonde and the tall and curvy brunette. "And those two running out the back door are their kids, Kat and Ray. You met my oldest son, Carlos, and this is his wife, Sara." Sara had short dark hair and a delicate face. Mrs. Aquino put a hand over Sara's very pregnant belly. "And this is my next baby."

Sara grinned and kissed her mother-in-law's cheek. "I'm starving. I haven't eaten all day."

Mrs. Aquino's eyes widened. "Carlos," she admonished.

He rolled his eyes. "She had two breakfasts, brunch, lunch, and fries in the car on the way here." He smiled at me. "It's nice to see you again, Rosa." To Alex, his grin became teasing. "Hey, bro, you finally show up for family dinner."

Alex groaned. "This isn't family dinner. I never said this was family dinner."

"How was I supposed to know it wasn't for everybody?" Mrs. Aquino sounded innocent, but I knew that tone. Mimi used it often.

"She's very pretty," Emily commented.

"Stop talking about her like she's not right there," Alex said.

His sister was a taller version of their mother with warm brown skin and nearly black hair that fell in soft waves. I wondered what it was like to have an older sister. Probably a lot like having my mother minus the maternal expectations.

"Thank you," I said to Emily. I desperately wanted to check my makeup and fidget with my dress.

"I've never been able to wear a matte lip like that," Fiona told me with a sigh. She had an athletic build and reminded me of a famous surfer I'd seen on TV.

"Lots of exfoliation," I said. "Also, video tutorials."

"Oh my god, I watch those just to relax." Fiona grinned. She subtly elbowed Emily, who looked pleased by our conversation. "I love the good eyeliner ones."

"And the contouring and eyebrow ones."

"Yes!" both Emily and Fiona said.

Mrs. Aquino was speaking quietly to Alex, her hands moving over his arms, clasping his hands and squeezing before letting go. He ducked his head and nodded at whatever she was saying. When she noticed my attention, she smiled brightly again and patted his tie. "Isn't he handsome?"

"Yes," I told her readily.

It was the right answer, because her smile grew even brighter. Mr. Aquino came into the room bearing a bottle of red wine. "I can't get this thing open," he complained.

Carlos took it from him. The older man spotted me. "Good to see you, Rosa." The awkwardness of earlier was gone. I didn't know if that was just his personality or the power of family dinner. Emily and Fiona were dragging more chairs over as Carlos pushed another table closer, its feet squeaking against the floor. Alex watched them with an annoyed scowl, offering no help. Javier gave Alex a happy smack to his shoulder. "Nice tie, son."

Alex shook his head, but he smiled a little now. "You guys are the worst."

❖

Dinner was a warm, rambling affair. It was also very good. I never wanted to stop eating, which was fine, because everyone else had stories and they all tried to tell them at the same time. It was like being in the back room with the Peña family where Spanish words were woven into the laughs, and the room hummed with affection. And it was easy to feel like the baby in this room with all the talk of jobs and children. I wondered how the stories sounded to Alex.

"What about you, Rosa?" Emily asked me. "What's the plan for Port Coral's brightest?"

"Oh, I'm not valedictorian," I answered by rote. She smiled, waiting for me to actually answer the question. "Uh, I'm not sure, but it's between Florida, Miami, and Charleston. I have to secure my spot by May first."

"That's less than two weeks away," Mr. Aquino said. "What's the holdup?"

"Javier," Mrs. Aquino whispered.

"No, that's fine," I said. "It's a legitimate question. Some factors changed pretty recently, so I want to make sure I consider everything and make the right decision for me and my future." That sounded a lot better than *I'm kind*

of avoiding it completely to indulge in an ill-fated crush on your
hot son and some occasional brujería.

"That's good," he said. "Better than making a decision
you'll regret and quitting early."

An awkward silence settled heavily over the table. I was
too nervous to look at Alex.

"Jesus, Dad," Carlos said. "Why do you insist on making
shit weird all the time. Leave him alone."

"Oh, because I worry about him, I'm the bad guy?" Mr.
Aquino argued.

"No, because you needle him," Emily argued. "He's not
married, he doesn't have kids. Let him breathe and figure
this out."

"This is why I don't go to family dinner," Alex said.
Everyone stilled at the sound of his voice. "Also, thank
you for ruining my date." He started to make the motions
of leaving, and I watched pain and panic swim in his
mother's eyes.

"There's a lot to say for taking your time," I blurted. My
hand shot out to grab Alex's thigh beneath the table and stay
him. "I mean, I rushed everything. Flew through my first
two years of college while still in high school for many valid
reasons, but now I've got to make a lot of big decisions very
quickly, and more than anything, I really just want a little
breathing room." I looked right at Mr. Aquino. "There's a lot
of pressure for immigrants and their kids when we want to
make good on the sacrifices. But sometimes the longer road

is the right one." Alex's leg relaxed. I let go and sat back. I had no idea what came next. Would I be kicked out? Lectured? This was a whole new dad dynamic that I had no experience with whatsoever.

Something like surprise painted everyone's expression in the ensuing silence. I glanced at Mr. Aquino again, who passed a searching look between Alex and me before saying, "As a parent, you simply want what's best for your children. And for them to be happy." He looked at his wife as if seeking her approval for his acquiescence. She appeared mildly appeased. Whatever argument was left unsaid between this family returned to its familiar place as Mr. Aquino raised his wineglass, perhaps his white flag of surrender, and his older children and wife followed suit. Alex nodded his acknowledgment, and under the table he grabbed my hand and squeezed it.

❖

Smaller conversations broke out as dinner wound down. Alex was pulled into one with his brother and sister, and I tried to listen in, but Mrs. Aquino started to describe her arthritis to me in detail. I was accustomed to this line of conversation from Mimi's clients, and I settled back to listen as she described the cream she'd bought from my abuela and all the miracles she inspired. It was like listening to someone describe a vision of la Virgen sometimes.

"She's amazing." Maria finished her wine and rolled her wrist back and forth. "It's fine. I can't believe it. A little cream and now nada!" She pushed her seat back. "Let me show you my ankles—"

"Mom, no," Alex interrupted. "I'm going to go get the tres leches cake. And, Dad—" He got to his feet and looked over at his father who was playing on one of his grandchildren's phones. "More wine?" Mr. Aquino shook his empty wineglass. "Perfect. Rosa, will you help me out?" Something in Alex's gaze told me not to question why he needed help grabbing two things.

"Of course."

"I'll show you when you come back," Maria assured me. "Wonderful."

I followed Alex into the kitchen. He closed the door behind us, then hurried over to the counter and picked up the milky sweet cake. He popped two forks out of the drawer, then jerked his head toward the back door. I swept out into the night after him. We were silent conspirators until we got to his boat, where laughter overtook both of us.

"How long until they figure us out?" I sat on the bench seat.

He handed me a fork. "A couple of minutes at best, but there's another cake in the fridge that will hold them over."

The sun had set, but the night was still warm. Beyond us, the sea stirred. The cake melted on my tongue, and I sank into this perfect night. "This is so good. You are so good."

203

"I like you, Rosa."

"I like you, too, Alex. You and this cake, my god."

He cleared his throat. "No. I *like you* like you."

The emphasis stopped my next bite. Alex's expression was so open and vulnerable. He jumped to his feet and began to pace in the small space in front of me. It was what I imagined watching me work through something looked like.

"What you just did in there? I've been trying to be chill about this, but I've liked you ever since I watched you draw beneath those oak trees at lunch and collect the acorns. I always wondered what you did with them."

"I put them on windowsills so lightning won't strike my house," I blurted.

This momentarily distracted him enough to stop pacing.

"They're also sometimes in my pockets for good luck. God, I sound like a little squirrel." I pressed my hands against my heated cheeks. "Why am I talking about this?" I held my hand over my racing heart. Alex was watching me from the other side of his boat, his hands in his pockets, a soft smile on his lips.

"Maybe because you like me, too."

"I do," I whispered, hoping the sea didn't hear my confession. I got to my feet and walked into his arms, because I was scared and a little cold and he was exactly where I wanted to be. He wrapped them around me and dropped his chin to the top of my head. I clutched the fabric of his shirt. This was terrible. I slid my nose against his tie and breathed as much of him in as I could. His arms tightened. Tears threatened. "I like you too much."

"That's not possible," he said.

He didn't understand. The dark waves beyond us did. The haunted boat slip and collection of unread letters at the bottom of the sea knew better than my cursed heart, because when Alex lowered his lips to mine, I kissed him anyway.

23

As the sun rose on Saturday morning, I was the busiest bee fluttering across the square while Spring Fest came to life around me. We had two and a half hours until the official start time, and I'd spent my predawn morning on ladders and had already nearly fallen out of a tree, but it was worth it. Tourists would soon—hopefully—pile into town to spend their money on Papá El's Popsicles, Mr. Peña's cubano sandwiches, and the dreamiest desserts baked by the hottest Ravenclaw. A sound check crackled through the speakers at the stage as I plunked Oscar's signs into the dirt to direct everyone from the food to the music and down to the boardwalk and harbor. The viejitos wore bright orange vests that made them puff out their chests. They were in charge of parking until the dominos tournament started and the soccer team took over. Xiomara was already strolling between tables and booths with her flamenco guitar. Jasmine climbed lampposts, violets spilled down window awnings, daffodils and hyacinths sprang from any pot with even a spit of dirt.

Our town square had fully bloomed into the whimsical garden of my favorite first memories of Port Coral.

"Do you think people will come?"

"God, you're asking me that now?" Mrs. Peña laughed. "We did good. Really good. I remember Spring Fest from when I was younger, and it was always a good time, but I look around at this"—she paused, her gaze full of wonder—"and I finally see us. The bodega, the viejitos, our food and music. All here, in this square. I've lived here for most of my life, but these last weeks were the first time I felt this connected."

Mrs. Peña gestured to the still-shuttered tent. No one went in, and no one came out. "Any idea yet what she's doing in there?"

Mimi had left every night this week, but no one knew why. "I have no idea."

"Well, I guess we'll see when we're meant to. I'm going to go get another one of Alex's doughnuts before he runs out. They're like warm lemon meringue pies. I've already had two. Come to think of it, this sugar high is probably why I'm not freaking out right now."

I really wanted one of those doughnuts.

"Rosa!" Clara paused in her preparation for the cake walk and waved me over. There was a big spinning wheel with cartoon cakes beside her and chalk squares with matching numbers. "What do you think?" she asked.

"Is that a pineapple cake?"

"No, about my dress." She gestured at her baby-blue, off-the-shoulder summer dress. Her hair was pinned into a retro updo. It was barely eight in the morning and she looked fantastic.

"You're already wearing it? Don't you want to save it for the ceremony?" I had on my gardening clothes again, prepared for the relentless heat.

"Definitely not," she said and popped a hand on her hip. "I plan to look this great all day. It's my wedding day. And Spring Fest!" She smiled, happiness shining in her eyes. "Find me later. I'll be the one with the handpicked daisies making eyes at the cute fisherman."

"I wouldn't miss it."

I called the officiant to confirm their arrival time and headed to the bodega to double-check on the cases of wine from the orange grove. My hope was to have a sort of reception as the festival wound down. The morning sky was brightening into a softer blue. I checked my watch. Ten minutes until nine.

My phone buzzed with an unfamiliar sound. I'd downloaded a walkie-talkie app per the viejitos' instructions. "Yeah?"

"You have to say *Ten-four, over*," Mr. Gomez said. He sounded winded. He and the others were at the soccer field two blocks over where we'd made the parking lot.

I rolled my eyes. "That's at the end . . . Forget it, what's up?"

"We have a whole line of cars! People are coming! Over!"

The relief nearly winded me. This hadn't been for naught. We'd done it. Applause sounded from the few around me who overhead him.

"Well, send them over," I called.

"Now you say *ten-four*, Rosa. Over."

"Ten-four, Rosa," I sang out and clicked off.

I hadn't gotten to see Alex since our date, between him baking and me spending every last moment with Clara making sure everything was ready. When I reached his dessert table, his sister, Emily, stood behind it. She smiled at my approach. "You just missed him."

"Oh, uh, no! That's not . . . I just came to see . . ." Emily's smile grew the more I tried to play it off. I rolled my eyes and gave up. "Do you know where he went?"

"Not sure. He got a call and headed toward the marina. He did tell me to give you this if you stopped by, though." She handed me a small bakery box. I unfolded it just enough to peek inside. He'd saved me two doughnuts. One with lemon and marshmallow, and the other had a golden caramel frosting. I dipped my head to inhale and closed my eyes as the scent of dulce de leche hit me. Emily laughed at my dreamy expression.

"Rosa!" Mike called, phone up to his ear, a cup of neon-blue shaved ice in hand. "We have an emergency. Ana can't find her sticks."

Cold panic seized me. "Where is she?"

"In front of the bodega with her aunt who is trying to

have a yard sale. I don't know, but they're worried she put them in with her secondhand stuff."

I asked Emily to hold the bakery box for me and ran across the square. All I could think of was Ana twirling her lucky sticks after she spent her savings on the drum set. Her parents arguing upstairs, she'd looked at that sparkle set and was so sure of what she wanted. She needed those sticks, and I would shake this whole town loose to find them.

I found her in a complete panic surrounded by her family, who all sounded very tiki-tiki as they dug through their stuff. "Did you check the van?" Mrs. Peña was elbow deep in a box. I couldn't even see her head.

"Why is Titi Blanca having a yard sale right now?" Ana demanded.

"Foot traffic," the older woman explained, with a matter-of-fact shrug.

"What about in all that hair of yours?" Junior asked Ana, unhelpfully.

Ana whipped around and looked ready to strangle him, but caught sight of me. She leapt forward and grabbed me by the arms. "Help me."

"That's why I'm here," I said. "Where did you see them last?"

She shrieked and let me go. "If I knew, I'd have them! Listen, I need you to help me. Give me some brujería, Rosa. Throw down some shells, fire up some smoke! I need that tracking-lost-things spell!"

Titi Blanca crossed herself.

"Okay . . . okay, I got this!" Excitement surged through me. "I need a string."

"A string!" Ana shouted at her family. "Someone get her a string!"

Titi Blanca and Junior searched through one of her boxes.

"And a candle."

"Found them!" Mrs. Peña breathlessly popped up from the box on the floor, waving the drumsticks in the air.

Titi Blanca raised her hands innocently. "I have no idea how that got in there."

Ana grabbed the sticks and took off. I was right on her heels. "Help me get set up," she heaved. Both of us were terrible runners.

"Always," I choked out.

Her set was packed away, sitting beside the stage. Tyler and Lamont stood nearby with their minimum amount of baggage. Tyler was on the phone, but Lamont smiled at me. "Hey, Rosa. Excited to get this semester over with?" he said.

"It'll definitely be nice to just go to one school again."

He agreed readily. "I gotta go find my mom. I'll see you guys in a bit." He knocked fists with Ana before heading past us.

Tyler clicked off his phone. His smile was bright and outrageous. My instincts warned me that at some point, this guy was going to try and sell me something. "Ruby, right?"

"Rosa," I said, rolling my *R* dramatically. I passed him and got down to the business of helping Ana carry her drums to the stage. Their first set wasn't until this afternoon, but Ana was going to provide a beat for Xiomara's upcoming salsa lessons. Tyler left to take another call.

"Such a lead singer." She sighed.

She was setting up her kick drum when Mike climbed up onto the stage. "Need anything?"

I knew Ana was nervous when she nodded instead of playing it off like she had everything under control.

"What's up with Alex?" Mike asked me. "Saw him arguing with some dude."

The idea of him arguing with anybody shocked me. "What dude?"

He shrugged as he tightened a cymbal into place. "I didn't recognize him, but they were over by the marina."

"You good?" I asked Ana. She shot me a thumbs-up, and I hopped off the stage and hurried to the marina. The festival was bustling with foot traffic now. At the marina I spotted a small crowd. Alex was on one side of it, his arms crossed, his dark brows low. He looked ready to fight, but his expression softened into an almost-smile when he saw me. "Did you get the box from Emily?"

"What? Oh, yes. But what happened? Eli said you were arguing with someone, which sounded so unlike you I almost ran here."

"Almost?"

"I try to run only in emergencies."

"My brother left because Sara is in the hospital."

My hands flew to my mouth in shock. "Oh my god! What happened?"

Alex looked at me. "She's having her baby."

"Oh." I took a breath. "Okay. Great! So what's the problem, then?"

He jutted his chin toward the man ahead of us. It was the older fisherman from my first day at the marina. Alex explained, "Skipper Pete over there said I'm out of the regatta."

Pete spied us and held his clipboard to his chest like a shield.

"I can sail by myself," Alex called, annoyed.

"It's a two-person race and we're heading out now." Pete side-eyed me.

Alex shrugged. "It's not that big of a deal."

But it was, because his dad was out there, watching him, and Alex had a trip on the horizon. He'd quit college, on his terms, but after having dinner with his family, I knew he wanted to prove he could do this.

"I'll be your second."

Alex's brows shot up. "What?"

"What?" Pete shrieked.

"If you want," I said and tried not to throw up or faint.

Alex's smile was wild and bright. He kissed me quickly and then defiantly looked at Pete. "I have my second."

24

Perhaps Pete wanted to ward the dock against me again, but I ignored him as I hurried after Alex. "We won't be gone too long, right? Ana's first set is at one."

"We'll be back by then," he assured me as he released the ropes. I tripped over one of them. There were so many. This was a highly precarious mode of travel.

"Do you remember what I told you about sailing?" he asked as he came aboard.

I wished I could scan my notebook and cram before the big test. "Of course I don't." I buckled my life vest. "I was on a pontoon boat for the first time with a very cute boy. You're lucky I didn't pass out."

"Very cute, huh?" He checked a few things before stopping behind the wheel. We began to motor out into open water. "We're in the first race, so we can get it all over with quickly."

I checked the buckles of my life vest again.

"The start is the hardest part, but it's not everything.

This isn't a long race, but we'll have time to make something happen."

I could see the group of boats in the distance. "Why does it sound like they're all yelling at one another?" We were too far to make out words, but it sounded like they were all squawking into the wind.

"The wind's shifting, so they changed the mark."

His words were easy enough to understand in theory, but not knowing how they fit into what we were about to do was frying my every instinct. I'd just jumped on this boat to go race it like the baddest Pink Lady, but I was a total Sandy. Before leather. Way before leather. There was no leather in my future, only cardigans and gel pens and hopefully not drowning.

"Don't worry, Rosa. This is a super mellow crowd, and I can do it all myself. I've been updating this boat and rigged almost everything so I can get to it without leaving the helm. I just need you to sit, relax, lean down when that big stick flies past."

"The boom?" I asked, remembering. Ever the student. I counted my breaths and kept my gaze ahead. "How deep is this water? Theoretically, could we swim back from here?" I shouted, but the wind was too loud now, and Alex couldn't hear me over it.

"It's fine," I murmured. "Look at all those people over there in their boats. I have a life vest. I am not going to puke. This is fine." My ears roared, and despite all the air flow, my skin prickled sharply with sweat beneath my shirt. The next gust of wind was too wild, too out of control. I felt the same. This was a terrible idea.

"I gotta be quick to catch up, so if you could steer us a bit while I unfurl the main sails . . ."

I gaped at him. "Say what, now?"

He gestured for me to come to him. We traded spots and he set my hands on the wheel. With subtle and gentle nudges, he helped me adjust. "Stay here. Hands at ten and two. Easy breezy." And then he just left me there with way too much trust. I turned the wheel, but the boat went the opposite way.

"It wants to go back over to the rocks!"

"You see that buoy? That big red balloon? Just point us at it." He pulled at ropes and released the sails. It looked like an intense game of cat's cradle as he moved with certainty across the boat, bringing it to life above us. He returned to my side. "Okay, so we're basically going to be sailing in a big triangle. The starting line is up ahead, marked by that buoy. Everyone has to be behind it before the race starts." His next words were drowned out by a deafening horn.

"What was that?" The wheel jerked in my hands.

"A warning. We've only got a minute."

He was buzzing with energy, but the words sounded like a bleak threat. Only a minute left. My clammy hands gripped the wheel. Alex was saying something as he loosened my hands and took over.

"It's going to be everyone clamoring for a spot in

the beginning. We'll hang back and take our time."

"Don't you want to win, though?"

"Of course I do, but messing up in the beginning is not the way to do it. We'll stay with the fleet, watch the wind, and see what happens." The line of boats was still ahead of us, but each one was shifting in place like a kid waiting for the recess bell to ring.

I glanced at Alex. His entire demeanor was steady and easy despite the wild winds shoving us around. "Where did that nervous guy go?" I wondered aloud.

He squinted against the sun to look at me. "He finally got out of the harbor."

Another horn screamed and the boat beside the buoy waved a flag. Every boat ahead of and beside us set off.

Alex tried narrating as we went, which did nothing to settle my nerves. He called out something about attacking.

"What?" I turned, terrified, to check the other supposedly innocent boats. So much for a mellow crowd.

"We need to go that way." He pointed left. We were tipping wildly to the right. Another buoy floated ahead of us.

I dramatically gestured to our current situation. He grinned. How could he be smiling at a time like this? "Exactly," he explained. "I can't go straight at it, so we have to go in a sort of zigzag. I'm tacking to turn us about."

"What am I doing then?"

"When I say 'coming about'"—he paused at the blankness in my face—"when I say 'go,' watch your head." He turned the wheel in one hand and loosened the rope with the other. "Go!" he shouted. I muttered a prayer and hunched down as the boom flew toward the middle. The sail whipped angrily above us as he pulled another line tight and turned the wheel even more.

The boom shot past, and the sail caught as everything shifted. My heart was still somewhere behind us. Alex was laughing as we sailed past a few other boats. Still hunched down, I glanced over the edge cautiously.

"You can sit up," he called to me.

"I'll take that under advisement," I shouted back and held on as the boat bounced and hit along waves, sending water over the front of the boat. "Is that okay?" Water pooled at my feet. "Is this okay?" I screamed louder, gesturing wildly at the deck.

Alex leaned over to check. "Yes, that's fine, Rosa." He glanced up and then, without warning, shouted, "Go!" again.

I threw myself to the floor as we did the awful attacking thing again. Once the boom was stable, I got up from my graceful belly flop into two inches of water, and returned, soaking wet, to the bench.

From behind the wheel, I could see Alex chuckling.

"Okay, next," he called. "We're going to make a hard right turn, and go around that orange buoy." He pointed it out in the distance. "The wind up there is coming from a different direction, so when we turn I need you to come over and sit on this side and—" He paused, looking like he regretted his next words. "Hang your feet over the edge."

"*Of the boat?*"

"Yes. It's fine, I swear. Just to balance us out."

I was going to die today. There were no other options. This boat was going to make some death trap of a turn, and I needed to go hang off it. Like a woman condemned, I ducked under the boom and went to the other side. I crossed myself and sat on the edge, hanging on to the railing.

"Are you ready?" he called.

"No," I shouted, then muttered, "but that's never stopped me before."

"Turning!"

I screamed as my side of the boat rose from the water. I squeezed my eyes shut against the sharp wind pummeling me. Shouts rang out from nearby boats, and my eyes flew open to check they weren't yelling that I was about to die. In front of me, sea met sky as the boat leveled back down to earth.

I hadn't died. I was soaking wet, my throat was sore from screaming, and my pounding heart had possibly broken one of my ribs, but I was terribly, amazingly alive. I gripped the railing and laughed into the wild wind. Behind me, Alex was laughing, too.

"Where are we today, Rosa?" he called over all of the noise.

We were sailing and I *loved* it. "What's next?" I asked.

"Another turn," he said. "Head back to the other side, and do the same thing again until we level out."

I took my spot and grabbed the railing. And this time I kept my eyes open the whole time. When the boat rose, I watched the boardwalk come into view. People were lined against it, watching the race. Their cheers were growing now that we were close to the end. There were only four boats ahead of us. Somehow we had passed eight others.

We sailed past another. I couldn't help it; I cheered, too.

"Where's the finish line?" I called to Alex.

He pointed with his outstretched left arm. "Over there where we started."

The starting line was pretty close to the left of us, and yet we weren't headed there. "If that's the finish line, why are we going away from it?"

"We have one more buoy," he explained.

In the wildest twist of fate yet, I was excited to do it again. I watched the three boats in front of us and realized the leader missed the buoy.

"They're going to have to circle around again," Alex explained.

"So we might pass them?" I asked.

Alex laughed. "I shouldn't be surprised the competitive spirit got you by the third tack."

Up ahead, the next two boats were rounding the buoy. From our vantage point, we were able to watch them go around the mark. Alex said, "After the turn, we're going to have to zigzag to the finish line, because we can't go—"

"Into the wind," I finished as I pulled my legs back in and righted myself on the bench.

As we watched the two leaders turn toward the finish line and start their own zigzag, Alex said, "Holy shit."

"What?"

He was looking at something up on his own boat now. "The wind shifted. Look at their sails." They were flapping erratically. "They have no wind," Alex went on.

"What does that mean?" I asked, and his grin sharpened. He looked the way I'd felt when I found the Golden Turtle beneath my foot.

"It means we could win."

Alex turned us around the last buoy, and instead of tacking like the others, he adjusted course for a nearly straight shot to the finish line. He did his cat's-cradle dance with the lines around him, and we sailed past the other two boats. Feedback squealed from a megaphone as the name of a boat that sounded like *Wallflower* was called.

"We won!" I shouted, then put together what the announcer had just said. "Wait. What did he just call you?"

Alex was grinning as he spun the wheel. "The name of my boat. My family has always teased me for being the quiet baker, so I named it the *Wallflour*."

"That is the most delightful thing I've ever heard," I told him and sidled up close.

"You were amazing," he said proudly and slipped an arm

around my shoulder. He pulled me against him and dropped a hard, grateful kiss on my lips. When he pulled back, it was like looking at the north star.

"I was amazing," I agreed, awed. The crisp turquoise morning was melting beneath the midday sun as we docked. When I pulled away I couldn't help but glance at our bench, the one we'd sat on the night I'd come to the marina.

Mimi sat there, watching us.

A curse slipped past my lips in Spanish. Mimi's eyes narrowed like she'd heard it.

"I have to go," I told Alex and turned to search for my backpack. But I hadn't brought it. I was still in my gardening clothes. And they were soaking wet. I hurriedly tried to unbuckle my life vest, but my fingers were too clumsy.

"What's wrong?" Alex was clueing into my panic. He gently pushed my hands aside and unbuckled the vest for me. I saw him as Mimi would. Alex wasn't a boy. He was leveled up. He had a beard and tattoos. Here was the first person I wanted to introduce to my abuela, and I already ruined everything.

"Mimi is sitting over there."

His brows furrowed as he glanced over. Realization dawned with an ice-cold side of panic. "You didn't tell her."

"No, I didn't tell her I was going sailing today with a boy she doesn't know about."

He looked at me again. "You haven't told her about me?"

"Not because of you. Because of us and our ghosts." And because this was supposed to be my secret crush. The one I had just been screaming and sailing with in front of everyone during a very busy festival. I was obviously terrible with secrets.

Alex looked confused but said, "I should go with you." He was ignoring everything he needed to do for the boat right now, forgetting that his father was out there somewhere on the boardwalk having seen his big victory. He was wholly focused on me and my panic. But I didn't know how long Mimi had been sitting there, and the longer I waited to go to her, the greater the chasm would be between the last time I told her a truth and this lie.

"Find me later," I told him and hopped off the boat. Alex called after me, but I couldn't stop. Mimi was already walking away, and I rushed to her side.

"I can explain." My heart raced. I had no idea how to be in trouble with her.

"With lies," she said coldly. "No quiero mentiras."

"Good, because I'm fresh out of lies. I didn't like them one bit."

"You did not like getting caught. There is a difference." She glanced both ways, and we crossed the road. The festival was in full swing now, and there were so many new faces around us, but the familiar ones were watching us instead of the entertainment. Gladys in line for a Popsicle, Ms. Francis walking her dogs, Mike playing at the dominos table with

224

Simon, Xiomara strumming her guitar in the midst of a bolero. They each stopped at the sound of Mimi and me sweeping through the festivities like a sudden rainstorm.

"I want to tell you about Alex."

Mimi laughed gruffly. "Ay, no. I do not want to hear about your secret boyfriend now. You lied to your abuela once, how many times did you lie before? Do you have classes on the computer? Do you still work at the bodega? Yo no sé."

"You're being ridiculous."

She stopped on the sidewalk. Her eyes were wide. Dangerously wide. *I'm-about-to-unleash* wide. I stopped breathing.

"Mimi, please. His name is Alex—well, Alejandro actually." I paused to see if the Latino name won me any points. "And yes, that was his boat."

She shushed me, but I hurried on, at my own peril.

"We went to school together but really only just met. He's very kind and sweet, and I care about him."

Mimi marched forward, parting crowds as everyone moved aside for her. I couldn't even see the festival anymore.

"We were working on the wedding together. You know this. His parents own the marina."

Feedback whined from the stage. Ana's band would start soon. I had to hurry. I chased Mimi, desperate to tell her everything. She hushed me and muttered curses, and I couldn't tell whether she was getting more mad or if maybe, hopefully, her anger was dissipating with every rushed confession. If I could just hand her everything now, then maybe I could save all of us. Her from the disappointment, Alex from her bad opinion, and me from the anxiety trying to swallow me whole.

She stopped and I nearly crashed into her. She turned to look at me. "¿Y esa cara?" she asked, her voice quiet, spirit tired.

"What's wrong with my face?"

"Igual que tu madre." Everything came back to my mother. It was a fight I was forever losing.

"This isn't about her," I said.

She huffed a humorless laugh, and her hand went to her heart. "¿Por qué, Rosa? This is not you. That girl on the boat? I do not know her."

The shot hurt. It was unfair. Was it such a terrible thing to change? Yes, I'd handled things poorly, maybe even childishly, as out of my depth as I'd been, but it had been in the pursuit of something great. I stood there, the same windswept girl. I still didn't know her either, but I wanted to.

Mimi searched my gaze. "You stop going to school and who is this? Who are you?"

"I'm me," I burst out, and her eyes widened again. "This doesn't erase all my work, and it's unfair of you to say so. I'm figuring it all out, but I'm still me, Mimi. I was lost and I met someone and started to care for him and had no idea how to do that."

Her eyes closed, pained, and I immediately wanted to take the hurt back. I hated this fighting and yelling. Maybe I was changing, but this still wasn't us.

"Ay, Rosa," she whispered like a prayer to one of her saints. My throat tight, I walked into her arms, and she enveloped me in them. I pressed my nose to her shoulder. She smelled of her delicately perfumed powder and the charged note of her oil and herbs. Here was home and my harbor. Welcomed, I could weather anything.

"I'm sorry," I whispered against her neck. She said nothing, but her soft, strong hand rubbed my back as gently as it did when I was a kid who climbed into her bed those first nights I couldn't sleep for missing my mother.

"Will you meet him?" I asked.

"I know who he is." We were still hugging, and I put my chin on her shoulder. "I remember everything." She sighed and pulled back. Her smile was tender. "I hear Ana's drums. Come back after the wedding."

"Where?"

"The tent. I will show you everything." Before I could ask what that meant, she turned and disappeared into the crowd.

❖

I crashed to a stop beside Mike, who toasted me with a neon-green snow cone. "I heard you not only sailed, but won."

"News travels fast in this town."

"Not as fast as you, it sounds like." Mike grinned.

I pointed at the two cigars in his shirt pocket. "Looks like I'm not the only one winning today."

"My prize for cleaning up at the dominos table, but these are for Jonas," he said. "A wedding gift for the nervous wreck."

"It's going well, right?" The crowd was smaller in front of the stage, but there were plenty of people walking around the square, following the signs down to the harbor.

Mike tapped his cigars. "Luck's on our side today."

Good luck usually didn't want anything to do with me and mine, but I hoped he was right. The band walked out onto the stage and took their places. "Welcome to Spring Fest, y'all," Tyler screamed into the microphone.

Mike rubbed his left ear. Paula came over to us and jerked her thumb at the stage. "Who is that joker?"

"Tyler Moon," I told her. "Are you here for Ana?"

She heaved a sigh. She wore a white crop top and her pants were bright blue with a flattering high waist. "I'm not much for this hipster music, but family is family." She cupped her hands around her mouth and screamed. I followed her bold lead and did the same. I was so going to lose my voice tomorrow. Mike crunched on his snow cone.

"We're Tyler and the Electric!" Tyler called. Judging by the rest of the band's confused frowns, the name was a surprise to them.

And it threw Ana. The beat was off. The song started without her, and she fumbled forward. Not knowing what else to do, I started to dance.

"What are you doing?" Paula asked after some of my best moves.

"I'm offended you have to ask." I knew they were playing popular covers, but I didn't know this song. I really had to update my playlists.

Still, I danced, and I did it hard. I was already huffing and puffing, but there would only be five songs, and the small crowd was somehow thinning. I tried to take up as much room as I could, but by Paula's and Mike's faces, it was not impressive. Before I became terribly embarrassing, Mike joined me. He hopped into my makeshift circle, and we punched the air together. Paula finally gave in, and we made an awkward triangle, but we went all in.

"Hipster music," Paula complained as she danced along with us.

Maybe it was the power of our mini dance floor or my whispered prayers to the spirit of Celia Cruz, but Ana found her rhythm with a clatter of thunder. There were no clouds in the sky, but the ground shook beneath our feet.

Our eyes lit up, and dancing became the easiest thing in the world. I wanted to chase the beat down. Swirl my hips and throw my hands in the air just to feel the wind Ana electrified to life, even if it was still only the three of us losing our minds.

Until Benny crashed the party.

"Hey, assholes," the charming Cuban maestro called. A crowd followed him. The area in front of the small stage filled with what I was sure were all the members of the dance team, judging by their impressive moves. Benny stopped in front of Paula and me and dropped a flower crown on each of our heads.

"What's up, Captain Rosa," he said with a wink before melting into the crowd of dancing girls.

"What does that mean?" Paula asked me.

I didn't stop dancing. "I drizzled the caramel."

Paula threw her head back and laughed.

When the next song started, Ana grabbed hold of the new burst of energy and powered over it. It vibrated up our bones. The crowd moved like a wave. We were the tide, she was the moon, and like any good salsa song, she held us in motion for as long as she wanted us.

26

"*I didn't think* I'd be this nervous." Clara paced in front of the mirror in the bodega's break room. "Is he out there? Can you please check again, Ana?"

"He's out there," Ana told her. She swirled around the room in a long yellow skirt and white tank, still buzzing from her performances.

Mrs. Peña swept into the room. "There's a pretty good crowd out there. We announced there would be a small wedding, and folks are sticking around to watch."

"But we're strangers to them," Clara said.

"It is romantic," her mother said and kissed her daughter's cheek. Clara's mother wore her hair in braids and her dress was a darker shade of blue. They held hands and tipped their faces closer as they shared soft words. My heart clenched and I looked away. Part of me had thought Mom would be back by Spring Fest. I shook off the gloomy disappointment and leaned in close to steal a corner of the mirror and apply my lipstick. I'd gotten out of my sea-soaked clothes and now wore a cap-sleeved tomato-red wrap dress. I'd given my flower crown to Clara.

"My abuela once told me it was good luck to get married in spring," Mrs. Peña said to Clara. "You'll make strong babies or something."

"Gross, Mom," Ana complained.

The bright afternoon was fading, spilling warm golden light into the room. We were reaching that perfect hour between day and dusk. Clara nervously checked her reflection again. She turned one way, then the other, her lacy skirt dancing across her dark skin. She was the sweet, tender picture of romance in spring.

"How did you know?" I asked her.

"Know what?" She readjusted her flower crown.

I shrugged, feeling embarrassed. "That he was the one. That . . . I don't know what I'm asking. It's your wedding day." I tried to laugh off the awkward nerves.

"Well, I fell in love with this shop first. Port Coral second, and then a very dedicated fisherman with a wicked sense of humor and soft heart." Her smile felt like a private thing to witness. An unexpected gift. I didn't understand romantic love that lasted, but it was a thread in my favorite stories. I liked to believe.

Alex stopped at the open door and shot me a quick thumbs-up before disappearing. It was go time.

I turned to Clara. "I wish you the best wedding ever."

Clara, halfway to tears already, hugged me tightly. "Thank you for being such a wonderful friend."

Honey-sweet emotion rushed over me as I squeezed her back. "Let's get you hitched."

Ana left, and a few seconds later the Electric kicked into a fun doo-wop song. That was our cue. I went out ahead of Clara and her mother and tried not to kick up the flowers too much as I joined the others lined up around the square. Clara, holding her handpicked daisies, stepped out of the bodega, and her hand flew to her mouth. Pink, yellow, and white petals marked her path to Jonas. She was all the way to crying now. I waved at Oscar, who flipped the switch for me.

Every tree around us sparkled with soft twinkle lights.

A collective sound of awe sang out, and Clara cried out in joy. My heart was going to burst. This baby bruja of Port Coral could make magic, too.

Clara floated all the way to the driftwood pergola decorated with magnolias where Jonas was waiting for her. The big, cheerful fisherman was in tears, too. This was the first time I'd ever seen him in a suit. We all moved in closer to make a tight circle around the couple, and beyond us, curious tourists watched. I wondered how we looked to them. If this moment showed them more about Port Coral. I hoped so.

Jonas and Clara tangled fingers, and the officiant got the ceremony under way. This was my first wedding, and the words were familiar enough because of TV and movies, but this was so much more. Unexpected tears flooded my eyes.

Across the crowd I found Mimi. She watched the ceremony with a faraway look.

Her love story hadn't been long enough. I wondered if her broken heart had ever healed. Even just a little. Her gaze met mine and softened.

"I now pronounce you husband and wife."

We erupted in applause, cheers, and the viejitos' sharp whistles as Jonas and Clara sealed the words with a kiss. Somewhere beyond us Benny's bottle rockets exploded in the sky.

"Let's go get the wine," Ana said as Clara and Jonas were enveloped by their friends. Ana tugged me away and blew a quick whistle—sounding so much like the viejitos. Several of her cousins pulled away from their groups to come help. We hurried to the bodega for the buckets piled with ice and chilled pink bottles.

As we hauled the buckets out to the square, I glanced at Mimi's white tent. It was still closed off. "The festival is over. What is she even doing?"

"Who?" Ana said, her voice tight from carrying the metal buckets.

"Mimi," I said. "With her tent."

"You don't know?"

"You do?" I demanded.

She laughed. "It's the reception."

With a heave, I set the bucket down on the grass. I studied the mysterious tent for the hundredth time that day. "So what, is there a dance floor in there? Then why all of this secretiveness?" I marched across the square, through the laughing crowd, everyone growing giddy with romance, twinkle lights, and champagne bubbles. The tent was fairly large, but I should have put two and two together. I'd never considered my abuela would be so enigmatic about a reception.

"Mimi!" I called, hands on my hips. She told me to meet her here, so she had to be in there already. "I know this is for the wedding! I'm going inside."

Nothing. I glanced around. Ana was stopped by her mother.

"Enough with the secrets. I'm here, let's get this party started already."

This was ridiculous. *Just open it.* The sun finished sinking into the horizon, and the tent's flaps moved a little, as if there had been a breeze. I frowned, confused.

"Mimi?" I called again. I checked behind me, but Ana was gone now.

At the top of the tent, knotted string began to loosen. I took a quick step back but didn't look away. The ropes gave with a sudden sharp tug. One by one, the panels along the sides fell, and my abuela's magic spilled out.

It wasn't just a party.

It was a party in Havana.

27

I faced a bustling city street with café tables, palm trees, and candles on every surface with twinkle lights spilling over the green leaves overhead. I crossed the invisible line between the familiar square in Port Coral and onto the tropical city street. Trumpets, drums, the rhythmic slide of beads against the gourd of a shekere played from somewhere farther inside. Papá El stood at the entrance with his cart. Smiling excitedly, he offered me a mango Popsicle.

"How?" was the only word I could get out. How had this happened? How did it all fit under the tent?

Papá El laughed. "Your abuela is very creative." He handed out more Popsicles to the people walking past me. "Good thing we didn't ruin the surprise, huh?"

There were plants everywhere. Green and wild, even in their bright pots. The sea breeze stirred palm leaves, and the air was sweet with coconut. Pop-up shops offering small slices of wedding cake and sparkling wine sat along the pathway filling with foot traffic from the festival. Others strolled past me like all of this was part of the planned festivities. How could that be possible when we weren't in Port Coral anymore? The sun had disappeared, and with it the square I knew.

"Xiomara!" I called, and she turned but continued walking backward as she strummed her guitar.

"Hey, Rosa!"

"What is going on?" I stopped. People walked around me. "Have you seen Mimi?"

She tipped her head, confused. "Around here somewhere." She continued on her way.

Maybe I didn't know my own abuela, because the woman I knew never even *spoke* about Cuba, but here it was around me, seducing my senses. Color, sounds, scents. The music grew louder until finally, up ahead, surrounded by a rapt audience, I found the beating heart.

Ana stood behind her congas from jazz band. Her curls were a glowing halo, and her smile just as bright. She played a fast, demanding beat and called for the other drummers— all older men—in the circle around her to keep up.

Xiomara danced into their circle, already singing, her voice deep and vibrant.

Jonas led Clara out onto the dance floor to the cheers of a delighted crowd. They didn't follow practiced salsa steps but instead swirled and shimmied, cracking each other up. My wonder gave way to a big smile.

The song ended and swept right into the next with the call of a trumpet. Mr. Peña sat in one of the chairs with his trumpet, his foot tapping as he played near Ana. My best friend laughed, radiating joy. Oh my god, by some miracle, Mimi even got *Mr. Peña* to play. How in the world did Mimi make all of this happen? And why?

My hand was grabbed, and I was smoothly spun into the middle of the floor, where I found myself in Benny's arms.

"Ready?" he asked, grinning.

"Why do people keep asking me that?"

I put my hand on his shoulder and dove hip first into the song. I'd danced hundreds of times with Benny at Peña family gatherings, and we were good together. He led me left and spun me once before I snapped back into position. I forgot all of my questions and disbelief and lost myself to the music. The rhythm wrapped around me and guided my feet. My hips. My pulse. My next breath. Here I was fluent, and always on beat as I swayed through time.

Benny spun me away again—I was going to get dizzy in a minute—and I stopped in a different set of arms. Alex smiled down at me. He looked all Ravenclaw again as he held one of my hands, the other resting carefully on my waist just above my hip.

"Hey," I said, breathless. "Fancy spinning into you here."

He laughed, but his hands tightened a little, that soft, nervous look in his gaze. But here he was, ready to dance. My heart was surely glowing in my chest.

The song slowed and we drifted closer. This was different than dancing with Benny. His hands gripped me tighter.

"The wedding was beautiful," I said. He made a sound of agreement that rumbled against my ear. He dipped his head down, and I pressed my nose against his shirt. Warm sugar and mint. He was both a danger and balm to my senses. Just beyond us, I finally spotted Mimi waiting at the edge of the dance floor. I stopped dancing and Alex looked down at me with concern. At my expression, he turned around. I reached for his hand, and his chest rose and fell with heavy breaths.

Mimi watched us as we walked toward her. Tonight she wore a midnight-blue dress, and the hem danced softly in the breeze. I wondered how we looked to her. Was I still sweet baby Rosa in her eyes?

And that's when it hit me.

I wish I could show you my home, our home, but I will try.

"Oh, Mimi," I said when we stopped in front of her. I let go of Alex's hand and grabbed my abuela's. Her smile was small, but emotion rolled like waves in her eyes. She brushed my hair behind my ear and laid a gentle hand against my cheek.

In Spanish, she whispered, "I should have used my pain better. You and your mother deserved that."

She let go and I felt bereft. I didn't know what to say.

Mimi looked at Alex. I wiped my eyes and hurried to formally introduce them. "Mimi, this is Alex. Alex, this is my abuela."

"Hola, Doña Santos," he greeted in smooth Spanish. He leaned in close to kiss her chastely on the cheek. Mimi softened and a faraway look came into her eyes. She smiled, squeezed his shoulder, and said something too low for me to hear as Celia Cruz's "La Vida Es Un Carnaval" began to play. With a wistful smile, she reached for Alex's hand and tugged him to the dance floor.

"Hey, that's my date," I called playfully, my voice hoarse from all the screaming and crying today. I was emotionally spent, but it was such a joy to watch Alex dance with my abuela, her smile lighting up the night. I begged time to slow so I could live in this moment for a little longer. Gather all of this up and press these memories between pages like flowers.

Tonight was a homecoming alive with music, life, and joy.

"Look at her go."

I started at the voice beside me. My mother smiled at the sight of Mimi dancing. She wore a white shirt and jeans, and looked tired and rumpled from travel. Paint stained her shirt and hands. "She do all this?" Mom asked without looking away. The dance floor filled with couples: Dan and Malcolm, Clara and Jonas, and even Ms. Francis, laughing delightedly with wine in hand, with Simon. I grinned at her, because I knew he definitely liked dogs.

"Yeah," I said. "I don't know how, though."

Beyond us, fireworks burst over the harbor. Yellow,

golden, and red. We'd done it. Spring Fest, a wedding, and a real chance for the harbor. There was so much I wanted to say to Mom, but instead I asked, "You want to dance, too?"

Mom's sigh was soft with relief. "Always, baby." She took my hand, and we disappeared into the music that sounded like longing, pain, and love all wrapped up into one song.

28

The party ended with the sky dark above us. Vendors packed up and the crowds went home. Jonas and Clara bid us all a grateful good night, and we did the same. We would know the total made for the harbor in the coming days, but for now, my friends helped us pack up a few important things from the tent. I wanted to linger beneath the stars and dance to another song. I wanted Alex's hands wrapped around me as we spun and spun until time finally stopped for us.

When we were almost home, all of us carrying boxes, rain began to fall.

"Of course," Benny complained. Mike cursed. Alex checked the sky like he was measuring the threat.

Lightning struck and the streetlights around us flickered. We all froze, then sighed with relief when they stayed on. Until a transformer blew in a thunderous boom and sizzling spark of blue lights. We screamed and booked it home in the darkness, lit only by the full moon.

"Is this a good time to admit I'm afraid of the dark?" Benny said through heaving breaths as we ran.

The rain began in a torrent. We crashed inside and tried not to wipe out on the tile in the entryway before setting the boxes down.

I looked at Mom. "You brought quite a storm with you."

She rolled her eyes and shook the water from her hair. "I always do."

One good thing about losing power in our house was there were always plenty of candles around. Mimi and I collected the ones we could find in the dark. Mom went to find matches. Soft light flickered throughout the house.

"Very romantic," Benny said.

"Not my worst date," Mike agreed and showed me the weather radar on his phone. The wash of green, yellow, and ominous spots of red didn't look great. But that was Florida for you. "It's a tropical depression that just turned for us," he said.

I shot a look at Mom, who rolled her eyes.

"It's moving pretty quickly, though."

Ana called her mom. "Yes, I left the square. . . . No, Mom, I'm not in the rain. . . . My hair is barely wet! . . . I'm at Mimi's. . . . Okay, okay." She rolled her eyes and lowered the phone from her ear. "She told me to get off the phone or I'd get electrocuted, and then hung up on me."

Mimi swept into the kitchen, surrounded by candles. She set the metal coffeemaker on the gas stove. The pilot light sparked into a small blue flame.

243

"Ah, you're a genius, Mimi," Benny said.

She smirked. "We all did not have electricity our whole lives."

"The wind's calmed down," Mom said. Her wet hair was braided over her shoulder. She looked so young. "Let's open windows before it gets stuffy." The cross-breeze that swept into the dark house was cool and sweet with rain. The candlelight allowed us to see one another and the steps in front of us but not much else.

"What do we do now?" I asked. My friends were pretty much stuck until the storm blew over.

"Be quiet or you'll make more thunder," Mimi said, a smile in her voice. It was something she always told noisy children during storms, i.e., me.

Mom grabbed mugs and waited for coffee. The night was preventing whatever fight she and Mimi would have had otherwise. The soft hush of evening soothed away their sharp edges and allowed them to move in sync. The rest of us settled down in the living room together. I stretched out on the floor beside the coffee table. Alex leaned back against the wall beside me.

An idea sprang to mind, and I jumped back to my feet. "Be right back." I grabbed a candle and went to Mimi's shelf, and from the bottom I pulled out what would have looked like a suitcase to anyone who didn't intimately know her Cleansing Sundays. I set it on the coffee table and opened it. "Ta-da!"

244

"The hell is that?" Benny asked.

"A record player," I said. "You crank it. No electricity." Mimi and Mom watched from the kitchen, amused by my eagerness.

Alex leaned over and did the honors. I carefully slipped a record into place. When he stopped turning the crank, the music began.

Magic engulfed us—the crackle of the record player, our windows open to a wild, salty breeze that rustled past palm fronds outside. Mimi returned with coffee for each of us. She gave me a soft smile as she curled into the chair by the window.

"I heard him sing this song."

"Really?" I asked, surprised but hopeful for more. Maybe the night wasn't over. There was still so much I wanted to know.

Mimi looked at Mom. "The night I met your papi." I'd never heard Mimi call him anything so familiar and present. Mom stood at the window, watching the storm outside.

"My sisters and I went to Havana with one of our mother's sisters for my birthday. Tía was young, and let us go to the concert. Alvaro was there because he knew the trumpet player, and he came up to me and said I was the most beautiful girl in Havana."

"And what did you say?" Ana asked.

"I told him I wasn't from Havana."

We laughed. My mother stood with her back to the room.

245

"Falling in love was so easy. I never wanted to leave." She worried the button of her dress. Without turning away from the window, Mom offered Mimi her hand. My abuela took it and brought it to her lips, kissing it twice. *One from me, one from him.* Old memories grew wings as I remembered Mimi always kissing Mom twice when I was a little girl.

"Tell us more," I begged.

"When I met him, Alvaro was a student in Havana. He wanted to be a professor and had books everywhere. Even his furniture! He asked me to sit on a chair, but it was just a pile of more books. I came back to Havana many times that summer."

Benny murmured, "Scandalous."

"In the fall, Alvaro came home with me and asked Papi if he could marry me. 'What can a teacher give my daughter?' he asked, and Alvaro said, 'Good love letters.'" Her laugh painted her ghost story in brighter shades. It broke through the old shadows with love and light. "Alvaro had never been to Viñales, but we married at the church and dreamed of starting a farm, just like my family. But he loved Havana. The music and people. He loved Cuba so much."

Mimi's mournful gaze came to me. In Spanish, she confessed their hunger and fear. Their determination to see their child free.

"Alvaro tried to get me a ticket to leave, because—" She paused as her hand fisted against her middle. "They went

246

to arrest him instead. He could not go back to school, and I could not risk my family."

Outside, the lemon trees swayed in the stormy wind. The chimes played a gentle song.

"Cuba is about so much more than the land, but the land means so much." As quiet as a whispered prayer, in Spanish, she said, "If her cities fall, if we're all gone, may God watch after her." The sweet, sharp scent of lemon blossoms swept inside and wrapped around us. The pain of her loss bled through everything, because she loved her island. Despite everything, her love lived and breathed, still tangled with an eternal hope for freedom.

"I'm sorry I could not show it to you," she confessed. She looked at Mom and reached for her hand. Mom gave it and bent down and kissed her mother's brow. Twice.

"You did," I told her and moved closer to sit at her knee. She had carried and protected and nurtured it. It had always been there for us to find.

"Ay, mis niñas." Mimi held both of our hands, clutching them against her chest.

"Viva Cuba libre," I said with conviction.

"Pa'lante," Mimi whispered. *Forward*.

29

The lights flickered on, and I blinked hard as the room around us came back into focus. We snapped back to the present. Phones buzzed and coffee mugs were returned. No one really knew what to say, but Mike, Ana, Alex, and Benny stopped by Mimi's chair to offer a grateful good night. It wasn't out of place for my friends to kiss my abuela's cheek in greeting and farewell, but everyone was lingering. Ana's phone rang—her mother making sure she hadn't been electrocuted—but she was hesitating to leave, too. We'd found something thought lost tonight. A story and memory of Mimi's love in the face of exile.

I walked them outside but lingered on the front porch with Alex. The night was sticky as the streets and sidewalk steamed from the rain. Alex stopped at the first step.

"What is it?" I asked.

"I've been thinking a lot about something. I wasn't sure if you'd want to, but after today . . ." He reached into his back pocket and drew out a square piece of paper. I knew what it was before he unfolded it.

My stomach twisted at the sight of his map. He handed it to me, wordlessly, and I carefully looked over it again. I expected to see the same lines and coordinates, but everything was different. I followed the path and my heart nearly stopped when I realized that this time his trip was taking him to Cuba. My gaze shot to his.

"You talk about going, even when you're not talking about it, and I know how disappointed you've been about study abroad, but I researched sailing to the island, and with my dad's connections we could sail into the marina there, and stay somewhere on the island this summer. You can see everything you want." He rattled off all the laws and regulations he'd researched. He'd done this the way I would. For me. Something close to panic made me take a quick step back, leaving Alex on the bottom step.

"I can't."

He stopped talking. "What?"

"I can't go." This wasn't panic. It was a hollow frustration edged with a desperate sort of anger. How could he show me this map like it was a possibility for us? It was a dream I couldn't have, one he had no place offering me. "How can you ask me this?"

He drew back, confused. I hated it. "Because you were going to go."

"That was different. That wasn't me sailing into the

middle of the ocean." *I climbed out of that broken boat and*—I shook my head to clear it of Mimi's voice. The night was so humid, and my skin felt too tight.

"But we got onto a boat today," he said, genuinely confused.

"We didn't even leave our harbor. And like you said, that's not the ocean."

"And like you said, semantics." He dragged a rough hand through his hair. "If you don't want to go with me, fine. I would never . . . I just don't understand if it's because of my boat or me or—"

"I have school and work, and then I have to get ready to move, and I can't just leave on a sailing trip. I'm not going to Cuba anymore, okay?" I nearly shouted it. Had the wind heard me? I'd defied so much. Played pretend too long. And yet I couldn't reason with this flash of bitter anger. I exhaled sharply and tried to think past it. "And I saw your first map. Your trip is so much bigger. I won't take that from you because of my neuroses."

Alex's dark brows were low. "Plans can change."

"*No*. She said when you start to change plans for each other that's where it all goes wrong." Ana's words flashed through my mind.

"What? Who said?"

"It doesn't matter." I gave him his map and clenched my hands as I stepped back. "A sailing trip? God, Alex. Look at me. I've spent two years preparing to leave, and at the last minute, my plans fell apart, and what have I done to fix it? *Nothing*. I'm procrastinating and forgetting, and I won't stand at your empty dock and scream at the sea."

He gripped the railing and stared at his feet. He didn't understand. I looked up at the moon and gritted my teeth against the tears burning my throat. I wiped my eyes and exhaled in a gust. I had two women in that house gutted by the loss of love, and I wouldn't do it. To me or them. I was repeating something, and I had to stop this. I wouldn't put another picture on my table.

When I said nothing more, Alex carefully slipped the map back into his pocket. "I'm sorry."

His apology fractured me further. "I have to leave." The words sounded low and harsh. I had finally lost my voice.

"Okay." He nodded slowly. "Maybe I'll see you tomorrow, then."

"No, Alex. We can't do this anymore."

He watched me, and I knew that vulnerable, searching look. I'd seen it in so many mirrors. He was trying to understand how we got here, what signs he'd missed when someone he trusted didn't give him the chance to prepare for a good-bye. "I'm sorry," I whispered just before I jerked open the door and went inside. I stayed with my hand on the knob and prayed he didn't knock. Because I would open it. I dropped my forehead to the door, and my body shuddered. I was such a mess.

I found Mimi and my mother sitting together, their voices low. The lights were dimmed and the candles still lit. Life and love buzzed between them, complicated and vibrant, their connection a tangled, beautiful mess. Together they were a battle in concert; happy and sad, lost and found, here and somewhere else.

When they looked up, concern marred both their expressions. "What happened?" Mom sat up at once.

"He asked me on a sailing trip." My hands fell uselessly at my sides. "And I told him no, because I don't want him to die."

Intimate knowledge shadowed their faces. Their shoulders caved from the weight of carrying it. I sank between them. Mimi slipped her hand into my hair and brushed against my scalp gently while Mom rubbed her hand up and down my arm.

"Nela told me not to leave Cuba with Alvaro," Mimi confessed.

I stilled. "Tía Nela?"

Mimi gave me a look. "So impatient. Yes, Tía Nela."

"Is she the one who took you to Havana for your birthday?"

"No, Nela was everyone's tía. It's difficult to explain, but she knew Cuba more than all the angry men who spilled so much blood. She knew the island's spirit and understood it was in pain. She warned me our land was bleeding and the sea would demand a sacrifice. I left anyway."

"Because of me," Mom said, sounding so achingly tired of being everyone's bad omen.

"Because of love." Mimi's hand went across me to hold Mom's.

All of my careful planning, but these winds had set us on this path long before tonight. These same winds had once fluttered through the dark strands of hair of the women before me as they looked to a horizon and set off into the unknown. Where did that leave me? Daughters carried legacies and curses as deftly as their inherited hearts. It was a delicate, demanding balance.

"Tell me another, Mimi." I leaned my head into her neck, comforted by the smell of lemon and rosemary. She brushed her empty hand through my hair and laid a long, soft kiss on the top of my head. "Uno más."

The three cursed Santos women huddled together as Mimi told us one more story.

30

Curled in bed, unable to sleep for more than a few hours, I waited to watch the sun rise from my open window. The morning air was chilly as I watched the sky lighten into a soft robin's egg blue and imagined the sea of Alex's maps. The impossible latitudes and longitudes.

I already missed him, but a new day waited for me. I just had to get out of this bed.

The kitchen was empty and the coffee cooling. I warmed a mug and stopped at the threshold of the garden room. Mimi wasn't here, but I settled in her chair to wait for her. Several sprigs of rosemary were drying, as well as sage and thyme. I opened my notebook, determined to create my outline for May. It was less than two weeks away and I would meet it with a decision.

I uncapped my marker and remembered my first journal. Mimi had given it to me. *It's important to write things down,* she'd told me as she handed me a composition book after my mother left the first time. Those blank pages had felt like hope. I'd hidden in her garden and filled them with all the wild, welcoming plants that kept me safe.

As I traced a line along a ruler, separating my days from my goals, I thought about my grandfather. What had he wanted to teach? What were his favorite books? Authors? Did he dog-ear pages and talk with his hands when he got excited? Wind and steel sang out as the wind chime danced. Between two pages, I shaded the stem of a sprig of rosemary with swift, sure strokes. If my father had come back, would I have been brave enough to go with Alex? The chime's song became louder. Outside, the sky was still bright blue; there wasn't a single cloud. It was a perfect day.

But my abuela's wind chime was wild with panic.

My skin prickled with sweat, and ice swam in my blood. *Instincts,* my mother's voice whispered from somewhere in my memory. *Listen to them.*

"Mimi?" I called, but there was no reply. The silence felt hollow. I slowly got to my feet and watched the wind chimes dance. I sprang out of her chair. "Mimi!" I swept into the house, sure she was in the kitchen stirring coffee. She was going to be mad about me shouting. But the kitchen was empty.

"Mimi?"

I found her in her bedroom and the relief made me stumble against the doorjamb. Mimi went to sit on the side of her bed. But she fell from the edge. I rushed forward to catch her, and her eyes met mine for a second, or maybe a lifetime, maybe both of our lifetimes, before I held her still, small body on the floor. In the next beat, my mother was there, pushing me aside. She kneeled beside Mimi and began CPR.

I was frozen, but Mom didn't slow. Her movements were strong and vigorous as she pushed down, over and over, on my grandmother's chest.

"Rosa! Nine-one-one! Now!"

My mother's gaze was flooded with unshed tears. But she didn't stop. Caught in an angry, unforgiving storm, she fought Mimi's heart.

I ran out of the room and dialed 911. The operator spoke, and from underwater I begged them to come. Her heart, I said. Her heart was so strong, but something was wrong. I ran out of the house and bounded across the street. I slammed my fist against Dan and Malcolm's door. Dan opened it, carrying his daughter, and his annoyance turned to concern. "Rosa, what's wrong?"

I couldn't say it. I needed to, but I couldn't. I choked out, "Mimi."

Dan's face changed. My easygoing neighbor shifted into a determined paramedic. He handed me Penny, rushed back into his house, and a second later was running back out with what looked like a duffel bag. I ran after him. In Mimi's room, he dropped down beside my mother and abuela's still chest and took over. My mother fought him for a moment, but Dan didn't relent or explain. There was no time. My mother curled into herself and wept. I couldn't go to her. I couldn't move. I needed to hold Penny. I needed to keep her from sinking.

Red-and-blue flashing lights spilled into our windows, and the front door flew open. Firefighters and paramedics swept past me, filling my grandmother's lace-and-lavender bedroom with too many people and all of their foreign equipment.

Penny began to cry, and I tried whispering the song to her that Mimi used to sing to me, something about a frog in Spanish. I fumbled with the first verse as my grandmother was slipped onto a stretcher. Dan walked with her, still performing CPR.

Mimi still hadn't taken a breath on her own.

I followed them through the fog. Neighbors stood outside their houses, hands to their mouths in shock. Dan climbed into the back of the ambulance with my grandmother, and the other paramedic looked at me. I looked at my mother.

"Go," I told her. She didn't hesitate. She rushed into the back of the ambulance and the doors slammed. A moment later the noise and chaos rushed away with them until it was just me and Penny on an empty sidewalk.

I was alone.

My neighbors rushed to one another, everyone trying to understand and comfort. Mrs. Peña jumped into her van as Ana ran past to Dan's house. She broke into his car for Penny's seat. Everyone was in such purposeful motion on this impossible day.

Penny whimpered and dropped her head to my shoulder. I rubbed her back.

Ana was at my side. She didn't say anything. What use were words, anyway? You could never find the right ones when you needed them. Words were islands that sank into silence like forgotten songs. With a hand on my arm, Ana led me to her mother's car. The doors slammed shut, and we raced to the hospital, where the last pieces of my family fought to survive.

31

My sorrow was a steady companion that sat beside me in a hospital waiting room where my mother would have been had she not been pacing the hallway, breaking down, or being the adult representative of what currently stood for the Santos family. *Cardiac arrest*, they said. My abuela's heart had failed. It didn't make sense. That heart was my shelter in every storm. That heart was my home.

I can never look back, Mimi's voice whispered so long ago.

He never came back, my mother cried when I was too young to understand.

The woman across from me answered a phone call. I watched her try to keep it together as she told someone too far away that their chance to say good-bye was gone. I wanted nothing to do with good-bye. I wanted to find a way home with Mimi. That was the only way I could leave this room. I wished for Penny again, and the weight of her in my arms to ground me, but Dan had taken her home hours ago. He promised to return later with Malcolm. I would still be here, in this chair beside Ana and her mother. They held hands and I looked at my own empty palms as her mother began to pray.

I was adrift, dry-eyed and empty of words but trying to hold still enough so maybe this terrible moment wouldn't find me. If I stayed hidden, maybe that next terrible phone call couldn't reach me. If she got up and breathed again, if *she* found me again, the rest of the world could have me back.

The door opened and I steeled myself, expecting my mother bearing the news that would break me, but it was Benny. Ana got to her feet and hugged her brother tightly. Their mother wrapped an arm around both of them.

Maybe if I had a sibling. Another parent. Did pain feel lighter when there were more hands to carry it? All these hypotheticals swirled like dreams. The door didn't close, because behind Benny, Alex rushed into the room.

His hair was a mess. Flour dusted the apron he hadn't taken off. Panic in his eyes, he found me almost immediately. My name escaped his lips like a prayer.

The tears finally came; they spilled and choked me as I stood and slowly went to him. I buried myself in his arms. He smelled of the sea and brown sugar. I gripped his shirt, pulled myself above these waters, and inhaled a desperate lungful of air.

❖

Mimi was in the ICU unable to breathe on her own. She'd coded twice. I filed this information away because if I tried to look at it too long I would break. Ana and her family finally left in the early hours of the next morning after I reassured them I was okay. They had work and school, and I needed space. Alex stayed. His quiet presence was strong and steady enough to lean against, even in the awful waiting-room chairs. He brought food and coffee my mother and I barely touched, but after so many hours without improvement, Mom sent me home.

"I want to stay," I told her.

"I need you to go. Check on the house, shower, and sleep. I'll be here with her if anything changes." My eyes burned with exhaustion and I badly wanted to disappear into a hot shower, but I couldn't just leave. Mimi was here. Mom's voice was quiet but strong when she said, "Please let me be your mother and her daughter right now."

After driving me home, Alex stood on the threshold with me. The house was achingly quiet. Candles weren't lit, the radio was silent, and coffee wasn't brewing. Everything was so still. I hated it.

"Let me make you something to eat."

He flipped on lights and went to work in the kitchen. I watched him for a beat, but time was tangling with all my desperate hopes. I glanced at Mimi's bedroom door and strained to hear the music of her; her beaded slippers shuffling against the tile floor, the jangle of her bracelets, her whispered prayers to her saints. Could they hear her tonight?

"Hey." Alex's voice broke into my thoughts. I focused on where he stood in the warm glow of the kitchen. The rich smell of caramelized onions and peppers tickled my consciousness. "I'm here."

"I know." I was grateful, but my voice rattled with weary grit.

I went to shower and peeled off my clothes. The sting of hot water was welcome, and I stood motionless beneath the spray. I was too hollowed out to cry anymore, but as tired as I felt, I craved the release and purpose. I wanted to be the one who sank to my knees and knew to perform CPR. I longed to capture the steady look Dan had given me. I pressed my hand against the tiled wall and tried to count my racing breaths. I'd sat on her bedroom floor and in that waiting-room chair and changed nothing. I fisted my hand and leaned against the tile as dry, useless sobs wracked my body.

The water soon turned cold. My skin broke out in goose-flesh and my exhales felt hot. I wished the tile could give beneath my hands, because I was freezing and alone and the world was spinning too quickly away from me.

A knock sounded. Startled, I inhaled sharply and coughed on the water. "Rosa," Alex called. I could practically feel his concern pressing against the door, but from how long I'd already been in the shower, I knew he was fighting himself to give me my space.

"I'll be right out." Whether it was a shout or a whisper, I didn't know.

I shakily shut off the water and dried myself. I dragged a hand across the mirror to find my reflection beneath the fog. *There I am.* My mother's eyes, my grandmother's mouth. *There they still are.* The other angles and edges were shaped by ghosts I never got to meet.

I ate for Alex's sake and because it was important to sit at the kitchen table and go on as usual. Meals were meant to be shared here. If I did this, that would be a good sign. A positive affirmation judged to be enough to save her.

"Do you want me to stay?" he asked. I didn't say, *My abuela would kill me,* even though it was my first thought. Being alone tonight felt like facing a void on my own, but I needed to lose myself in inherited rituals. I needed candlelight, oil, and a hissing flame. I needed to whisper prayers as smoke reached for those who looked after me and mine. Stricken with doubt, I hesitated, and he said, "I'll come back. Later tonight or in the morning. Call or text me, and I'll be here."

Grateful, I nodded. He cleaned up the dishes and kitchen and then, with his arms around me, he pressed a gentle but firm kiss on the top of my head. He bid me a solemn good night at the door. I couldn't watch him go.

I went right to her garden room. I scanned her shelf and found white candles and her treasured saint medallion of Caridad del Cobre, patron saint of Cuba. I grabbed a pin and one of her oils. I found three of her pennies and slipped them into my pocket. I returned to my room and dropped everything on my desk and poured the perfume in my hands and dragged Florida Water through my wet hair. The citrusy scent filled me with a sense of protection. Guiding hands always smelled of this when they gently brushed over my forehead and showed me how to honor and grow my practice. I grabbed matches and lit every candle I could find, and with the pin, I carved Mimi's whole name into the wax as more flames sparked to life.

Finally, before my ancestral altar, I fell to my knees. I dropped my forehead to my grandfather's picture, and like a child, I begged for her life from the man I never got to know, but who loved her as much as I did, and fought an angry sea to ensure her safe passage.

"Bring her back to me." My pulse drummed a steady beat and my abuela's name fell from my lips like a chant.

There was no answer. Only my stubborn hope.

Hours or maybe only moments later, I got off the floor. It was like moving through wet sand, the air around me heavy with stirred energy. I was exhausted.

I fished my journal out of my backpack and fell into bed. I turned to an empty page to start making lists of everything we needed for a prolonged hospital stay and all I needed to learn about the human heart. A small white square slipped out from between the last pages. It was a folded piece of paper, flattened by my book. With a touch of my hand, it opened and became a boat. In small, neat letters, *S.S. Rosa* was scrawled on the side.

In those lost hours, Alex had made me a boat.

I climbed out of bed and went to my open window. The perfumed air was cool as I leaned against the sill and held my paper boat up to the moon, imagining it finding the right winds and reaching home.

We try with all we have. We fight hands we can't see. We stomp against the earth and whisper all the right prayers, but sometimes it isn't meant to be. You believe life will always be as it is, and you make plans, but the next thing you know, you're climbing into a sinking boat in the dead of night because the land you love is no longer safe. The sun sets, the man you love doesn't swim above the water again, and time runs out.

The phone rings to tell you the worst.

As I lay awake at 3:17 in the morning, my life cracked in two as Milagro Carmen Martín Santos slipped away from this life.

Mimi was gone and I was too far away to say good-bye.

32

For a family so well acquainted with death, we had no idea how to have a funeral.

The bones of our dead were lost to the sea, not buried in cemeteries. Mimi would be cremated, according to her wishes, and my mother and I returned home from the funeral home with nothing. We had to wait a week to receive her because of paperwork. It had only been two (or was it three?) days since the festival, but it was the strangest void of time and we had no idea what to do next. We stood in the entryway, aimless and lost. Maybe this was what life would be like for us now without Mimi. A knock sounded, and I opened the door to find Mrs. Peña, teary-eyed and bearing Tupperware.

"I have soup," she choked out. "It's tomato, though." She cried harder. Mom and I got out of her way.

People just kept coming. Most we knew, but some we didn't. The door didn't get a chance to close as more deliveries of food filled our kitchen, and emotional neighbors offered us somber words of mourning I didn't know what to do with yet. Mrs. Peña kept order in the kitchen as soup containers battled for dominance against the many casseroles. Next came Mimi's patrons. They were all in tears and offered us beautiful flower arrangements and harvests from the gardens Mimi helped them grow and save. When someone tried to give us a live chicken, we politely declined. Mrs. Peña asked us if it was okay to open some of the food, and we told her yes, of course, there was no way we could eat it all. Conversation drifted around our silence as people found others who needed to share their grief and say my abuela's name. The smell of coffee reached us like an old memory.

"Is this a funeral?" Mom asked.

I hadn't slept in too many days and the numbness left me a spectator. "Mimi probably figured we'd be terrible at it and did it herself."

Mom's laugh was rough. "Typical."

Mr. Gomez and the rest of the viejitos broke through my fog, sounding like my found collection of abuelos. My throat tightened as they wrapped me in their cologne and cigar smoke. They served rum to toast our family, and even I was given a small glass.

"To Mimi," Mr. Gomez said solemnly. "Tell our island—" He paused and when he tried to continue, emotion strangled him. He shook his head and tried again but couldn't.

"Tell her hello for us," Mom finished with a gentle hand on his arm.

I carried so much faith in things I couldn't see, but now I had to apply it to someone I knew and deeply loved. Someone who was gone but was still as much a part of me as my next breath. Could her spirit already be miles and years away? She was so unreachable to me now.

I escaped outside and found my friends coming up the walk. Benny had sunflowers and Alex carried bakery boxes. Ana and Mike were trying not to cry, but once they saw me the war was lost. Oscar followed them. He wore dark jeans and a black shirt, which was typical, but they weren't faded or splattered with paint and sawdust.

He raised his gaze past me. "I'm sorry about your mom, Liliana."

"Thank you," Mom said, standing beside me now. She took my hand and Oscar glanced at us. Smiling a little, he shared a long look with my mother.

"I saw it. . . . It's really good. Looks just like him. It gave me an idea, and"—he paused to check his watch—"I need to show you both something." Without another word, he turned and headed back down the sidewalk.

I didn't understand anything he'd said. I checked Mike, who sighed.

"He forgot to ask you to follow him."

We followed, as did my friends, and after a moment of curiosity, everyone gathered in our house trailed after us. Our small group expanded as we moved down the street.

"What's happening?" Dan rushed across the street, still straightening his tie. Malcolm followed behind with the stroller. "We were on our way over."

"Oscar's showing us something," I told them as they fell into step alongside us. "You both look really nice." They were in dark formal suits. Dan squeezed my shoulder as Malcolm pulled me into a hug.

Almost to the square, I sidled up close to Mom. "Was it like this when my dad died?"

"There was this collective shock and a big search for him, but after they found the boat, they gave up. There was nothing they could do, and I had to stop hoping or I'd have been lost when you needed me."

Our group became larger as more neighbors fell in line with us. "You moved forward and kept going. Because of me?"

"Because of . . ." The memory of our last conversation with Mimi bloomed between us. "Love," she finally said, and took my hand again.

The storm had made an impact. We reached the square where soft pastel snow covered the ground. The vines and garlands of spring flowers had been no match for the battering wind and rain. Our collective steps kicked up the petals as we followed Oscar to the farthest corner of the square where Mimi's tent had recently stood. It now held the Golden Turtle and a brand-new bench. I didn't understand until I read the plaque that bore my abuela's name.

I couldn't say a word. Mom tensed, and squeezed my hand.

Oscar stood beside the bench, silent. Mike stepped up and explained, "He's been working on it since yesterday. It's wild he got it done, I mean, I wouldn't sit on it yet because the stain might not be fully dried." He shot Oscar a proud grin, and his mentor crossed his arms. "But the plan is to build a garden around it. All green and wild. Like Mimi."

Oscar shrugged, but the corner of his mouth tipped up in a small smile when he looked at Mom.

The tent was gone, and with it our perfect night. But this bench would stay.

This wasn't Cuba, and it wasn't her farm, and so much life and family had been taken from her, but despite loss and a raging sea, she reached this shore with my mother and her story hadn't stopped. She made something real and her life counted here, too.

"Thank you," Mom whispered to everyone.

Flowers would grow freely here. They would bloom and die and rise again beside a bench that invited you to sit and stay. Beyond us was a sea you could watch and imagine you were anywhere else. Or perhaps, you could just be here in Port Coral where the wind sang softly and wildflowers bloomed.

On the way home, Mom led me toward the boardwalk. I thought she wanted to avoid the crowds in the square, but when we stopped beside the fire station, I understood Oscar's earlier words.

"You finished it."

Her wall was complete. Calm blue waters met an indigo-blue sky, and there in the middle was a simple boat. The white sail billowed out and blended into a soft cloud. At the helm was a brown-skinned boy with short black hair and a bright smile. He looked happy, healthy, and eternal. And there on the side was the name of his boat: *La Rosa.*

"Was that really his boat's name?"

Mom nodded, smiling. "Your name was his idea. I thought it was weird to name a baby after a boat, but he said it was perfect and a good omen." Her laugh was edged with an old, dark humor. "Mom thought it would be terrible luck, but everything was, back then. I wanted to give Ricky at least that."

"I didn't know."

"Turns out I didn't learn my lessons from Mimi." She sighed. "I don't want him to disappear or become some haunted memory we can't talk about. It's not fair to you, me, or him."

I regretted every question I'd been too scared to ask

Mimi. I didn't want to make that mistake for the rest of my life.

❖

One week later, Mimi returned home.

The house was somehow even quieter. Mom and I had spent the last few days eating takeout from the bodega and curled up on the couch watching the fluffiest movies we could find. We sat outside at night to track the stars and imagine what might come after death. We found no answers, but sometimes a lemon-blossom breeze hit us just right and felt like one.

We stood in the foyer with Mimi's urn.

"Now what?" I asked, needing my mother to give me something: direction, purpose, surety we could survive this. She took her mother's ashes down the hallway. I followed her into my room where she stood, facing my small altar.

Mom offered me the urn. I shook my head. I couldn't do this.

My grandfather looked back at us from his picture. He stood beneath a mango tree, his arms crossed. His gaze was now just beyond the camera. Had it always been that way? He was smiling at what he saw. Or perhaps who he finally saw again.

With a shaky hand, I took the heavy urn. This spot had always calmed and grounded me, but I now felt faint. For the first time, after years of honoring my family, I was placing someone I knew upon this table. My abuela would look back at me from a picture, because she was somewhere in this dust and not in the kitchen stirring her love into a soup or bottling potions to heal baby gums. She wasn't in her garden room, tending her plants and finding me again and again. She wasn't shuffling across the hallway on her way to tell me another day was beginning. She was here in my hands, and soon on my altar, which meant she was forever gone.

I dropped to my knees. Through my tears, I placed the urn beside my grandfather's picture. "I hope she found him," I whispered, my voice small.

My mother sat beside me. She held a hand over the urn, then reached for my father's picture and pressed a gentle finger against it. "Me too."

The last two Santos women curled into each other and cried for home.

33

The next morning, I skated across town in the early morning light to the bodega for a to-go order of breakfast—my new routine. But the window was empty today. No Peña in sight. I leaned up on my toes, and the familiar smell of breakfast greeted me. Bacon, eggs, pan tostado slathered in butter. I went to call out for Mr. Peña, but the low and haunting sound of a lone trumpet stopped me.

Each note squeezed my heart tighter. I checked the viejitos. They were gathered at their usual table, and Mr. Gomez glanced over and gave me a solemn nod. The song ended on a somber, heartbreaking note, and Mr. Peña appeared a moment later. He looked surprised to see me and checked his watch. Grief had a way of throwing everything off, including time. Without a word, he prepared two breakfast plates, and when I tried to pay him again, he refused. I thanked him, but when I went to leave, he stopped me. "Rosa."

I turned, surprised. "Yeah?"

"She was one of the best people I knew."

I wasn't ready for past tense. I jerked my head in a short nod. "Me too."

He returned to work and I rode back home wondering how many people my abuela had made feel like they belonged.

❖

I found Mom in Mimi's bedroom, her fingers trailing over ceramic figures, opening small, delicate drawers, searching for her mother in memories stirred by a forgotten trinket. Or maybe she wanted to have the last word somehow. I knew them as adversaries, polar opposites, two ends of a magnet destined to forever oppose the other, but now without Mimi's south to fight her north, would Mom leave? Would this still be home then? I didn't want Port Coral to become one more home to lose.

In the garden room, those same herbs dried, waiting for a purpose that wouldn't come. I opened the window to let in the breeze and listened to the quiet song of the wind chime. The dirt around the lemongrass was dry. I picked up the metal watering can as the ache of missing her crushed me in one sweeping rush. I dropped the can and sobbed into my hands.

I still had so much to ask her.

"Tell me what to do," I whispered to the empty room and pressed my hand against my chest, counting my breaths.

Missing her would be agony. Time would only make this worse. The further I got from this terrible moment, the further I would be from her.

I hated this. I hated it so much. I wanted to bargain with fate. To fall asleep and wake up the morning of the festival. I would find Mimi, and we could save her heart and stop this terrible turn. I could fix this.

"I can fix it, just let me fix it, just let me . . ." On the desk in front of me was a small stack of pennies. I counted four. The three I'd found the night she died had been in my pocket since that night. I carried them in a silent, desperate hope for something I couldn't name. Seven pennies. I had enough for an offering.

I jumped out of the chair and ran to get my skateboard. It was a race to the boardwalk, and then even farther beyond it. I picked up my board and carried it as, for the first time ever, I walked across the sand.

A sharp gust almost knocked me sideways. My abuela taught me to listen to the world around me. Sometimes there were answers in a spread of cards or in the tea leaves at the bottom of a worn mug, but sometimes they were in a sudden breeze and waning moon.

Sometimes they were in the thing you feared most.

I dropped my board, navigated my way down the empty beach, and slipped out of my shoes. In bare feet, I walked right up to the shore. The warm water rushed over my skin in reply and I gasped.

I gripped my pennies. The sea. *I was in the sea.* I walked in a little deeper.

The next wave crashed and reached for me. Spilling forward, it washed over my ankles. My pulse pounded in my ears as blood rushed beneath my skin. Oxygen, I thought. Water, blood, fire. I waded in to my knees. The water now reached the bottom of my dress. It pulled at the fabric with sure hands. A surprised laugh bubbled up in my throat.

My first time in the sea felt like returning to something. I thought of my mother and abuela, the image of them sharp and sudden. I wanted to see what was on the other side. I wanted to find what was lost. I wanted to know how to move forward. I knew the old prayers, but now I stood in the sea, and carried no fruit or honey. My only offering my heart, humility, and these coins. My tongue was heavy with the wrong language.

The water reached my waist now. I closed my eyes and tossed the pennies into deeper water. There was only me, the never-ending ocean, and the horizon where the sky met it now.

"Rosa!"

"Mimi?" I shouted. I searched around but found Ana back at the shore, waving her arms.

"What?" I called over the riotous ocean.

"Rip current!"

"What?"

Before she could explain, I was consumed—thrown and

277

pulled beneath by forces I couldn't see. Swallowed whole by a rough sea, I kicked and pushed to find air. When I couldn't, panic filled my lungs instead. I swung my arms, but direction meant nothing.

I couldn't hold my breath any longer.

Light flickered in front of me. I moved toward it, my chest burning, and in the next wave I was caught and dragged above water. I gasped and came face-to-face with a very wet Ana-Maria.

"Didn't you see that red flag?" she yelled in my face as she pulled me back to shore.

I looked around and spotted it. Had that meant something? I had gotten so much farther out than I thought. "Holy shit."

Ana was breathing hard from swimming for us both, but she laughed. "I don't think I've ever heard you cuss before." She grabbed hold of my waist, and we carefully moved with the waves back to shore. Shaking, I fell to the sand, coughing hard as I tried to catch my breath. I rolled onto my back and looked up at Ana.

"I'm alive," I declared, wonderingly.

"You also owe me a new phone." Her jeans and shirt were plastered to her skin. "What the hell were you doing? You're not the strongest swimmer, and since when do you go in the ocean?"

"I don't know." Grief was exhausting, and I was a mess covered in salt water and sand, stretched back on the beach. I squinted against the sunlight. "I hate this so much."

She didn't tell me she was sorry for my loss or say she understood how I felt. She dropped down beside me, leaned back on her elbows, and tilted her face to the sun instead.

After a while, I finally asked the question knocking around in my heart like a mournful ghost. "Am I still Cuban?"

Ana blinked. "I'm skipping school right now and it's way too early for this." She sighed hard at my sincerity and sat up to shake the sand and water from her hair. "Of course you're still Cuban. That doesn't just go away because someone . . ." She hesitated and slid a worried glance over me. "Passes."

I watched the horizon. In the distance, boats dotted the line between sky and sea. "I gave myself all these markers. If my Spanish was better. If I studied in Cuba. If Mimi could go home again, but now she's gone and I don't know. Maybe it all went with her." Mimi was my island, and now she was gone. I had no map and I could not go back.

"I remember my dad saying that when he died, he still wanted to be buried there." Ana shrugged and messed with the drying curls of her hair. The idea clearly bothered her, but she was trying to downplay it. "It was so heavy with regret. Like he's always going to love the other life he didn't get to live more." She picked up a piece of driftwood and drew a line in the sand. "Diaspora is weird. So is exile. We're going to be different on this side of it. That's not a bad thing."

I imagined the generations of women living in my blood. The times they must have sat like this and considered their plights. Their heartache and dreams. Their whispers swam through my veins regardless of where I was on a map. The sun was so warm on my face.

"Hey, did you hear? The festival raised enough money."

I shot up. "Are you serious?" I'd checked out so hard I hadn't been in the loop on the final count.

"Yup. The university okayed the program, which halted the sale. Jonas said the first bunch of biology nerds should be here as soon as this summer."

"Wow." Relief stubbornly pushed its way into my heavy sadness. Down the beach, I could see the busy harbor. Watching movement on the docks filled me with dizzying anticipation. I wanted to see the changes and possibility. For the moment, and maybe for a long time after, we all saved something. This all would stay and hopefully become even stronger. "I should have come out to the beach more."

"You definitely made a splash for your first time." Ana stretched out and crossed her feet at her ankles. "So, made a decision about college yet?"

I laughed, the sound rough and just a little bitter. "I have no idea what I'm doing anymore. I was so sure, and now I'm just . . . tired." Everything was so heavy now, and trying to think through the fog just winded me more.

"Take a nap, champ." Ana's eyes were closed. She looked happy to lie back in the sun as it slowly dried our clothes and hair.

I missed my certainty. Before the study-abroad program

was canceled I'd been so *sure*. "Mimi always said she'd never seen water as blue as Cuba's."

Ana made a noise of agreement. "Dad says the same. That's the Caribbean Sea for you."

I wanted to see it so much, but god, I just wished Mimi could have seen it again.

My pulse picked up. For the first time since losing Mimi, conviction kicked the door open and cleared out some of the fog. I knew this feeling. I *missed* this feeling. Ana was halfway to a nap when I leapt on top of her and hugged her, hard. "Thank you," I whispered fiercely against her ear.

"For what?" She yawned and patted my shoulder.

"Finding me." I pulled away, jumped to my feet, and grabbed my board. "I have to go. Come see me later."

"As long as it's not in the sea, weirdo," she called after me, but I heard the smile in her voice.

Salt water dripped from my hair and the cotton of my dress as I raced home. In the square, I slowed. The Golden Turtle was still in place right beside Mimi's bench. I touched both for luck.

"Rosa!" the viejitos called in unison. "¿Qué pasó? Where are you going?"

I didn't stop. I couldn't until I got home, where I burst through the front door. Mom looked up from the table. A jewelry box sat open playing a soft song.

"We're going to Cuba," I declared. She closed the music box with a snap. "And we're taking Mimi with us."

34

"What?" they all shouted at once.

Ana, Mrs. Peña, and Malcolm all sat in my living room later that afternoon. Mom carried Penny to the window. This was my moment with my Port Coral family.

"Mom and I are leaving for Cuba tomorrow," I repeated.

Ana leaned forward. "Oh god, Rosa, were you going to try to swim there?"

"What? No. Well, metaphorically, maybe."

Ana turned to her mom. "Will you talk to her? Do you have your passport? We should go with her."

"You have school," Mrs. Peña pointed out to her. She stared at my mother and asked, "You're really going to go?" Mom nodded. It felt like a private conversation was happening between them. This hadn't even been a possibility when they were my age.

"I don't understand," Malcolm said, hands on his hips. "Why are you leaving so suddenly, and for how long? You

282

still have three weeks of classes and—" Understanding dawned and his hands fell to his sides. "Mimi."

Her name held weight for us. Here, in the place she was meant to be, speaking it felt like saying a prayer.

"It'll only be for a few days. I'll only miss a couple of assignments, I swear."

He sighed, his eyes soft and tenderly exasperated with me. "Rosa. It's your last term. I'm not worried about that, and you shouldn't be either."

The door opened and Dan rushed inside in his uniform. "I'm late, I know, but catch me up."

Malcolm said, "Rosa's going to Cuba."

Dan grinned. "Finally."

❖

The next morning, just before dawn, I set our plane tickets and my packed bag on the kitchen table. Inside was my notebook along with Mimi's. I wanted to bring everything of hers I could, but the notebook felt most prudent. With careful hands, I wrapped Mimi's urn in one of her silk scarves. The kitchen was silent. No bracelets. No shuffle of her house slippers. No peppermint soap or Sunday sage. The laundry room window was closed, and I didn't know if it would ever open again.

Before my flight, I had one last farewell.

Alex sat on the back of his boat with coffee and watched

me as I walked up the dock toward him. The sun was rising in a pink lemonade sky, and the marina was mostly still around us. I reached his boat and noted all the new supplies around him. He was preparing for his trip. I tucked my hands into my pockets, afraid to get too close. *I'm letting him go*, I wanted to scream to the universe. *Please keep him safe.*

"I'm going to Cuba today," I told him.

He looked down at the rope in his hands. "It was the big story on the viejitos' Insta. They're attempting to track your whole itinerary." He held up his phone. "They posted three minutes ago that you were headed this way."

"My god, they are relentless." I glanced over my shoulder. "Well, we don't have a real plan," I admitted. "Grief offers a lot of panicky momentum once you realize how quickly this all can end. We're just sort of running with it."

I smiled, but it fell away in the next sea breeze. I wanted to say something significant. I wanted to offer him important words so he knew how much our moments together meant to me. I was running on sorrow and uncertainty, but looking at him on that boat, I remembered how I'd shouted wildly into the wind and believed anything was possible. He ducked his head before looking up again with his shy gaze that always warmed for me, and I wanted to forget everything. Walk into his arms and fly away with him. I knew I could give him the words, but standing here, with that empty slip beside us, I would not speak them.

"I hope you find what you're looking for, Rosa."

"Me too."

He got to his feet and grabbed something off the table. We stood together on the dock. I wanted to reach for him so much, it hurt to hold myself this steady. After a moment of hesitation, he offered me the map again.

"Alex—" I looked at him, confused.

"This was always your trip. It changed around you, but I don't think that's a bad thing. Because I did, too." He shrugged a shoulder, still holding the map. "Just do me a favor and look at it once you get there. See how far you've made it." He held it out between us.

I took it, my hand gently brushing his. The contact stirred a small, surprised inhale from me. Our gazes held each other before dropping away. When I looked down at the map I realized a string was tied around it. His rope.

"Oh, no, I can't take this." He'd had it so long and it meant too much to him. I started to take it off.

"It goes with the map, Rosa. They're kind of a set. What you're about to do is a big deal, so when you get nervous, on the plane or after you land, just look at both and remember you're a great sailor."

I started to open the map, but his hand shot out to stop me. "Later."

I smiled. These gifts were subtle, but important. Just like Alex. These last days had reshaped us. I folded the map and put it in my pocket. The rope went around my wrist like a bracelet. Alex smiled, pleased.

"Now I wish I had something to give you," I said as I looked at the boxes in his boat.

"You gave me plenty. You were my second."

I laughed. It felt like a hundred years since the regatta.

"Where are you today, Rosa?" he asked.

I smiled past the tears blurring the beautiful sunrise and the dreamiest baker and sailor I knew. I would miss him so much. Without Mimi, I didn't know where and how Port Coral fit in my life anymore. I would be gone after this summer, but maybe I would get to come back one day and see him down on the docks. He might look up and smile, and we'd both remember a spring that went by too fast, but tasted of tangerine lollipops.

I squinted past the brightness and told him, "I'm on my way across the sea."

❖

For all the panicked worries and lists of possible problems, everything came down to a piece of paper. I already had my passport because of study abroad, but it was still technically illegal to go to Cuba as an American tourist, so we needed to declare a reason for traveling. The rules were in constant flux with new confusing restrictions and a list of prohibitions of where we could stay, shop, and eat. And once we reached Cuba we had to navigate two different currencies: one for Cubans, another for tourists. Cuban citizens were mostly unable to travel across their own island, so I could put up with this.

"Can I really check family visit?" I stared at my travel visa, anxiously doubting the spelling of my own name. If I messed anything up, I'd have to buy another one. And that would be another hundred dollars. My shoe box of savings was crying.

"Yes. We're just bringing our family with us," Mom said. She was already done with hers. "Do you want a coffee before we board?"

"What? There's no time." I glanced at my watch again and muttered a prayer as I checked the box. We were ten minutes ahead of the schedule I'd made. There hadn't been much of a line at the desk and we'd already checked our suitcase filled with supplies I'd read were needed. Things like shoes, toothbrushes, and tampons, especially outside of Havana.

"It's early and I know you scheduled a preflight coffee break. You underlined it twice."

"Yes, but our cushion keeps shrinking. We need to get ahead of it." I adjusted my backpack as panic hit me. "I don't know enough Spanish to do this." Mom laughed at me. "I always respond in English and don't always know how to translate!"

"Yes, welcome to being bilingual. You're fine." She checked the signs around us. "You need the coffee more than me. Let's go."

We got our cortaditos and went to our gate. While we sat and waited for our boarding call, I charged my phone again and Mom patted my knee every few minutes.

"You keep bouncing it like that and you're gonna be the one to take off."

"Don't forget, Pedro will be at the airport to pick us up," I told her. I slipped out my notebook from my backpack and double-checked my list. I checked off *Drink coffee*.

Mom flipped through a magazine. "I remember. From the casa particular."

"It's cool that they're okay with strangers staying at their houses."

"Tourists make for good income when most Cubans make less than twenty dollars a month," she said.

My knee took off again. Mom gently soothed it again.

When it came time to board, I shifted to school mode. Get in line, follow directions, wait your turn. It was almost a relief, but before I knew it, I was in my designated seat bound for the Caribbean. The pilot announced our destination, and I still couldn't believe it. I wanted to cement this moment somehow. I, Rosa Santos, was on an airplane headed to Havana. Mom was busy chatting with the older woman in the seat beside her. I stared out the window and watched as we started to roll down the runway. When we began to ascend, I clutched the Caridad del Cobre medal I now wore around my neck.

Mom clutched my other hand. I expected to see her easy

smile, but her eyes were shut tight and her jaw clenched. I squeezed her hand, and she spoke without opening her eyes.

"All my flying, and I've never crossed the sea," she whispered.

I forgot all of my panic. "But you already had your passport." I didn't know everywhere she went on her travels, but I'd have bet anything she'd gone overseas.

She took a slow, measured breath. "I always wanted to be brave . . . or defiant enough, but every time I considered it, all I could picture was lightning striking and someone telling you I was lost at sea." She finally looked at me, and her hand squeezed mine again.

My fixation on seeing Cuba had never allowed enough room to consider what it meant to Mom. I brought her hand to my lips and laid a quick kiss against her knuckles. "My brave mother, returning to where she first sparked into existence."

She exhaled slowly and smiled. "Such a poet," she complained, and relaxed a little.

The energy on the flight was charged. People vibrated with vacation excitement and wonder. But some carried ghosts too. It was such a short flight, the Caribbean Sea already below us. All that blue made me think of Alex. I touched the bracelet at my wrist.

When the island appeared, I put my hand to the glass. My eyes raced over roads, clusters of towns and buildings, and so much green.

The pilot announced we were reaching José Martí International Airport.

Getting off the plane was a haze. I shuffled through lines, straining to look past the shoulders in front of me, my heart racing. I climbed down the steps, and the language and heat felt familiar. Palm trees, concrete. Green, brown. I knew this landscape. Even the airport bustled in a way I understood. There was way more Spanish and everything broadcasted Cuba, but it didn't feel that far off from Florida.

We got our bag and headed outside with the other travelers and waiting cars. We found an older Black man with our names written on the paper in his hand.

"Hola," I greeted with a big, nervous grin.

Pedro's eyes warmed. "¿Liliana y Rosa Santos?"

In friendly, rolling Spanish that sounded like home, he welcomed us to Cuba and led us to his car. It was an old blue Cadillac, and he opened the door and helped us with our bags. He merged into the traffic and the warm, salty air blew through my hair. A rumba song powered through the static on the radio. My excitement edged out my fear.

Mom leaned forward between the seats and asked him about the smaller towns around us as he drove to Havana. Beyond the window, everything looked like middle-of-nowhere Florida, and yet my mind kept screaming, *You're in Cuba.*

I swept my hair out of my face. Pedro said something I

didn't catch as he smiled at me in the rearview window.

Mom explained, "We're taking the scenic route."

We drove alongside the wall that bordered the sea. Huge waves crashed and broke over it, one right after the other. The sidewalk was soaked. I stuck my head out the window and inhaled deeply. Pedro laughed warmly.

He brought us to his house in central Havana. It was a yellow building sitting between a green one and gray one. It was three stories, with balconies on the top two. An older woman opened the front door.

"Mi esposa, Marisol," he told us. His wife came forward and greeted us. When she heard my mother's Spanish, we were embraced like long-lost family. The questions came fast: about who Mom's parents were, what part of Cuba they were from, when they left, and what we thought of Florida I was grateful to have Mom with me, because my Spanish felt clumsy and insufficient, even though I understood most everything. As Marisol led us through the house, the tile, decor, and open windows felt achingly familiar.

Marisol showed us to our bedroom on the second floor. There were two twin beds and a small fridge. Mom went to get coffee with Marisol while I headed outside on the terrace, where I faced the blue sky, buildings, and sea beyond. A warm breeze kissed my skin. I'd done it. I'd made it to the other side. I placed the urn on the small metal table and set my hand on it. I wished it hadn't taken this long to come. That my abuela could be here, too. This breeze would sift through her hair as she closed her eyes to breathe it in deep. When she opened her eyes again home wouldn't disappear.

I just wanted to feel my abuela and know she was okay.

"My house is your house," Marisol told me in English, startling me. Her gaze touched on the urn with a look of understanding. I wasn't the first to bring someone back, and I wouldn't be the last.

"Gracias," I returned, grateful and determined.

35

"*Stop writing things* down," Mom ordered.

We ate a breakfast of eggs, bread, and sliced bananas. There was no butter, and the portions were small, but it was delicious. We were only staying in Havana for the day before finding a way west to Viñales, where Mimi's family had once lived and farmed. Mom and I really didn't have a plan beyond getting here. We had three days, and it felt as if we were hoping for some grand sign from Mimi to tell us what to do. Spread her ashes? Take her back with us? We were flying by the beat of our grieving hearts.

But I was still Rosa Santos, so of course I tried to make a plan.

"We're going to Old Havana today," I said. I wanted to see the streets Mimi had woven together beneath her mysterious tent on our last night together.

"Solamente en español," Mom said, making Marisol laugh.

"Vamos a visitar la Habana Vieja," I said in a formal tone. Marisol clapped.

The sidewalk outside was bleached white from the sun. Older cars cruised past alongside buses teeming with passengers. Laundry hung from the balconies above us, and kids kicked nearly deflated balls in rowdy games. Older teens— maybe my age—walked past, wearing backpacks, and didn't even bother to look at us or the other tourists slowly trying to take panorama shots of the street.

I fumbled with my camera.

"Where are we, Rosa?" Mom asked.

My head snapped up. Did she remember? I couldn't see her eyes behind her dark sunglasses, but her smile was soft with memory. Somehow, against all odds, I was in Cuba.

I wanted to fit an entire semester—life—in one day and see everything. I wanted to stay long enough to learn my way around and have someone sitting out on their porch recognize me as Milagro's nieta and call me by name. I wanted to go to the university and sit in on a class before searching for some trace of my abuelo.

Are you already here, Mimi? I tightened my hands around my backpack's straps.

"Let's find a map somewhere," I said.

"Look at you still trying to plan our day," Mom returned with a half smile. "Let's find a shop first."

"You buy it, though. My Spanish feels clumsy."

A bicycle-drawn taxi drove by, with more tourists leaning out of it to take pictures.

"Your Spanish is fine. Should we take a taxi?"

"Tired already, vieja?" The morning was already warm. It would be hot soon.

"Come mierda," she cursed, grinning, and took off down the street.

"Wait!" I was the one carrying the heavy bag.

"¡Solamente en español!" she tossed back without slowing. My mother was ruthless.

Several crumbling buildings were under construction, and the narrow streets surrounding all of that work were crowded with people. We passed older folks on plastic chairs in animated conversation, kids hollering about a game—some in shoes, others not—teens holding hands and disappearing down alleys. The tourists were easy to pick out as they posed against faded buildings, finding their best angles. A group of them stopped to sit beside and take selfies with women in bright dresses smoking cigars. They were reveling in the timelessness and beauty, and their pictures would be posted—once they found an internet connection—and everyone would see those shots as the story of Cuba. I knew this because these were all the photos I'd seen when I obsessively researched Havana. But standing here now, on this hot, humid street, I watched the stories happening around those pictures. The ones living beyond the photo filters.

Mom was also watching the activity around us. She slipped her sunglasses up into her hair. "What's wrong?"

"I don't know," I said. Another large tour group turned down the street. The guide held up a red umbrella, and he sounded Cuban. "I've been so focused on my place and whether I fit, and now I'm here." I stepped back to let the group pass. "I worry at the end of all of this I'm just going to have more questions than answers."

"Sounds like you."

We found a city map and after roaming together for several hours, we stopped at a walk-up window to get something to eat. The man behind it was slicing a huge piece of roasted pork he was then splitting into small sandwiches. Mom bought us two, and as she paid, I glanced across the street at a small flower market.

Mom handed me my sandwich, already biting into hers. Something about the flower market felt familiar, like I'd once seen a picture of it.

Beside the market was a building with a small numbered sign that read 306. There was also a blue door with a papaya tree. The door had been painted onto the wall, and the graffiti was bright and wild with color.

Mom gravitated closer and I followed. We'd passed several murals. A city controlled by so much censorship still exploded with art. Mom's hand hesitated over the painted door. "I don't think I could paint this."

Farther down the wall, another older woman sat at a small table. Her dark hair was pinned back and a lit cigar was clenched between her teeth. No one was taking a picture with her.

"¿Estás buscando a alguien?" she asked us.

"Oh, no, we were just looking," I answered automatically in English. The woman cocked her head, and I burned with embarrassment. And sadness. This wasn't Mimi who knew our bilingual rhythm. "Perdón—" I started, but the woman cut me off, and said, "It's fine." She shot me an enigmatic smile. "I can do both."

Mom was still wondering over the painting. The woman watched her for a moment before ashing her cigar. "You're looking for her." She exhaled a wall of smoke.

Mom froze. I slowly looked at both of them, my mouth suddenly too dry to swallow my next bite. Excitement and disbelief rolled in my stomach with the sandwich. *Just give me a sign.*

"You are looking for your miracle, no?" The woman continued to smoke. A skinny orange-and-white cat slunk over and stopped at her feet. My pulse picked up, heavy and fast. I was afraid to take my gaze away and find her gone or drawn from my own desperate imagination.

She put down her cigar again. "I will take you."

"Where?" Mom asked, her voice rough.

"I will take you to her."

36

It turned out that hope and grief could lead even a type A planner down some pretty strange roads. Mom and I were now driving into the setting sun while riding in the back of a Cuban cowboy's truck, headed for who knows where.

Mom, stretched out beside me in the bed of the truck, had been quiet ever since we grabbed our suitcase from the casita, followed the older woman to this truck, and climbed in against the advice of every travel horror story and Ana's favorite murder podcasts.

"Ana would kill me right now if she knew where I was."

Mom stared up at the sky and scoffed. "You're with your mother."

"Exactly."

I glanced inside the back window again. The radio played Mimi's beloved guajira music—the twangy, earthy sound of their country music. The top of the old woman's head, now covered in a scarf, bopped along as the cowboy drove.

"Do you really think she knows anything about Tía Nela?" I asked Mom, then lowered my voice. "We might be on our way to *really* meet Mimi, if you know what I'm saying." I pointed my thumb at the driver, then mimed slicing my hand across my neck.

"Morbid much?"

I blinked. "I'm carrying my abuela's ashes in my backpack while riding in the back of some stranger's pickup truck at dusk, Mom."

"Latinx are exceptionally goth people."

City gave way to country, and beyond the dusty road were small towns with mostly one-story buildings, open fields, and tobacco farms. Rural, green, and open, it was another world out here. Mom sat up and looked out at the farmlands around us, too. She looked so strong and proud, like a mermaid at the helm of a ship, even in the back of this truck.

"Is this Viñales?" I wondered. I held back my wildly flying hair.

"I think so."

The truck jerked roughly, and we threw our hands out as the cowboy pulled over. "Let's not die," I said to Mom, who agreed as we both hopped out. It was almost dark, and the truck's back tire was flat. The old woman climbed out of the passenger side—she had to jump down from the seat— and ambled over to us. She sighed at the sight, thanked the cowboy, and turned for the field.

"Wait, where are you going now?" I asked, following.

"This way," she said. Panic simmered, leaving an acrid taste in my mouth. I was too reasonable to be okay with any of this, but I was desperate for all of this to actually mean something. I could be patient. Well, I could try really hard.

"There's a house up ahead," Mom pointed out. The squat yellow house was like a beacon.

I wiped sweat from my brow. "Do you think they might help us?"

The front door opened, and another older woman came outside. She wore dark pants and a pink blouse. I straightened my shirt and tried brushing my hair into less disarray. This poor lady was going to think we were tourists who'd lost their minds. Which, come to think of it, was a fair assessment. The greeting was humble but warm between the two women ahead of us.

The owner of the house turned to us and introduced herself as Gloria. She invited us inside, holding the door open for us to follow.

The old woman we came with said, "This family needs what you bring. Strong shoes, toothbrushes, the girls need help with their cycles."

I was tired, hungry, and wanted to cry, but more than anything, I wanted to believe. "What is your name?"

"No importa. The question is if you will help." She passed me to head inside.

I leveled a look at Mom. She looked as tired and overwhelmed as I felt. "I don't know, either," she said in answer to my silent question, "But I do know this is how Mimi would do it."

I thought of Mimi's mysterious tent. Her notebooks of answers she carefully fed me in small bites. Tinctures that took months and candles lit only when the moon was in just the right place.

Mom sighed. "Just once I'd like for something to be simple." She heaved the suitcase behind her into the house. "And she called *me* the bruja of the family."

Gloria also opened her home to tourists, although she didn't have any at the moment. She walked us through the airy home with open windows that offered a cool breeze and breathtaking views of the valley. She showed us to a back bedroom with a small bathroom.

With nothing else to do with this surreal moment, I took a shower. When Mom went to take hers, I sat at a small desk in our room to make note of our day in my journal. I was in *Viñales*. The golden hour was right out of a painting, but this wasn't a computer screen. I placed the urn on the desk beside me and opened the window. This was where Mimi had been born.

"What do you think?" I asked. Silence, because it was an urn. I used to hate that I was such a crier, but this last week had shown me how good crying could feel. I was always a little stronger and sturdier after.

301

Mom returned to the room, drying her hair. She stopped behind me and gazed outside at the green hills. The orange sky deepened into a bronze rust. "I wonder if I'd have liked being the daughter of farmers."

I imagined a younger version of my mother running through that valley. So wild, green, and alive.

Mom bent to kiss my head. "But then I wouldn't have you."

❖

The next morning, Gloria's neighbor brought over three horses.

I looked from them to our little old lady. "Are you serious?"

"Claro que sí." She somehow defied gravity and smoothly hopped right on. Surprised, I looked at Mom, who shrugged and said, "Guajiras."

We got on the horses and set off down the dirt road behind the woman.

"Stop making faces," Mom said, trotting along beside me. "You've been on a horse before."

"No, I haven't." I held on with a firm, but hopefully not panicky death grip. Animals could smell fear. "Be cool," I murmured just before the horse shook its head a little. I stifled a cry. "What did I *just* tell you?"

"Yes, you have," Mom said plainly. "We were in Colorado,

302

I think. You rode a pony. We spent the whole week on that cowboy ranch."

I sort of remembered purple cowboy boots and a cabin with a thick blue quilt. We'd cuddled beneath it by a fire while she'd talked to the cowboy. "Wait, was he your boyfriend?"

"Not really."

"Did he know that— You know what, don't answer."

"Forgive me for not getting serious about every Tom, Dick, or Harry that came around."

"Please don't say *dick*," I begged.

The valley around us was out of this world. Small, bright houses with thatched roofs surrounded on all sides by grassy hills that became mountains. The fields were alive with rows and rows of tobacco. Donkeys pulled farm equipment as the farmers walked alongside. Kids played and worked, and somewhere around here my abuela once ran.

There were more tourists, too. Lots of them. They traveled in groups on horseback as they stopped to visit the tobacco farms. Mom and I watched them move across the countryside as we settled into an easy pace.

"Years ago, I sold this painting to a woman who knew I was Cuban, and she told me she was planning a trip here."

"Let me guess, she wanted to come before everything changed?" I'd heard that line and it always made me want to gnash my teeth. "Yeah, we wouldn't want things like a failed economic system, censorship, and food shortages to change. Can't have a free press killing the vibe."

"Careful," the old woman said. "Cubans do not have the freedom to speak so loudly."

Guilt sank its claws into my chest. I wanted peace and dignity for the people of this island. Power to make their voices heard, even when they were dissenting. I wanted them to eat.

Pa'lante, Mimi had whispered.

Two hours later, I realized it was absolutely useless asking our old-lady guide where we were going next. I asked her when we stopped to get water for the horses and then at the stand that sold sugar cane juice. I asked her when she stopped at a riverside for rocks, and then in a field to pick wildflowers. We were running out of time. Our plane home was tomorrow night, and still this impossible woman only pointed ahead of us and said, "That way."

"Are you really picking flowers again?" I demanded, sweaty and delirious.

"Impatient," she growled, and lit her cigar.

I marched back to Mom, who was digging into a ripe mango. I paced in front of her. "You think she's just taking us back to Havana?"

"Well, this is an island. Sometimes you have to go back to go forward."

It was the story of my life these days.

We returned to the horses and set off again. The island

grew wilder around me and I gave myself up to it and stopped trying to track our direction or time. I could be wild, too.

Finally, we reached the end. Somewhere beyond the tree line ahead of us, the ocean roared. We carefully navigated our way through the trees, and past the last ones I gently pulled my horse to a stop as I faced the bluest water I had ever seen.

I wanted to cry but laughed instead. "Mimi was right."

The old woman climbed off her horse, and we followed. She stopped at the water's edge and said, "She left from here."

My gaze shot to the empty beach in front of us. "What?"

"The one you carry. He waits for her."

I took an automatic step back. My next breath whooshed out of me, and I looked at Mom. We had come to find some kind of peace over Mimi, and I thought I'd been prepared to spread her ashes. It seemed the Thing to Do when faced with death. But after traveling with her like this, I didn't know if I was ready to give her back. I was still trying to find her again.

Mom's eyes watered, and she looked at the sea before marching right up to it.

I stayed where I was and glanced at the old woman, who was also watching Mom. "You could have at least warned her we were coming here."

She sighed. "Warnings never help."

Mom paced the beach. She kicked at the sand before stomping into the waves. When she began to scream, the wind picked up, fast and strong, and swallowed her words.

I stumbled in the sand, then crouched down and watched, full of worry, as my mother unleashed. When she finally stopped, the wind settled. She turned and looked at me.

Her chest heaving, she asked, "Now what?"

The sound of an engine broke the silence. In the distance I spotted a boat headed toward us. My nerves took flight. It couldn't be Mimi. I logically understood this, but as I stood on that beach and stared out at the blue waters, something tickled my consciousness, sounding so much like Mimi's wind chimes.

I swallowed hard as the boat came closer. I was so light-headed I wasn't sure whether I would throw up or pass out. When it reached us I saw it was just a young boy on a single engine boat he steered from the back. The engine stopped and he directed us to climb inside.

I held the urn, but the decision wasn't mine. "What do you think, Mom? What you say goes."

She stood stiffly and bit her shaking lip. I didn't know if she or the sea would look away first. "I want to know who's out there," she finally said to the old woman before looking at me. "Come on."

We waded out into the warm water, and the young boy helped us climb aboard. The engine kicked on, and we were off. The momentum nearly knocked me sideways, but Mom caught me and said, "I'm on a tiny dinghy with my daughter, helmed by some eight-year-old boy, to toss my mother's ashes into the sea."

"I am thirteen," the boy corrected.

Mom's laugh was wild with emotion.

The boat coasted as the engine turned off. According to our guide, we were now three miles out. I wasn't sure what came next. Did we just spill the ashes and say a few words? I needed a cue from my mother, but she held the urn to her chest and watched the horizon. Her dark hair played in the soft sea breeze. The boy looked away from us, offering what privacy he could.

Facing the wide-open sea felt a lot like sitting in front of my altar. Ancestors wanted to be remembered. "We're bringing her back," I said, breaking the heavy silence.

Mom glanced at me. I felt nervous and unsure, but pressed on.

"Milagro built us an incredible life with love and magic, and never, for one single moment of it, did she stop loving you." Mom was still watching the sea, her tears falling openly. "I'm Rosa, by the way," I said past a tight, teary laugh. "I'm Liliana's daughter, and Milagro's granddaughter. And yours, too."

The boat moved softly as the sun slowly sank into the golden horizon offering us the last of its light. Mom opened the urn and spilled her mother's ashes into the sea. The calm waters gently rocked our boat. And there on the salty sea breeze, I caught the scent of lemon and rosemary.

To the sea, my mother whispered, "Nos vemos, Mami."

We'll see each other soon.

37

It was nearly fully dark when we got back to the beach. I kicked up sand in my rush to return to the old woman's side. When I reached her, I blurted, "You're Tía Nela, aren't you?"

She looked me square in the eye and said, "If her cities fall, if we're all gone, may God watch after her."

It was like a punch straight to my solar plexus. Grief seized me. Cold, sharp, broken.

Finally I exploded.

"Why couldn't you have told us? Why this wild-goose chase? You could have stopped at any point and said, *Oh, hey, by the by, I'm Nela,* but no. God, it's never a real answer. *Be patient, have faith.* I'm exhausted."

The young boy settled against his boat and watched.

"Why was she cursed?" I wailed. "She lost everything, but that wasn't enough? That wasn't enough payment, so you made Mom pay into it, too? Am I next?" The image of Alex sailing into a storm was a knife stabbed into this bleeding wound. "How many people do we have to lose before our check clears and we're allowed to live and love again?"

Nela watched me. I tried to breathe around the ache of missing Mimi.

"Sometimes a mother gives birth to the mirror her great-grandmother lost," she said.

I was so tired of poems. Of essay questions and bad omens. I didn't know my great-grandmother, didn't know her name or how she died. I just wanted Mimi.

"Who are you?" Nela asked me.

"That's rich." A bitter laugh escaped me. "You ask me this now?" I jerked a finger toward the sea. "I'm their grand-daughter. And her daughter, but that's not enough." My voice small, I turned away and muttered, "It's never been enough."

"You are Rosa de la familia Santos, and it is time to return to the sea."

"What?"

Tía Nela whistled to the boy, who returned to his boat, revved the engine, and drove away. She picked up my back-pack from the sand and unzipped it, but when I expected her to reach in and grab my notebook—or Mimi's—she instead pulled out the herbs and flowers she'd picked on her way here. When had she put them in there? After that came a dark bottle and a coconut. I didn't want to look away from her even as I wondered what else in the world I'd been carrying around. She cracked the coconut against a nearby rock and drank a sip from both halves before splitting the contents of the dark bottle between them.

She offered each of us a half.

Beneath a setting sun, Mom and I drank from the coconut. It burned my throat, but turned nectar-sweet at the end. Next, Nela handed both of us a white shift. We undressed and the cooler night air danced along my bare skin. She lit a bundle of leaves and the sweet smoke rose between us. It filled my nose and made the night hazier. She nodded to the sea.

"Wait, you want us to go? *Now?*" It was dark. The water was mostly still, but it was the *ocean* at *night*.

Nela waited.

Mom shook out her arms like she was preparing to go for a swim. Or fight the ocean.

"Okay," I whispered under my breath and bounced my shoulders in an effort to loosen up. "I can do this." This was Mimi teaching me what words to whisper over a hissing candle. It was her hand over mine as she showed me how to pour anointing oil and crush herbs. This was just me sinking into a warm bath she prepared with flowers and salt to cleanse my energy. I could do this.

Mom and I walked into the sea as Nela's chant built with quiet intensity even as her voice never became louder.

"You know what's weird?" Mom asked as we walked in deeper.

I looked between us and the picture we currently made. "Where do you want me to start?"

"We just spread Mimi's ashes. So, technically, all three of us are in the sea."

As the water reached our waists we stopped. The sea was calm. Were we meant to just dunk ourselves or keep walking? Nela was still chanting, but I didn't understand the words. Also, why did the air suddenly smell as green and wild as Mimi's garden room?

"What do we do now?" I called over my shoulder.

Nela stopped chanting and gave me a look. She shouted back, "Patience!"

"It's like a lecture from Mimi," I muttered, slicing my hands through the dark, still water. Moonlight shimmered across it, and I watched the small ripples I made.

"Your ancestors are very proud of you," Nela told us, a smile in her voice.

My head jerked up and whipped around. "What?"

A wave broke in a deafening roar and consumed me.

I disappeared. One moment I was in the ocean, and the next I was nothing. My lungs burned from holding my breath, guarding the air I could, but soon I would have to let go. Maybe this was drowning. This was another rip current, and Ana wasn't here to save me. My chest and throat were on fire, and my arms and legs moved me nowhere. I was dying.

Breathe, Rosa.

I gasped and didn't choke. There was no water. There was nothing. I caught the sound of drumming and smelled the sweet potent scent of night jasmine blooming beneath the moon. My skin warmed as something nearby clattered.

"Hello?" No response, but I tracked the sound and finally recognized it when the rich smell hit me. I hungrily inhaled. It was Mimi's soup simmering on the stove and there, right there was the music of her record playing, soft with the crackle of distance and longing. The ache of those familiar sensations were too much, even as the new weight I'd carried in my chest grew lighter.

Don't cry, Rosa.

"Wait!" I ran and moved nowhere. Was I still in the sea? Flashes of voices swept past me in conversation. It was like standing in a never-ending hallway and hearing snatches of words as doors opened and closed around me. Pieces of a language I didn't know. I was lost and alone until I recognized a voice.

Mimi's brushed past as she called out for Alvaro. A deep voice received her with joy. I laughed, delighted. The sharp sweetness of lemon tickled me as I caught the sound of her saying my name. Everything was happening behind doors I could not see, but my name floated past. Once, twice, again. Guiding and arguing. The chimes of soft laughter. A determined defense and inspired pride. They were remembering me. Just as I remembered them.

Something rumbled. It sounded far away, but was

moving fast like a train. Or storm. The air felt heavy with it. Humid and salty. It was getting closer. The pressure was changing as the rolling thunder grew louder and light broke through the inky darkness.

Lightning cracked and I choked on salt water. It rushed into my nose and mouth, burning my chest and lungs. Air. I needed air. Just when I was sure I was lost or dead, I broke the surface.

And realized I was still standing on the beach.

It was daylight, and Mom and I, wracked with desperate coughs, were two drowned sea creatures standing in knee-deep water. The low tide rushed forward over the sand before returning to the sea. The very calm, very blue sea.

We stumbled onto the sand and crashed down on our backs as we both made a heroic effort to catch our breath. Mom looked as dazed as I felt. She brushed the wild tendrils of her hair out of her face, met my gaze, and said, "I'm never drinking from a coconut again."

We burst into delirious laughter as an older fisherman with wrinkled brown skin passed us, shaking his head. "Santeros," he mumbled, and we laughed harder.

38

The only one waiting for us on the beach was my backpack. Tía Nela was gone. Just as suddenly as she'd appeared, she disappeared. We smelled of oil, herbs, and potent magic, and our dresses were drying in the early morning light. I checked my bag. It only held what we packed. I heaved it onto my shoulder.

"Do you have any idea how to get back?" I didn't know if I should ask Mom what happened to her, but I didn't want to try and explain what happened to me. I simply wanted to hold on to this very real warmth and lightness and carry it forward.

"I don't even know where we are," Mom returned, but she didn't look all that concerned. She smiled and glanced back at the sea like she missed her camera.

We walked to the road and found a car waiting. The driver was young, dark, and watched us with wide eyes as he climbed out of it. I feared we would have to explain.

"¿Están listas?" he asked simply.

Were we ready? Ready for what?

Mom asked him where he was offering to take us.

"Havana," he said.

"Of course." I wondered if Nela would be back by the painted blue door. A realization hit me, and I stopped walking.

"Oh my god," I said. "She Yoda-ed us."

Beside me, Mom laughed so hard she had to grab me to keep from falling. Her laugh was lighter than I'd ever heard it.

The ride to Havana took a few hours after stopping for a lunch of papaya, rice, and roast chicken. It was a small restaurant off the beaten path, and everyone was friendly and kind, but we must have radiated some serious lingering woo-woo, because they watched us eat almost reverently. We changed back into our clothes in the bathroom. Luis, our driver, realized we were from America, and talked to us the whole way back about baseball and Tom Petty. When we got to the city he dropped us off in the middle of Old Havana.

"American girls," Luis said, flashing a big smile and a thumbs-up, before driving away.

Mom and I faced the wall where this all began. There was no Nela and there was no door.

But there was a big, beautiful mural of a blue wave.

"Life, man." Mom half laughed. "I've got to stop being so surprised by it. Come on." We grabbed a cajita—a small box of roasted pork, rice, and cucumbers marinated in a vinegar dressing—for each of us and walked down to el Malecón, the big seawall separating Havana from the sea.

"How long until our flight?" I asked as we hopped up to sit on the wall. I crossed my legs and faced the sea as we ate our food.

"Four hours," Mom said. After finishing her meal, she leaned back and tipped her face to the sun.

I took the moment to jot down the memories I'd made in my journal. They were still so bright, sharp, and mine. I uncapped a marker and added my lost family to them. A little girl exploding with laughter as she chased a goat in Viñales. The grandmother who always slipped her extra sweets, when her world was alive with peace and possibility. I added a grinning Alvaro, in full color, rushing up the university steps, a book under his arm and hope in his heart.

"Not too bad," Mom said, peeking over my shoulder. After a moment, her voice small and vulnerable, she said, "You don't have to tell me everything, but just . . . tell me something so I know he was real."

He? "I didn't see anything." Her face fell. "But I heard them. I heard Mimi find Alvaro. She called my name. And I think I heard Dad. Wherever we were, whatever that was . . . they were there, too."

Mom's smile bloomed.

I had to ask, too. I couldn't wait any longer. "What's going to happen with the house? I know you never want to stay in Port Coral, but now that Mimi's not there, is it still home? Will it still be ours?"

Mom went to say something but stopped as she struggled to explain. "I'm not her, and I can't promise to be for you what she was. But that house is ours. It will always be ours, and Port Coral will always be home." She swung her legs and shrugged. "Maybe I can fit my easels in the garden room and open the window every once in a while."

It was the release of my last fear. It floated away like a dark cloud as the sun finally warmed me all the way through.

"What about you? According to that little journal of yours, tomorrow is May first."

"I know." I took out my phone. I hadn't charged it since Viñales, and it only had 5 percent battery left. Luckily, el Malecón had Wi-Fi now. It had been a big deal for the people of Havana. I hurried to secure my spot.

Mom was leaning over my shoulder. "You're killing me, Rosa."

I opened the draft of the only unsent e-mail in my outbox. I hadn't been totally sure of my answer, but of course, I'd had my acceptance letter all queued up. It waited for the answer I finally found here. I took a deep breath and hit SEND. There it was. I was going to Florida.

"Really?" Mom asked, curious. "After all of this drama?"

I twisted my wildly blowing hair into a knot. "It *was* dramatic for me. Staying and leaving are both big deals. Charleston is great and the campus is beautiful, but it was only about study abroad for me. Being only a few hours from home may not sound exciting, but staying in-state allows me to save money, and that's important, too. Plus, I can combine my Latin American studies with a minor in sustainability. Learn about places I love but also *do* something about it."

"You're so reasonable." Mom smiled.

"And maybe next semester or year they'll offer study abroad to Havana or Camagüey or Viñales. Who knows? It's only two years. Either way, I'll come back." I unzipped my backpack and searched for the map of Havana to plan our way to the airport. But when I opened the map, it wasn't the one of Havana we'd bought. It was the map Alex had given me.

"Where'd you get that?"

"Alex," I told her. A blue line sailed from Florida across the Caribbean sea to where I stood now, just about.

I looked at the state of Florida and imagined my hometown, where flowers bloomed, fireworks burst over the harbor, and perceptive black cats led you down boardwalks. You could buy mango Popsicles in the park and some of the best guava-and-cheese pastelitos from a quiet sailor. I traced the lines leading here and my finger came to the coast of Havana. It stopped on a shiny spot of gold.

That hadn't been there when Alex first tried to give it to me. I was sure of it.

I brought the map right up to my face and stared at the spot of gold, expecting it to disappear. It didn't.

"What's the matter? Are we lost again?"

Words were written in a small, inky black scrawl next to the gold spot. *On your last day, I'll be at the Marina Hemingway.* My shocked gaze shot up to Mom's.

"What happened?"

I could barely hear my own voice over my hammering heart. "He's my Golden Turtle."

39

With my heart in my throat, I dropped the map before snatching it right back up again so it didn't fall into the sea. This was too wild. Too impossible.

But the mystery of it. It's the sort of mess I would have made if anyone left me in charge of the yearbook.

I remembered my words as we headed to find the turtle. More importantly, *he'd* remembered my words.

Mom studied the map, smiling. "Aw, I remember hiding that thing. Your dad and I loved that little island. Very secluded."

"Gross." I checked my watch and then put together what she just said. "Wait, *what*? You lost it?"

"We didn't lose it. We hid it, and then I drew the map and snuck it into the yearbook."

"Why didn't you say anything?"

"Because life happened. After your dad, I wasn't thinking about adventure and quests." She smiled. "Not until you. Come on, let's go."

We jumped off the wall and ran. It was my last day, but my flight left in a few hours. Could he really have sailed here? We raced down alleys, navigating through the traffic with surer steps. Waves crashed into the seawall, and we took off toward the marina. Maybe he knew I was ready and maybe this was all real and last night really happened. I ran faster.

And remembered I hated running.

"This is terrible." I coughed and stopped.

Mom hailed a taxi. "Just remember that you're the vieja and not me." A bright pink Oldsmobile convertible pulled up. Another classic car. Despite our rush, we stood on the street and gawked at the impossible shade of pink. Mom laughed, hard.

"Who knew my magical seashell would be a hot-pink vintage car in Havana?"

"I'm always right." Mom jumped into the car. "Remember that, because it's here to take you on your next adventure."

"¿Pa' dónde van?" the driver asked us.

"The Hemingway Marina, and step on it!"

He jerked around. "¿Qué?"

"Forget it." I shrugged at Mom. "That's what they say in movies at this part."

He pulled into traffic and drove down alongside el Malecón where waves broke against the seawall. Crowds were gathering beside a small band. It was too much: the wild ocean, the chant and drumming of the rumba song, the smell of the driver's sweet cigar smoke. I threw my head back and, like a bird who sighted home, I let out a wild cheer. *Here we are,* I said to my family's island, *alive.*

The taxi arrived at the bright blue building, and Mom paid the driver as I jumped out and ran. From here, I had no map. I rushed past the pool and what looked to be a small hotel. There was a canal beyond it with boats parked along the sides. Sailboats, yachts, older and newer, but no Alex. My feet faltered and I held my hair back from the strong breeze to peer down the row one more time.

My hammering heart settled. Silly, and mad, but it had been one hell of a maybe.

Mom caught up to me as I scanned the rest of the boats.

The door of a sailboat farther down opened, and a very cute sailor stepped outside. Beside me, Mom was still looking the other way.

Alex's head was bent over the book in his hands. He dropped it onto the table and crossed his arms. His chest rose and fell in a heavy, worried sigh. The water and sky were so blue behind him. My heart restarted.

He glanced over and met my gaze. I couldn't control my smile, but then, neither could he. I ran to him. He climbed out of the boat and hurried to meet me halfway.

I couldn't wait. I jumped right into his arms and kissed him. He caught me and said against my lips, "I was so worried you wouldn't come."

"I almost didn't. I thought the map was a metaphor."

He laughed and my heart sang. His strong arms tightened, and I kissed him again.

"You're here to whisk my daughter away, aren't you?" Mom asked, suddenly beside us.

I slipped down from Alex's arms. "Mom!"

He tucked his hands into his pockets. I knew he wasn't looking for his rope, because it was around my wrist. "I wanted to see you before I left for the summer. When I get back to Port Coral, you won't be there, so I had to take this chance."

"How spontaneous," I said.

He smiled. "You inspired me. I mean, look at you. You're glowing right now."

What could I even say? I wasn't sure what I had experienced these past two days, but I did know that the girl standing in front of him was not the same one who left Port Coral. Something within me had expanded beneath this sky and in these waters. I was still me, but more. I was a horizon and I was enough.

"Does the invitation to sail with you still stand?" I asked. It was bold, but I had a map in my bag and I was ready to fly. "Because I learned it's proper maritime etiquette to be invited to board," I said.

His eyes widened, and after a confused beat, he hurried to say, "If you wanted to, of course I am. I'm always inviting you onto my boat." Alex focused on me, his expression earnest and open. And excited. "You want to sail the Caribbean with me?"

I wanted to so much. The picture of it unfurled like his sails in my mind, but I worried my lip as I remembered school.

"You only have classes for a few more weeks," Mom said, interrupting my train of thought. "Wi-Fi. Find a computer at a library. I'll tell Malcolm your senioritis finally kicked in. Just be back before graduation." She looked at Alex. "Graduation," she repeated, sounding like such a mom. Memories rushed me as I met her bright gaze. Long car trips with broken antennas and open windows. Her soft fingers brushing my hair as I fell asleep in her lap again. Violets and country radio stations and the jangle of keys when she swallowed her pride, faced her ghosts, and brought me to where I longed to be.

I hugged her and whispered against her ear, "Thank you for getting me here."

Her arms stayed tight around me for a long moment.

"They're proud of us," I whispered.

"I am, too."

When she stepped back, her eyes shone, but she stood tough and kissed my brow. Twice.

I checked my watch and looked back at Alex. "I need to buy a few things before I set off onto this great big adventure with you, sailor. Do you want to see Havana before we go? I could show you."

His smile bloomed bright and tangled with the new things growing in my heart.

"Definitely," he said and took my hand. He slipped a reverent finger under the bracelet at my wrist. As we walked back to Havana, he asked me, "Where are we today?"

Surrounded by the bluest water, I smiled and told him.

Acknowledgments

I wrote this book for a girl who sat in her purple bedroom with the big daisy her mom painted on her wall, and watched love stories that took place in soft, small towns and dreamed of living there, too. A bilingual place that welcomed and accepted all of her while cheering her on as she figured out who she was and what she wanted. This is my love letter to her and you.

Thank you to my agent, Laura, who, just like Rosa, proves some of the fiercest champions are bookworms in cardigans. You've been there for me and all of my flower girls, and I can't wait to see what story we'll tell next. Thank you to Uwe for the home base you created in #TeamTriada and welcoming and believing in me from the very first.

This story would not be what it became without my editor, Hannah. You walked into Port Coral and made a home. You understood Rosa, honored my magic, protected my voice, and helped them bloom so much brighter. You ensured I had space to heal after tragedy, and this story became a book because of you. I wish I could build you a bench. Thank you to Mary Claire for the cover of my dreams. And to everyone at Hyperion who championed this romantic, sometimes heartbreaking, but—like magic and love—ultimately hopeful story. I am forever grateful for the shelf space you carved out for me.

To my Plus One and captain, Kristy. We'll build this tree house all the way to the next galaxy. Thank you to Jaye, my first yes and the first to read Rosa when she was an entirely different story. I'm so grateful you ran away with me to an orange grove. Alicia, who wrote the name of my first book that never sold on her door, I love you forever. To Dalia, who keeps all of my teenage stories safe and always knew I could do this. Ali, thank you for reading and loving Rosa when I didn't think I could anymore. To my hermana and diaspora love, Tehlor. Thank you for every candle, card, and protecting this coven with me. You guarded my spirit and healing heart this year, y te quiero siempre. When the announcement of my book dropped, I was overwhelmed with so much love from fellow Latinx writers and readers, and I love and appreciate every one of you so much. Gracias a las Musas. My kingdom of croquetas forever belongs to Alexis. Thank you for drawing Rosa and Alex first, for the letter after I lost everything, and becoming my long-lost prima.

Rosa is a story of my heart, but when you try to paint your spirit on the page, it's tough not to break it. While writing this book I spent many afternoons by the pool, my dad's cigar smoke in the air, his eyes a little faraway as he offered me his last memories of the boy he'd been. The one who cried good-bye to his beloved tía and island through a chain-link fence knowing he would never see them again. All in the name of freedom and hope. My father's heartbreak and sacrifice guided me like a lighthouse. I wanted to do right by it. I wanted to earn it. As I worked on this story I hurriedly wrote the names of his cities and lost memories, desperate to keep them safe. Camilo Carlos Moreno was a lover of books and learning, and my first library. He loved science and asking questions. Our moon and map, he was a man who endured so much, and his story was one of miracles and love.

On the longest Sunday morning of my life, my dad left us to sit with his father and our ancestors. He waited for me in that hospital room where his circle sat beside him and held his hand as he left. My last words to the man who gave me mine were that I hoped the waters are as blue as he remembered.

Later that week, I went to work editing this book.

With clumsy words and a broken heart, I reached for a hand I could no longer find. In this pain, I went home. To my brother and sister, Carlos and Victoria, I am at my best beside you two. This loud-as-hell triangle saves me every day. We are the stewards of this story, and I know he's wildly proud of us. And to Mom, my harbor and home.

You built this heart that could hold and create so much. I'm so grateful to the bold girl who climbed out of her window, the young, fierce mother who kept me safe while a hurricane raged, and the one who held my hand as my own daughter came into this world. I am so proud to be yours. Dad, I miss you so much and owe you a first edition. How are the stars? We'll keep our magic strong and hear your song.

Abuelo y Abuela. Yeya y Abi. You crossed miles of sea and land for your children. To my whole family and our ancestors: I am here because of the story of all of us.

Thank you to my babies, Phoenix and Lucia, who showed me I could make magic, too. And finally, to Craig. You're not supposed to meet your soulmate in high school, but here we are. You read every word and listened to every story and always believed, even when I was ready to throw it all away. You searched the skies for signs of good luck for me, but as you did, I was always looking at you.

To all the next-generation kids with old maps who fear they're losing something even as we create new things. You are magic. And you are enough.

Viva Cuba Libre.